Mark Taylor's Checkered Past

THE LOTTERY HEIRESS

BOOK TWO

ANGELINA ASSANTI

Cover created in Adobe Firefly

E-book ISBN: 978-0-692-59484-1

Paperback ISBN: 978-0-9979843-9-2

DEDICATION

To the staff at Betty Ford Hazelden
in Naples, Florida

Acknowledgments

This book would not have been possible without the following people: my family and friends for their constant support; my editor, Karen Auriti, from Jacobs Writing Consultants; and Betty Ford Hazelden in Naples, Florida.

CHAPTER *One*

MARK TAYLOR RECLINED in his seat at the most exclusive French bistro on Fifth Avenue in Naples. He looked around at the exotic cars and ageless people going by. There were a lot of people there for July. It was eight o'clock, and things were just starting to get exciting. Music was playing, and crowds were forming. Mark's group was seated outside – where you want to be. Because in Naples, you want to be *seen*. Mark had dropped by Naples Recovery Center to visit and wound up giving an impromptu speech. Afterward, the staff and some of the residents took Mark to eat at the new French bistro in town. He was making conversation with the group when a new, red Mercedes careened out of control. It barely missed a black Maserati parked in front of the restaurant. Fingers pointed as the crowd gasped at the loud screech and near-miss of pedestrians walking on the brick crossing.

A man jumped out of the driver's side and yelled, "Please, someone help my wife. She's not breathing!" Then the man ran over to the passenger side and opened his wife's door.

Without even thinking, Mark jumped out of his chair, knocking it to the ground, and ran towards the woman sitting unconscious in her car. He pulled her out and carried her to the sidewalk. As Mark gently laid her down, he needed something soft to rest her head upon. He yelled to a woman spectator, "Can you take my shirt off?" he asked, cradling the victim's head in his arms.

The woman looked at him longingly and, in a breathy voice, said, "Yes, please." She took his shirt off and held it out, but she was reluctant to give it to him.

He frowned at her, knowing every second counted. "Put it under her head for me." Mark said, "Hurry up. I'll let you *have* the damn shirt."

The spectator folded the warm shirt and set it on the hard concrete sidewalk. Then Mark laid the victim's head down and began CPR. The crowd thickened. It's one thing to see a car out of control on Fifth Avenue and come to a screeching halt. And it's not unusual to see celebrities on Fifth. That's where they go. But to see Mark Taylor racing to the aid of a helpless woman – that was impressive. To see him do it without a shirt on, that was just divine intervention!

As Mark continued the chest compressions and blew into the woman's mouth, her husband crouched by her side, watching her for any sign of life. And as her chest rose and fell with the air from Mark's lungs, finally she let out a huge gasp, and her hubby sighed with relief and a hysterical laugh. The woman came to under a bare-chested Mark Taylor, sitting back on his heels and smiling at her as the real EMTs came to her aid. "Are you okay?" Mark asked her.

"What happened?" she asked Mark as one of the EMTs started checking her vitals, and the other prepared the gurney. She lifted her head up, and her eyes followed Mark.

"You weren't breathing, honey. Mark Taylor saved your life!" her husband said, wide-eyed with disbelief.

"You need to relax and put your head down," the EMT said as he held her wrist and continued counting beats. Her husband shook Mark's hand so hard, it alone could have drawn attention. The crowd erupted in applause. Mark blinked and held his hands up to block all of the flashings from cameras. Spectators snapped tons of photos, and witnesses talked to a news crew who was doing a story down the block. The journalists had walked away from the person they were interviewing, without explanation or apology, and literally ran when they saw the ambulance and heard the commotion.

A reporter on the scene asked Mark why he helped a stranger, and Mark replied, "That's what you do when you see someone in trouble... you *help* them. I just did what anyone else would've done." Embarrassed, he did his best to shrug off the publicity. Mark autographed his shirt for the woman who'd taken it off and then walked away from the crowds as they started to disperse. Shirtless, he returned to the table.

Dane, a counselor from the rehab center, said, "Wow, there's never a dull moment with Mark Taylor around, is there?"

Mark just smiled and sat back in his chair. His waiter came up to him and said, in a French accent, "Monsieur Taylor, you simply cannot sit here without a shirt!"

"Oh, because of the health codes?"

"No! Because of the *husbands.*" The waiter nodded toward all of the men scowling at Mark as their wives batted their eyes and said how wonderful he was. Mark grinned at the men and waved to the women who smiled and waved back.

A fan came up to Mark and asked him to sign a tabloid magazine she was holding that had a picture of Mark on it. As he was signing it, she said, "I can't believe I'm meeting you! This is the greatest day of my life!" Mark just smiled as he scribbled his name with a little note to her. He gave her the magazine back, and she looked at him with a worried look. "I *used* to be a huge fan," she said. This confused Mark. She'd just told him that this was the most important day of her life.

"Used to be?" Mark questioned her. "What happened?"

"Oh, I *lost weight*!" she said.

Mark laughed and said, "Well, whatever you're doing, you look great!"

"Can I get a picture with you?" she asked.

"Sure!" Mark said as she handed Dane her phone, and he snapped a pic. She smiled and walked away.

Mark seems like a great guy, right? How nice to be the *good* guy. Mark truly wants to help people now. But it wasn't always this way. In fact, there was a time not so long ago when Mark couldn't even help *himself*. Let's go back seven years to where it all began, and you'll see how something beautiful can evolve from a huge, self-destructive mess.

Mark was coming right off the success of a TV sitcom called *The Trifecta,* where he played an EMT – good thing, huh? The premise of the show was three best friends lived together in a New York apartment and the one who could have the most meaningless sex won. Brilliant, huh? It takes real talent to write trash like that, but apparently, that's what audiences love, because it was a massive hit in over sixty countries. Gone are the days of intellectual shows or shows that let you use your imagination. Who wants people to actually think independently nowadays? It is far better to sway public opinion by beating people over the head with a message. Messages are everywhere: in song lyrics, TV shows, and movies. That's how you change the culture without people even catching on. Repetition is the key, and if you don't believe that, listen to how politicians speak. It's subtle brainwashing, but brilliant because you don't know it's happening.

Doing a show like that only gave Mark a worse reputation than he deserved. He was a ladies' man anyway, and why not? He was hot, rich, and famous. Women wanted him, and he didn't even have to work for it. I mean it. Women literally threw themselves at him and didn't even ask for dinner before *or* afterward. And why would they, when they could have Mark Taylor for dessert? Best "fast" ever! But that didn't make Mark happy, and he didn't know why. His character was always cheerful, never having to say he was sorry, never having to sacrifice or commit. Isn't that what every guy wants?

I mean, who doesn't want to be adored with no effort? Actually, Mark liked being in a relationship, he just succumbed to temptations. And there were a lot of temptations around. His friends weren't good role models either. They didn't know how to stay faithful, and they didn't want to learn. Let's face it, when you're young and hot in Hollywood, the clock is ticking. There will always be someone sexier and more youthful. You've got to take advantage while you can because it won't last forever. No one respects that old guy with a hot young woman on his arm, and if that's not offensive enough, she has to see him naked! It's not worth being a gold digger – is it, really? Our society has changed so much that now we're seeing older women with younger men. Everyone is trying so hard to recapture their youth. It makes you wonder if *anyone* is happy.

CHAPTER *Two*

DOMINIC WEBB SURE wasn't happy. After a five-year run, the star of *The Trifecta* ended his life with no warning. The network canceled the show almost immediately after. Mark had been close to Dom and had a hard time dealing with his death. But instead of grieving and seeking counsel, he threw himself into another project as soon as possible. Mark wanted to do movies when the show wrapped up anyway, but he never imagined it would end like that.

At least there was plenty of movie offers when the network made the announcement. No more waiting for a hiatus to explore the opportunities that awaited him on the silver screen. Mark was free to move on. Besides coping with the horrific and unexpected death of his close friend, he had a lot of pressure, narrowing down his next project. It would literally make or break him. Out of a few scripts he liked, he chose one based on the other actors who had already committed. The movie he signed on for was *Don O'Malley*.

It was an action-adventure where the protagonist wasn't actually a good guy – only in comparison to the bad guy did the character have any redeeming value. But it had a brilliant director and the script was excellent. It starred Declan

O'Conner as the title character. He was a massive star and had been an A-lister for twenty years. It says a lot when you can stay on top for that long in Hollywood.

Claudia James was cast as the female lead – another A-lister. It was rumored that she was no stranger to the casting couch and didn't have a problem with it. Some people will do *whatever* it takes. She had a reputation for using men until she got bored and then moving on to someone younger and younger. Every year as she got older, she'd date someone more youthful than the last. She'd be breaking the *law* pretty soon at the rate she was going.

Mark admired Declan's career and wanted to have one just like it. And Claudia, of course, he only admired. Even though he hadn't met in her person yet, she was beautiful and appeared to be everything a man could want. Mark knew this was going to be an excellent opportunity for him. He hoped this movie would show his talent and pave the way for him to play a male lead in the future. It didn't hurt that the director was known for producing Oscar-worthy performances from his actors.

Mark was confident this would be the launching pad for a successful leap to film. Everything was riding on this being a hit. He signed on and got an apartment in Miami. The project was scheduled to last almost a year, with all the martial arts and hand-to-hand combat training for three months in Miami before filming began. The fight scenes and stunts would be very intense. It would be a longer time commitment than the other projects out there. But he had no ties, and living in Miami was no problem for a hot, single guy.

His apartment building had amenities like a luxury hotel. He needed a concierge and spa – he was going to be a movie star now. He was sure of it. Mark packed his clothes and some things he couldn't live without into his '69 Camaro, and as he left South Carolina for Miami, he thought about his parents. They didn't want him to be an actor. You want to talk about a profession where the odds are against you making it? He may as well have been a writer!

He'd intended to be a doctor. He had even gone to Clemson for pre-med. But he met a girl who wanted to be an actress. Mark auditioned for a play at the university, and that was the end of his medical aspirations.

The play was open to anyone who wanted to audition, not just theater majors, so Mark decided to try out. Wouldn't you know that he got the male lead – with no experience? As they say, "the rest is history." Mark got discovered by a talent agent during the week of public performances. And that was it. He was cast on a soap opera right after graduation. Ridiculous, right? That just doesn't happen. Things seemed to fall right into his lap – including the female lead when she found out he had been cast in a soap opera. Like most things in Mark's life, she was a fleeting moment.

Mark eased comfortably into the Miami nightlife. He liked eating at the restaurants on Ocean Drive and people-watching at Lummus Park. He was invited to a few parties on Collins Avenue, which is known as Millionaire's Row in Miami Beach.

Very few commitments and even less clothing became his norm. Mark and Declan were getting in great shape, working out separately with personal trainers for a few months before shooting began. Per their contracts, they had chefs preparing meals for them to ensure they would keep their bodies looking as perfect as possible. It's funny that people who care about their physical appearance would even take drugs or alcohol, but it was commonplace in the Miami scene and in their circle.

Mark's personal trainer didn't know Mark was using, but it probably would have made sense if he found out. It would explain why Mark was sluggish on some days. If diet and fitness level were being controlled, there should've been no reason for his inconsistent performance in the gym. But there was a reason. And Mark would continue to conceal it for the time being.

Mark felt empty, and to fill the void in his life, he added large quantities of alcohol to meaningless sex. That *had* to work. He was definitely missing something. His family drank, so it wasn't like he never drank before... but not to this extent. It was like he had a tapeworm, or maybe a tequila worm that he was trying to satiate. Truthfully, Mark was a nice guy, deep down – uh, deep, deep down. It was there, at the bottom, a glimmer of "niceness." He just got ugly when he had a drink or three in his hand. He was misguided, misunderstood, and missing out on life! He tried to make up for being lonely by filling the voids with broads and booze. Making it easier was the fact that his friend Jack Daniels traveled lightly and didn't judge. He held Mark's attention and was always there when Mark needed him. There has never been any woman or friend so loyal.

After a few months out of the limelight, Mark was excited to start acting again, especially since he was the second male lead in *Don O'Malley*.

That was a huge deal at this point in his career. He was already pretty much a household name, but people thought he was that character from *The Trifecta*. They thought he was a jerk and womanizer. Not wanting to disappoint, Mark wound up letting life imitate art. The sad part was most women had no problem with it. Well, women *said* they had no problem, and women *acted* like they had no problem until they started getting clingy and insecure. That is if Mark ever saw them twice, and they had the opportunity to do so.

He was nervous. This had to be a smooth transition; many actors have tried and failed to make it in the movies. It was all or nothing for Mark. He no longer had the comfort of a hit television series to ride on. At least the show was syndicated, and Mark was able to live quite a lifestyle from those royalty checks. But if he wanted to continue working, he knew this movie had to be a hit. It was all a gamble, and Mark knew it. Sometimes a script reads well, but if the right people aren't in the mix, it's not going to work. Mark hoped Declan would take him under his wing, for the sake of his career and his love life. It was a huge deal for Mark's first film to have Declan O'Conner and Claudia James starring in it. Mark was literally banking on the two of them to carry him to the next phase of his career.

Like Mark, Declan also had quite a reputation as a ladies' man. He was someone who liked to party… Claudia was never without a man – in fact, never without a *groom* – but lately, she was trying to project a new image as a mom. She had been married several times, and now had children. In fact, she was on magazine covers as the "it" girl who had everything. She *did* have everything, from nannies to boy-toys. How much time she actually spent with her children was a mystery, but the media built her up. And everyone loved her because she was "likable."

I think the trail of men left behind would agree – there was *a lot* to like. She was beautiful, charming, and smart. Even better, she wasn't into long commitments. If you wanted to leave, she had her divorce attorney on speed-dial. No biggie. These are just the morally bankrupt people that our society worships – it makes sense, right? If they fall too far off their pedestals, their publicists just blame addiction and make them go to rehab and make a mockery of people trying to actually get clean. But hey, it's good for business – "show" business. It was no secret that she always took one of the cast members as a lover on every set. Mark was hoping it would be him this time.

CHAPTER *Three*

AS THE ACTUAL production started to gear up, Mark got to the gym to meet with his trainer and hopped out of his car. It was really early, but better for celebrities when there's less of a crowd. He immediately was sent to a treadmill and started jogging at a slow pace. Mark hates running. Declan came over and got on the treadmill next to him.

"Hey, how's it going, Mark?" Declan asked.

"Good, man. What's going on?"

"I just wanted to see if you want to grab a beer later."

"Sure, man, that sounds good."

"How long are you here today?" Declan asked.

"At least two or three hours," Mark said as he sped the treadmill up.

"Me too," Declan said as he sped his treadmill up to match Mark's speed. This did not go unnoticed by Mark. A few minutes later, Mark increased his incline on the treadmill, and again, Declan did the same. Mark let out a little laugh. He figured since Declan was ten years older, this was his way of letting Mark know he could keep up with him. The competition was heating up, and it was only the beginning…

After all, Declan had been at the top of the box office for

the last two decades. His movies had grossed over a billion dollars. He had a huge fan base. Everyone loved Declan.

Well, everyone who didn't actually *know* him. He wasn't a good person. He was a liar, a manipulator, a womanizer, and just in general, a big, fat jerk. Mark didn't know that yet because every director interviewed always said how great Declan was to work with. He wasn't. He threw tantrums, harassed all the females on the set, and sometimes showed up inebriated. If you look at some scenes in his movies, his face is red, and his hair goes in different directions. That's more of a continuity issue and should have been caught in editing. Declan was also notorious for not memorizing his lines. In fact, in his last movie, they had cue cards for him. Contrary to Declan, Mark earned the nickname, "One-take Taylor" for being the consummate professional. Mark's always camera-ready.

Needless to say, Declan wasn't the sweetheart everyone would lead you to believe. However, he was a cash cow, and movie studios and directors knew it, so they looked the other way. After all, it's all about making money, right? That's the *first* priority.

Declan and Mark met at a restaurant on Ocean Drive - which is on South Beach - for drinks and lunch. They sat under a vast canopy outside, which hung over the sidewalk. Passersby looked at all the people eating lunch while misters and fans blew a haze of water onto the diners. It's always hot on South Beach. The action doesn't get started until late... really late. Ask anyone, it's well-known that beautiful people don't even come out until midnight. So, to spot Mark and Declan out at such an odd time was worth the gawking they were getting from the peasants. A young woman approached them with wristbands. She was so star-struck she could barely speak.

"Hi," she said as she slid each one of them an orange

wristband across the table that had the name 'Deceptions' on it without saying a word.

Mark put his drink down and picked up the wristband, "What is this for?" he asked.

"It's for a nightclub a block over," she said with a huge smile, "you can't get in without one."

Declan laughed as he handed her the band back. "Sweetie, do you think Declan O'Conner and Mark Taylor can't get into your club without a wristband?"

Mark looked at Declan and then gave her back his wristband too.

She was embarrassed. "No, of course, *you* don't need a wristband, but I just wanted to come over and meet Mark." She blushed. "I'm a huge fan. You're even better looking in person," she said, and Mark smiled.

"Mark wouldn't waste his time on trash like you so you can take your little wristbands and give 'em to tourists for all we care," Declan said as he dismissed her with his hand.

The girl looked like she was about to cry, so Mark followed her and apologized for Declan. When he came back to the table and sat down, he told Declan, "Don't ever treat my fans like that, man."

And then came the most insincere apology ever. "Sorry," Declan said as he shrugged his shoulders and tossed back his drink.

A few minutes and a few drinks later, Mark noticed that other people were handing out wristbands only to beautiful people. "Why do the nightclubs here pass out wristbands?"

"You're in South Beach, they only want the beautiful people in the nightclubs," Declan said.

"Wow. It's like a canned safari hunt."

"Less effort on our parts…"

"Yeah, but you can't meet a nice girl that way."

Declan laughed. "Are you trying to get married or laid, Mark? This is Miami life, enjoy it. It won't last forever."

When they were done eating and drinking, they walked down Ocean Drive and then crossed the road and walked on the beach. There were a few attractive women there but not as many as Mark was expecting. Mark had envisioned many beach bunnies with taut skin and small bathing suits. Mark realized that maybe midnight was the right time to find someone who would amuse him for a little while. There were so many little planes flying over the water with drink specials trailing behind them that Mark knew he was bound for trouble.

Later that night, the same parking garage Mark and Declan parked in earlier for twenty dollars was now charging one-hundred and fifty dollars. But it's almost impossible to find a parking space on South Beach. It didn't matter anyway, there were so many cars everywhere, you couldn't even move a car on or off Ocean Drive.

Declan was right though, the beautiful people were out. And they were misbehaving. People were drinking alcohol and smoking weed and doing other illegal and immoral things right on the streets and sidewalks. It was like anarchy. Mark had never seen anything like it. The cars were totally gridlocked, and pedestrians were walking right in front of moving cars. Mark observed some crazy stuff, but he laughed a lot because he was drinking and finding most of it funny.

When Mark and Declan got to a nightclub, they walked in, and women came up and hung all over them. Not that they minded. They'd set out for one purpose, and it couldn't have been easier. They just had to pick which one to take home…

For the first few weeks of the shoot, before the arrival of Claudia James, Mark and Declan prowled all over Miami, further perpetuating their reputations for drinking and hooking up with anyone who looked good. It was like shooting fish in a barrel for these two. The guys weren't exactly close, but they made a very dangerous duo. Mark liked it because it brought his favorite three things together:

drinking, sex, and publicity. Declan seemed unscathed by the reports of him leaving with a different woman every night. Mark was the one the media focused on, suggesting that he was a chauvinist pig, much like some of the characters he'd played.

Declan loved being Mark's primary bad influence. He was full of misguided advice, especially when it came to women and money. Mark bought a half-million-dollar car because Declan had one. Now, it wasn't a big deal for Declan. He was part of one of the highest-grossing movie franchises in history, so a half million wasn't much to him. Not to mention the fact that Declan had his own production company now and was raking in cash. Mark didn't have the kind of income Declan had. But that didn't stop Mark from spending every penny he made.

As far as women went, Declan was also an expert on them. Well, an expert in his own mind. Mark did enjoy the benefits of being friends with Declan O'Conner, but as with everything else in Mark's life, it was going to be short-lived.

CHAPTER *Four*

LATE ONE NIGHT, the guys went out to a popular sky bar on South Beach and drank the night away – so much so that Mark didn't remember *anything* that happened.

Mark woke up the next morning with Goldilocks in his bed. He didn't know who she was or how she'd gotten there. What he did know was that they were both naked, and there was more than one empty bottle of liquor on the nightstand. All he could smell was cheap perfume and vomit, and his head was pounding. He had to get this woman out of his bed.

If he couldn't recall who this person lying next to him was, what else couldn't he recall? He started to panic. Did he crash his car again? More bad press if he did. And what if he hurt someone this time? It wasn't the first time he'd woken up unaware of his circumstances, and it wouldn't be the last.

Mark slid out from under the covers so as not to rouse his bedmate. He put on his clothes from the little pile on the floor and raced down to the parking garage. It was killing him that he didn't know where his prized car was – the car that meant the world to him – the car that Declan told him to buy.

As he tried to slip out of the bedroom, the mystery woman

awoke and said, "Good morning, Mark." Well, at least she knew who *he* was. She asked where he was going. He turned around and realized it was Regina from craft services on the movie set. Hell, she'd be on the movie set for the whole duration of the project. What was he thinking? He'd broken his rule again. It never ended well when he got involved with people he worked with.

"I was just going down to check on my car," he said as he grabbed the keys off the table by the bedroom door.

"Oh, so you don't remember last night," she said. She sounded disappointed.

"What? Of course, I do!" He looked at the bed. "I mean, we spent the night together, how could I forget… that?" They both knew he was lying. Mark had a nasty habit of not remembering a lot of things when he drank.

"Then you remember that we took a cab from the club because you were too drunk to drive?" she asked.

"Right. Right," Mark said as he shook the car keys. "Yeah, what club was that, again?"

She flung the sheets off in disgust and started getting dressed in her wrinkled clothes from the night before. "Helen was right. I never should've spent the night with you!"

"Who's Helen?" he asked innocently.

"She's the one you were screwing *last week,*" she said as she shoved her legs into her jeans.

"Right… Helen," he said, realizing who she was. He tried to make it up to her. "Do you want me to make some coffee?"

"No, I think I've had about all I need from you," she snapped as she put her shirt on.

"This isn't going to be awkward now, is it? I mean, we're going to have to see each other, and I don't want it to be weird, okay?"

"Oh, don't worry about that, Mark. I'm sure by next week, you'll be on to someone else, and you'll forget about me, too."

She grabbed her purse and stormed past him to the front

door. He followed her. "Look, I had a good time last night." He looked back at the bedroom. "I think."

She laughed angrily as she went out the door and slammed it with a huge thud.

Mark looked for his phone and texted Declan. He came over to give Mark a ride back to his car and find out how the night ended with Regina. But he already knew.

They were almost at the club. Mark had hardly said a word to him the whole way. Finally, Declan asked, "So, man, what happened with Regina?"

"Nothing."

"It didn't look like nothing. You were all over each other at the club last night."

"I mean, we went back to my place…" Mark looked at the scenery out the window without really seeing it. "Don't you ever get sick of this?"

"Sick of what? Not having to commit and getting women to come home with me for nothing? I love this Women's Lib crap, I don't even have to buy drinks for them anymore, and they're begging me to take them home and screw their brains out. Real dirty sex, too. There's something *wrong* with you, my friend."

Mark then recited the drinker's pledge to Declan. "I swear to God, I'm *never* drinking again!"

"Yeah, me too," Declan said sarcastically as he laughed at Mark, holding his head.

They pulled up to the club, and Mark got out of the car. He made plans to go out with Declan again that night. Then he got into his beloved machine and drove back to his high rise.

When he got back to his apartment, he looked at his watch. He decided to watch some television before he was needed on the set. He sat down in the living room and looked around. He'd never noticed how empty the place felt. Even after a night with a companion, he *felt* alone. Something was missing. What was it?

He turned on the television, and a rerun of *The Trifecta* was on. It was an episode where Mark's character woke up not remembering anything that happened the night before. Sadly, in that particular episode, he was trying to sneak out of a girl's apartment without her knowing. As the laugh track echoed in Mark's head, he cringed at how close to home this episode came. There was a reason it felt like he had been there before. The media loved making jokes at Mark's expense when it came to his reoccurring one-night stands, and the public was no better. They believed all the hype. They couldn't get enough. People love to read trashy magazines and watch the news on TV – which had now become tabloid journalism as well.

He sat there, reflecting on his life. How could he have so much and yet feel like he had nothing? He gazed at the TV screen and didn't understand. Dominic looked so happy. Could he have been that good an actor? What compels someone to end it all? He decided to call his mother in Charleston, South Carolina. He liked calling home when he felt melancholy.

His father answered the phone. The two spoke for a few minutes, and then Mark asked to talk to his mother. His dad gazed at Georgia, slumped over the side of the couch with an empty highball glass in her hand. Passed out.

"Your mother's napping right now," Marion said.

"Is she feeling okay?"

"Sure, son. You know your mom; she stays up all night and sleeps late."

"Dad, I feel like maybe I should come up for a visit."

"When are you thinking of coming?"

"Maybe this weekend. I'm off for the next few days."

"Well, your brother asked us to go to Hilton Head."

"Oh." Mark drooped with disappointment.

"Maybe next weekend, son."

"I've got a tight schedule next week, Dad."

"Maybe next time. I have to go. I have a tee time in thirty minutes. Love you, son." And he hung up.

Mark looked at the phone and put it back on the base. He sat there for a while, elbows on his knees, just looking at the floor. Why wouldn't his brother have asked him to go to Hilton Head, too? He should've just flown up. But he didn't.

The next couple of months of Miami nightlife left Mark empty and literally in pain. It wouldn't have been so bad, except Declan did everything to excess and encouraged everyone around him to do the same. In fact, one night, Mark drank so much that he fell asleep and almost didn't wake up again.

It all started when Mark was at his apartment looking through the Real Estate section of the newspaper. He'd decided maybe it was time to set down roots somewhere. Mark liked Miami's vibe because it was a playground for the rich and famous. He figured he would always have a reason to come to Miami.

He wasn't on the call sheet for the next day, which meant he had no obligations on the set the next day. So, Mark contacted a Realtor and found a beautiful Mediterranean estate on the water in Miami. It was far from perfect. It was in serious disrepair.

Mark decided to hire a renowned local architect, Phillip Mason, to renovate the house. It would give Mark something positive to look forward to. It wouldn't be a quick process; he wanted everything gutted, a total renovation.

As a cash buyer, Mark closed on the house right away. He couldn't live in the house while it was under construction, but he had the apartment to use until the work was finished. Phillip said it would only take a year.

Mark was very particular when it came to restoring the house, which was a hundred years old. He only wanted authentic period fixtures and architectural details. The previous owners had tried to update the home to a mid-century modern theme, which looked ridiculous. Even worse, they'd clearly done the renovations themselves. Mark spent a lot of time looking at magazines and samples, trying to pick out precisely what he wanted in the house.

CHAPTER *Five*

AFTER THE FIRST phase of the renovation, Mark began moving small items into the house and would sometimes stay overnight. He liked sitting in the back yard, facing the water and relaxing. Sometimes he had a few "friends" over, including Declan, to show them the progress of the renovation. They usually drank a lot and left a massive mess for Mark to clean up.

On the Fourth of July weekend, Mark had some people over the house. After they left, he stayed and continued the party alone while he waited for someone from Phillip's office to come by with some plan revisions. It was Fourth of July weekend, and in Mark's patriotic enthusiasm, he decided to find out how much liquor his liver could actually process.

Before he knew it, he had passed out on the living room floor. In fact, he never did know until afterward. Fortunately, one of Phillip's employees arrived at Mark's house to drop off some plan revisions. She found him unresponsive in the living room. When she tried to wake him to see if he was still alive, he threw up all over her. Thank God she found him – he would've died if she hadn't shown up. Imagine throwing up while he was passed out. Surely *this* would be enough to make him quit drinking.

If you ask Mark about this incident, he doesn't remember a lot. What he does remember is the recessed lighting behind her head as she stooped over him. It looked like a halo. He smiled in his mind as he gazed at her through a haze. Surely he was seeing an angel. Her hands came down, sweetly to touch his face. She cared! She was so concerned about his condition that she stayed with him until he was wheeled away by EMS. Well, that's what Mark was *told*. At least this much is true; this woman saved his life.

Events after that were foggy. Mark remembers being surrounded by a medical team as they pumped his stomach and ran tests on him. All the sounds and sights were distorted, but the pain of getting his stomach pumped remained with him.

As he lay in the hospital bed, he thought about the path he was on. This was another mishap that was bound to be in the papers by morning. Mark vowed to himself that he would never have another drink again.

Phillip had to come by and give him the keys to his house. He was so embarrassed about vomiting on one of Phillip's employees. Mark dreaded the thought of having to go into Phillip's office ever again. How would he face that poor woman? Maybe he could avoid it. He was a celebrity, after all, and used to getting what he wanted. He could just send someone.

The next day, before he could feel too sorry for himself, Peter, the director of *Don O'Malley*, came to the hospital to check on Mark. Declan was in the hall, but Peter asked him to wait so he could have a word alone with Mark.

"How ya' doing, Mark?" Peter asked.

Mark just gave him a 'thumbs up.' His throat was still sore from where they put the tube down his throat. The nurse left a pen and paper on his nightstand until he felt well enough to talk.

"I have the name of someone; it's time you meet." Mark exhaled as Peter stuck the business card of a counselor at a rehab center in front of his eyes. Mark grabbed it.

Mark pointed to the pad and pen, and Peter handed them to Mark.

Mark wrote aggressively, *"I don't want to go to rehab. It was an accident."* He ended the sentence with a period that he stabbed on the notepad and then showed it to Peter.

"Accidents are unavoidable. This could've been prevented, Mark. Get some help. The studio didn't want you for this role in the first place. They're insisting you go or they're going to replace you. I like you, Mark. It's nothing personal." Peter didn't even wait for Mark to stab any more angry punctuation out. He just gave Mark a sympathetic smile and turned towards the door. "It's an outpatient program. It's only thirty days, and they'll work around our shooting schedule."

Mark frowned and looked at the card again.

"I've already made the call. You're going as soon as the doctors release you!" Peter didn't even pause; he just kept his back to Mark as he left the room.

Mark lay there, flicking the edge of the business card with his finger. Rehab! Great. Mark knew there was no way he was getting out of going.

Declan came in. "Hey, how you holding up?" he asked as he gave Mark a fist bump.

Mark picked up the pad and pen again and wrote, *"They're making me go to rehab."*

"I know. But, it's *outpatient*. Don't worry about it! It's just so the movie studio can pretend that they have control over 'the talent,'" Declan said with a laugh.

Mark was not amused.

"So do your thirty days, then we can go to Key West as

soon as you're done." Declan gave him a weird handshake that Mark didn't understand and made Mark feel weak and uncoordinated – probably deliberate on Declan's part. Mark tried helplessly to reciprocate the gesture. "See you, man!" Why did he always pick the wrong friends and women? He was alone... again!

One of his nurses rustled into the room to check on him. She inspected his monitor and made sure he didn't need anything. "Wow, how exciting to have celebrities in here. You're so lucky to have such an exciting life."

Exciting? Mark drank so much he had to have his stomach pumped. She was envious of *him*? Mark envied *her*. She probably had loyal friends who cared about her, and here she wished she had *his* "friends." What a joke! People just don't understand celebrities. They don't know that it's hard to find people you can trust. Was there anyone sincere in Mark's life? The only one who seemed like he cared was Peter, and that was probably because he was worried that Mark was going to screw his movie up, and re-casting now would just cause more production delays and costs.

The next few weeks were filled with hand-to-hand combat scenes, motorcycle stunts, and fighting scenes. Mark insisted on doing his own stunts because he thought it would be good for his 'tough guy' image. There were martial arts experts and retired special forces guys on the set, giving technical advice and working with the actors to provide realism to the action, as well as the stunt coordinator.

When Mark's time at the rehab was over, he and Declan drove down to Key West for the weekend. On the way, they spent a lot of time talking about Declan's on-again, off-again relationship with an actress named Katelynn Davis. She was pressuring Declan to get married because she really wanted to have children. Declan didn't like that idea. Children would totally cramp his lifestyle. And having a wife? Declan wasn't going to ever answer to anybody!

By contrast, Mark really wanted to have children. Oh, he liked to go out and party, but he also liked the idea of going home to the same woman. Would that ever happen for him? Would there ever be a woman that captivating to him – to make him want to keep coming back? He wondered if being married and having kids would be what he needed to get his life on track. But he knew he wasn't in any shape to be a husband or father. He hadn't gotten partying out of his system yet. It was convenient not having any responsibilities – no one to answer to.

They pulled into their hotel in Key West, and the valet took the car while the bellhop took the bags. The guys didn't even look around. They were ready to take to the streets and see what they could consume for the night – whether it was just alcohol, or alcohol and women. They left their cell phones behind in the room since they were just going a few doors down. Mark and Declan were both prone to lose them when they were drinking. This posed a real problem when you have famous people in your contact list. People love to get their hands on your phone, among other things.

At the first bar they went to, flocks of women came up to them asking to buy the guys drinks. They had several rounds, and they had both found women to spend the night with. It was getting late, and Declan asked Mark if he was ready because he was going back to the hotel with his "date." Mark said that he was going home with Tammy, the woman he was with and that he would meet up with Declan the next day.

The bar started to thin out. People were leaving. Tammy left Mark for a minute and went over to the table where her friends were sitting. They were having an argument. Mark turned around on his barstool, drink in hand, watching the girls argue. He couldn't hear what they were saying, but they were pointing at him and yelling. The bartender yelled, "Last call." Tammy came back to Mark and started kissing him. Her friends followed and screamed some more.

"What's going on here?" Mark's speech was slurred.

"They don't want me to go home with you."

"Why not? I'm a nice guy," he said.

"You're *Mark Taylor*. When am I going to be able to have sex with someone famous? Do you care that I'm engaged?"

"Do you care that I *don't* care that you're engaged?" Mark asked.

"No, let's go back to your room."

They got up and started to leave, but her friends wouldn't give up. One stepped up in front of them. "You're going to sleep with Mark Taylor? That's like screwing everyone in Hollywood – no offense," she said to Mark.

"None taken. Now, if you'll excuse us," Mark said as he tried to plow through those loyal friends of hers.

Another one stepped forward. "Mike would never cheat on you. I can't believe you're going to do this to him. I would kill to have a guy like him, and you're going to throw it all away for a night with *this*?" she looked at Mark, disgusted by him, and then she stormed out of the bar. Just then, Tammy got a text from her fiancé. It said, "I love you so much. I hope you're having fun in Key West. I can't wait to spend my life with you!"

Tammy read the text and started crying. She looked at Mark. "I can't leave with you. I made a mistake."

"You bitch! You waited for Declan to leave me here! The bar is about to close, and I don't have a way back to my hotel."

Her friend piped up. "Maybe I would've given you a ride if you hadn't called her a bitch."

They left while Mark hurled curses at them. The bartender slid a shot of whiskey to Mark. "I guess you got screwed in Key West, after all." Mark slammed the shot back, and the bartender offered to call him a cab. But, but Mark said he would walk – which would've been fine any other time, like *daylight*. He had no idea where he was going, and everything was closed.

CHAPTER *Six*

HE STARTED to realize he was lost. Really lost. And it was December, which is typically cool, but there was a cold front that made it about forty degrees in Key West. Dark and cold. He patted himself down and realized that he must've left the phone at the hotel or the bar. All he could do was keep walking. He had no idea how much time had passed. But finally, there was light.

The light was coming from a bonfire. Maybe there was a party on the beach. As Mark approached, he realized that the blaze was coming from some homeless people who were just trying to keep warm. They welcomed him to stand near the fire. This millionaire had less clothing on than people with nothing! They even shared their whiskey. And he drank it… from their *bottle*.

The same mouth that shared passionate kisses from a stranger with hopes of unknown pleasure was now sharing swigs of desperation with homeless people. Kind, homeless people who were worried that he might freeze. They didn't know who he was, yet they shed their own clothes to protect him from the cold gusts that were staved off by the warm whiskey. Imagine Mark Taylor being protected by homeless people? Maybe being protected from himself.

The next morning he awoke with the smack of a Billy club. The police were doing their morning round-up of the homeless, and this morning, Mark Taylor was one of them. "Hey, I'm Mark Taylor, what do you think you're doing?"

The cop who smacked Mark quickly came back to Mark. He yelled to the other cop, "Hey, Mark Taylor is sleeping with homeless people!" Then he turned back to Mark as he returned his club back to his belt and offered Mark a hand up, "What are you doing here?"

"Uh, what *am I* doing here?" He questioned it too as he took the cop's hand and climbed to his feet.

Then the other cop stopped smacking people and quickly walked over to Mark and his partner. "Oh, wow. It really is him! Are you doing research for your next role?"

Mark really couldn't remember how he'd gotten there. So, he did what any good actor would. He wiped the drool off his face and gave the performance of his life – which got him sober rather quickly. "Yeah, I'm doing research, and I'm a method actor, so I came here to see what it was like," Mark said, wondering if they would buy it.

"You picked a cold night to do research, man. And this is a rough crowd. You're lucky you didn't get hurt."

They helped Mark, who stripped the loaned layers off and returned them to their owners. He said thanks to the people who helped him get through the night, and he left with the cops. They gave him a ride back to the hotel, and he gave them both autographs.

Mark walked off the elevator and headed towards Declan's room. He couldn't find his room key, but he remembered the room number. He banged on the door several times before Declan answered it, wearing only his boxer shorts, holding his head like it was about to split open.

"Hey man," Declan muttered. "I hope you had a better time than I did."

"I doubt it. I spent the night with homeless people."

"So, you *didn't* get laid last night?"

"What's the matter with you? I spent the night on the street, Declan… with *homeless* people. And I woke up to a cop whacking me with his Billy club because he thought I was homeless too."

"What happened to Tina?"

"Tammy?"

"Like it matters," Declan said as he walked over to the bar. He made himself a drink and lit a cigarette.

"She was engaged."

"So?" Declan said as he took a drag off his cigarette.

"So, she started crying, and she left me at the bar."

"Nice," Declan said, laughing. "Oh, my head." He took a sip of his drink.

"So, what happened to you?"

"That whore I brought back here left in the middle of the night."

"Why are you angry about that?"

Declan blew out a breath of smoke. "She took my wallet and both of our cell phones."

"Great," Mark said. Why in hell's name did he go anywhere with Declan?

"Let's get some breakfast."

"I guess it's on me…" Mark said, and Declan laughed again.

"You know I'm good for it – since I'm worth more than you, Mark." It didn't seem like Declan meant that just from a financial aspect.

Declan and Mark showered and went down to the hotel restaurant and ate breakfast on the beach. Declan lit up another cigarette after they finished. "I've got to figure out what project I'm going to do after this," Declan said as he exhaled a big puff of smoke.

Mark was surprised. "What do you mean? I thought you were going to Toronto."

"The studio pulled the plug."

"Are you kidding me? So now what?"

"I just got a script for a movie shooting in Brazil. You ever been?" Declan asked as he took a drag off his cigarette.

"No, I've heard it's beautiful."

"Let me just say," Declan leaned in, "the women are a lot more liberated and progressive when it comes to sex."

Mark exhaled and looked out to the ocean, wondering why he had grown so tired of this life that he used to love.

Mark and Declan decided they were going to go out again because it had worked out *so* well the night before. Of course, Mark had to pay for everything because Declan's wallet had been stolen. They wound up going to Sloppy Joe's, a famous bar in Key West. It was quite a spectacle. The place was jammed with college-age kids, most without boundaries or common sense. Just the kind of crowd Declan liked.

Mark and Declan chose their partners for the night and didn't bother to get their names. Mark woke up the next morning, and his "date" had already left – not before she got some really sobering naked pictures of Mark on her smartphone. She knew someone would pay big money for the story and photos. Mark's life was a mess, filled with events that he could not recall, and his choice of friends was not helping his poor decision-making.

Declan's "date" did not leave. He had to kick her out of the room. She wanted to spend more time with him. Who knows why? Declan wasn't particularly nice or charming. He had a huge ego and didn't have the goods to match. There were better-looking guys in Hollywood. For that matter, there were more handsome guys on the set of *Don O'Malley*. And as far as talent went, Mark was a better actor, more natural and charismatic.

When Mark and Declan met up for breakfast, they shared stories about the women they'd spent the night with. They both lit up their cigarettes and smoked away as they stared off at the ocean before them, trying not to talk about anything profound or life-affirming.

The guys had another night of binge drinking and meaningless sex. When they met the next morning, they ate breakfast and started back to Miami. Halfway there, they stopped for gas. Mark pumped the gas while Declan went into the store. He came out laughing, with a newspaper in his hand. "Hey, Mark, what did you know about that chick you spent the other night with?"

"Which one?"

"The one who was holding this camera," he said as he held up a paper in Mark's face.

Mark released the nozzle. He had no idea someone had taken pictures of him while he was passed out. He grabbed the paper from Declan's hands. "This is funny to you, Declan?"

"A little, yeah. I mean, c'mon, man. You don't fall asleep with these women. You're not in love with these women, that's why you have sex and then kick them *out*. You don't fall asleep with whores in your bed." Declan thought any publicity was good publicity, and that's what they were about, making money and getting laid. Isn't that what they were supposed to be doing? I guess if women demanded more, maybe they'd oblige, but women are just as carefree nowadays, so what does it really matter?

Mark took out the nozzle and put the gas cap back on the car. He got in the car and slammed the door. They barely spoke on the way back to Miami. Mark didn't even have his phone. There was no way to do damage control at this point. It was going to have to wait until he got back to his apartment. One thing Mark did know, Declan not only liked watching Mark self-destruct but liked pushing his buttons.

When they got back to Mark's building, Declan tried to apologize for laughing at the pictures in the paper, but Mark had had enough and didn't even acknowledge him as he grabbed his weekend bag and got out of the car.

As Mark reached his apartment door, he heard the beeping of his answering machine. He immediately walked over and saw that he had thirty messages waiting for him. Some were women looking for a night of affection. Some were from his family, but the majority were from his publicist, who was angry. Not only was this scandal out for a whole day, but without his phone, Mark couldn't even talk to anyone and explain what happened. And, he'd allowed it to happen.

To make matters worse, Peter was trying to get hold of them and couldn't. They were needed on the set, and no one knew where they were. When Mark played back the messages, he got into his car and flew down to the set.

Peter strode over to meet him. "Mark, how is everything going?"

"Fine, fine, Peter."

"You know the studio doesn't like that kind of publicity. They already have their hands full with Declan," he said, giving the 'evil eye' to Declan.

"I know, Peter. I'm sorry; I spent the night with this girl and fell asleep with her. I didn't think anyone would do something like that. It was stupid of me."

"I think maybe you and I should have a talk, Mark. I like you, and I've been in your shoes. I know it's not easy. But your life could take a very dark path if you're not careful."

"I'm okay, Peter. I promise."

"We'll see. Meanwhile, some friendly advice… stay away from Declan," he said, pointing the finger at the source of trouble. Mark just nodded. But he remembered that old adage about keeping your friends close, but your enemies closer. Mark wasn't stupid; he knew Declan was no good.

CHAPTER *Seven*

DECLAN INVITED Mark to a party at a gorgeous mansion on Collins Avenue in Miami Beach, which is known to the locals as "Millionaire's Row." Mark was hesitant because of what happened in Key West, but he went because Declan informed him there would be a lot of high-powered Hollywood executives there. It wouldn't hurt Mark to be seen with Declan and be introduced to directors and producers. The night went off without a hitch, and Mark got a meeting about a new trilogy in the development stage, and no actors were attached to it yet. Because of this, Mark gave Declan another chance. But Mark was about to get entangled in something that would haunt him for years. Poor innocent Mark, he really never means to hurt anyone.

The day before Claudia James was scheduled to show up on the set, Declan asked Mark to go out for drinks after a late night. Declan and Mark met up at the house Declan was staying in. One of Declan's friends was a retired quarterback for the Miami Dolphins and had a gorgeous house on the Intracoastal Waterway. He and his family were living in Cape Cod, so Declan had moved in and made himself right at home. He was more than happy to show Mark how life was when you're on top. It was a Tudor style mansion with an imposing wrought-iron gate that had a "W" on each side. There was a six-car garage and a beautiful pineapple water fountain in the driveway in front of the main doors.

Mark pulled up to the circular drive and hopped out of his car. When Mark knocked on the door, Declan opened it to reveal a long, narrow hallway that led to an edgeless pool overlooking the water. He noticed the picture of a football legend on the wall with his wife and kids.

"Is this Terry Webber's house?" Mark asked.

"Yeah, we've been friends since I got my breakthrough role."

"What was that?"

"Uh, *The Terry Webber Story*," Declan said. "Come on, we're taking the boat." They walked to the pool deck and then down to the dock. Mark looked at the name on the back of the boat, which was aptly named *Guilt Trip*. It would be a name that Mark would never forget. I probably shouldn't even call it a boat, it was a yacht. Mark asked Declan what was up with the boat's name, and he said that Terry's wife named it. Something about Terry getting his way instead of her getting hers.

Mark had never been on such a lavish boat before. Every part of the inside was covered with mahogany. Every inch was handcrafted. The sound system was terrific – and very loud. It was a party boat designed to impress, and it did. Mark was very impressed. He wished he had a friend who let him use his fancy house and boat. Actually, Mark wanted it all for himself. Mark was always impressed by money. In Mark's family, money was equated with happiness – whether it was real or not. People never think money brings problems, just possessions. Truthfully, it brings both, but when you try to explain that to people, they always say they'd like to try it anyway.

As the guys pulled away from the dock, Declan already

had a beer in his hand. He knew of a secluded bar where the elite drove their boats up to the pier. Declan drove the vessel with no problem. He had his Captain's license because that's just one more fun thing for rich people to brag about. Being at the helm, he told Mark to grab a beer. As Mark turned to the fridge, he saw the corner of a sign they were passing. It had a manatee on it. "What was that sign for?" he asked.

"I don't know anything about manatees. But if they're too freakin' stupid to get out of the way, they're going to become speed bumps," Declan said with a laugh as he increased their speed.

Too bad Mark didn't wear his "I brake for manatees" t-shirt. Suddenly, he felt something slam against the boat. He ran to the stern and watched the wake to see if Declan's reckless driving was flinging manatee carcasses everywhere. Mark's shoulders drooped. Why did Declan have to be such a jerk? Imagine Mark keeping his mouth shut because Declan could destroy his career, and they both knew it. Aside from the other names Mark already had for Declan, he could now add *Manatee Killer* to his repertoire. And this was just the beginning of the intense hatred that would divide these two men.

Mark returned to the bridge just in time to see Declan slam the fridge door shut. "Hey, can you take the wheel while I go get more booze?"

Mark took the wheel and pretended he was captain of his own vessel. The wood shone, and everything looked brand new. He peered over the wheel at the endless ocean and enjoyed the views as he pulled the boat into the open water and left the city behind.

Declan came back and stocked the fridge. "Okay, I've got it from here," he said as he took over the wheel. "There's a place about twenty minutes from here that has some of the hottest women in Miami."

A little while later, the guys pulled up to the dock, and

Mark hopped out to tie the boat down. Declan came out a minute later, and they walked up toward the bar. There were beautiful people everywhere. Some were made by God, but most by science. Most people don't know when they've gone too far with plastic surgery. Here's a hint; if you look like The Joker from Batman, you know you've crossed the line. Imagine your face being so tight that you can no longer express any emotion. Personally, I love ventriloquists. But, etiquette says that when you're asked about someone's cosmetic surgery, you're supposed to say, "Yes, you look very natural." Very natural for what? If you resemble a villain from a comic book or a character from Star Wars, it's not a good sign. But it does give the rest of us something to talk about... so thanks!

When Mark and Declan strolled up to the bar, the bartender slung Declan a beer and said, "How's it going, Declan?"

"Good, man. This is my friend, Mark."

"Hey, Mark. What are you drinking?"

Before Mark could answer, a woman came up to the bar and slammed down a twenty. "Whatever he's drinking, I'm buying." Mark turned around to see Natasha West standing there in a peach-colored bikini and a smile. She was a beautiful plus-sized supermodel who was in every fashion magazine at the time. They had never met before, but they knew each other just from being famous. Just so I'm clear, she was only a *size eight*. I know, you think that's not plus-sized! Au contraire! A size eight model or actress may seem reasonable to you and me, but to the people who control our thoughts – Hollywood and the fashion world – that's considered *morbidly obese*! Poor Marilyn Monroe wouldn't stand a chance now! No. They want our actresses and models to look like those starving children on late-night TV that need a sponsor. I wonder if anorexic movie stars have flies circling them in person, too. Maybe that's why there are so many celebrities who are divas. Could it be that they're not pouty or difficult? Perhaps they just need a good cheeseburger and some fries.

"Hi," Mark said.

"Hi, Mark Taylor." She hopped up on a barstool. "So, tell me, are you like your character in *The Trifecta*, or are you nicer than that?"

"No, I'm nicer than that guy," he said with a coy smile as he told the bartender he wanted a Jack and Coke.

"Oh, that's too bad, I kind of like bad guys," she said.

"I can be as bad as you want me to be," Mark said as the bartender set his drink down. He threw it back almost as fast as he got it.

A couple of hours later, after many drinks and dancing, Natasha and Mark were drunk. Natasha was all over Mark, but her friend, Britt, who was a regular-sized model, wasn't really into Declan. Maybe she saw through him, or perhaps it was the fact that she had just been drinking Diet Coke all night while the others were consuming anything they could. When the girls went to the bathroom, Mark went to the bar to get more drinks while Declan stayed behind at the table. Declan looked around and then slipped something into Britt's drink before the others returned to the table. When they sat down, Britt downed her drink. A few minutes later, she slipped to the floor, unconscious. Natasha got down on the floor with her friend and slapped her face gently, but she was too intoxicated to understand what was really happening. "Britt, are you okay?" She looked at Mark, "She doesn't drink because she can't handle it. We have to get her back to our hotel."

"She *is* a model, maybe she passed out because she didn't eat enough," Declan said. "I can see you don't have that problem." Isn't he a charmer?

"You don't know anything about her, so why don't you shut up, Declan?" Natasha said.

"C'mon Declan," Mark said. "We need to get her back to the hotel."

Declan had another idea. "Listen, you guys are hitting it off, why don't you let me take her back, and you two can go back to my place for the night. Or you all can just stay at my house tonight, and we'll give you a ride back to the hotel tomorrow. Where are you staying?"

"Fontainebleau."

"That's right on Collins Ave, right near the set. We can drop you off tomorrow," Declan said.

Natasha looked at Mark and Declan as they carried Britt between them, with her feet dangling in white designer sandals in the air, all the way to the boat. "Okay, I guess we'll stay with you guys tonight."

They got to the boat, and Mark put Britt on her back on a white leather sofa. When Mark looked at Declan, he was starting the engine. Mark and Natasha went below deck and left Britt, passed out – with Declan. They weren't concerned at all about Declan being alone with Britt. She was unconscious. What could possibly happen? Declan heard Mark and Natasha having a good time, so he put the boat on course for the house. Then he pulled out his phone and moved closer to Britt…

CHAPTER
Eight

THE NEXT MORNING, Britt ran down the stairs and woke up Natasha. They went into the bathroom that was in the cabin that Mark and Natasha were using. They slammed the door.

"What is going on?" Natasha said with little concern.

"I had sex last night."

"So did I."

"*No*…I don't *remember* anything, Natasha."

Now Natasha was getting concerned. "What do you mean? Like Declan put something in your drink?"

"Or Mark? I don't drink. Why would I pass out? And I know I had sex last night," she said, tears running down her face.

"Mark wouldn't do that. Plus, he was with me all night."

"You think you know Mark after one night with him? We don't know *either* of them. I'm telling you – one of them did something to me."

"What do you want to do – call the police?"

"God, no! I don't want anyone to know about this. Let's just get the hell out of here."

Mark woke up to a very messy, empty bed and shrieking.

He sat up and rubbed his eyes and yelled to the bathroom, "What's going on in there?"

Crying, Britt came out of the bathroom with Natasha.

What the hell did Declan do to her? "What's the matter?"

"Nothing. We're leaving."

Mark got out of bed, pulling the sheets carefully around his abs. "What happened?"

As Britt stood there with her arms crossed, Natasha put her shoes on and gathered her things. She didn't know exactly what happened, but she knew that Britt thought something happened and she believed her.

"We're leaving, Mark."

"I'll give you a ride back to your hotel."

"Don't bother, we already called a cab."

Mark walked up to Natasha and put his hands on her arms. "Look, I don't know what's going on here, but can I see you again?"

She shook him off. "That's not going to happen, Mark."

"What did I do?"

"Ask your friend, Declan," she said. Then she and Britt climbed up to the deck and practically ran to the main road to wait for their cab, which came almost immediately.

Declan was nowhere on the boat. Mark went into the house and found him asleep on the sofa. Declan's phone started ringing as Mark approached the couch.

Mark picked it up. "Hey, you want me to answer this?"

That panicked Declan. "No! Put that down."

Mark thought this was a strange reaction. By the time Declan got up, it had stopped ringing.

"What did you do to Britt last night?"

"Nothing. She was a frigid bitch. You know nothing happened between us. Can you make some coffee? I need to hop into the shower; we're both on the call sheet for ten o'clock."

"Sure, Declan," Mark said, but he noticed Declan clinging

tightly to his phone. Mark had to see what Declan was hiding. Declan went into the bathroom and took his phone with him.

Mark made coffee while he tried to figure out what Declan did. Mark started replaying the night's events over in his mind. He couldn't remember some of it, but he did remember that Britt drank only soda. And then he remembered that she passed out. Why would someone who doesn't drink pass out? Declan must have drugged her. When Declan got dressed and came down from the shower, Mark told him he had a headache and asked if he had anything he could take.

Mark followed him to the medicine cabinet and kept asking if he had anything stronger. Finally, Mark just grabbed an unmarked bottle, and Declan snatched it out of his hand. "No, not those."

Mark stared at him.

"Uh, those are a prescription. And it would be illegal for you to take those." Suddenly Declan cared about the law. Declan handed Mark two ibuprofen, and he swallowed them.

They went back to the kitchen, and Declan got out two cups and started pouring the coffee. He pulled his phone out of his hoodie and laid it on the counter. Mark perked up. He had to see what was on that phone. So he pretended he couldn't find his own phone.

"Oh, man. I can't find my phone. Do you think I left it on the boat? I need it. It's got my schedule on it. Would you mind seeing if I left it out there?" Mark asked as he gestured to the boat. Then Mark looked at his watch. "Wow, man, we gotta go."

"Yeah, I'll take a look," Declan said and hurried out to the dock. But Mark picked up Declan's phone and started looking through the photos.

Mark was horrified at what he saw. He put his hand over his mouth. This man, this monster… so loved by the media, yet he was the devil himself.

"I swear to God, I'm really going to quit drinking this

time," Mark said out loud. He could've prevented the whole thing. But now what? Should he go to the police or confront Declan? This could ruin his career. He couldn't have Declan *against* him. But how could he go on, knowing what Declan did to this poor girl? If ever Mark was in a bad spot, it was now. Does he help this girl or save his career? He knew what the right thing was, but could he do it? Mark put the phone back on the counter in the exact same spot.

He went over to the living room and started looking under the sofa and behind the pillows. He'd faked losing his phone pretty well, considering it was in his back pocket the whole time.

Declan came back in. "It's not in the boat. Are you sure you took it out of your car?"

"Yeah, remember I got that text from my agent?"

"That's right. I'll just call you, and then we'll hear the ring."

Mark had to agree even though his butt was about to ring. "Yeah, good idea." The phone rang, and he grabbed it. "Oh, I'm such an idiot." He pulled his phone out and waved it. "Sorry."

"That's okay, you have it now." While they drank their coffee, Mark stared Declan down. What an awful person he was.

"What?"

"Nothing. We should probably go," Mark said. Declan and Mark both drove to the set. Mark was contemplating his next move the whole time. Should he do the *right* thing and ruin his career or keep his mouth shut and keep working... Hmm, tough choice, making movies, or performing the dinner show at Medieval Times? Mark never did care for horses very much…

CHAPTER *Nine*

LATER THAT DAY, Mark intended to head for his trailer to rehearse his lines. But when he hopped out of his car, that's when he saw *her*. He had never seen Claudia in person – she was even prettier than he had imagined. She noticed him and gave him a huge wave and smile. He smiled back, and they walked towards each other while Declan spoke with the Assistant Director. Mark heard barking as she approached.

She was only 5'3". She had long brown hair and green eyes. She was wearing a pink sequined top and jeans with five-inch heels that no one can walk in. She tip-toed over to him like a malnourished flamingo. "Hi, I'm Claudia," she said as she shook his hand. Her Yorkshire Terrier was yipping its little head off. It was in the bag hanging from Claudia's shoulder.

"Hi. Mark Taylor. How's it going?" he asked. He was nervous but tried to be suave and cool.

She smiled. "I need to go to my trailer, but I'll see you in a little bit."

Claudia's assistant came over to her and tried to feed Claudia's dog tap water because it was panting. Mark heard Claudia yell at the poor girl that her dog only drinks Evian.

Duh! Everyone knows that dogs can *taste* the difference. They have such sophisticated palettes. It's true; toilet-lickers know the best stuff. Okay, so Claudia's kind of a jerk. But Mark's just looking for someone who will help boost his career. She's the type that will give him much more than a boost.

As they walked their separate ways, they both turned around and looked back at each other. That was it. Mark had it in his head that they would hook up on the set. Not a bad catch for him right now. He already imagined what their combined name would be in the media. All the coolest celebrities had their names mixed.

She was fun, too. She liked to party. She was no woman to take home to Mama – only thirty-one and already divorced several times. She also had babies, but that didn't stop her from changing boyfriends almost as frequently as her nannies changed her kids' diapers. Yet she was thought of very highly by her fans. They didn't see anything wrong with her life-style. At least her kids would be screwed up by her nanny and not by her since she hardly spent any time with them.

Claudia had a new clothing line out and was trying to launch a home décor company. She traveled whenever she wasn't making a movie, always in different cities than her kids. Different states, even. Those kids were just a product of a short marriage – clearly the only kind she was capable of having. At least they didn't affect her lifestyle.

They finished their scenes and then made plans to have dinner later, blowing off Declan completely. Claudia and Declan had no scenes together as yet. Mark knew if he was going to have Claudia, he needed to close the deal tonight.

The two of them met up later at Larios in Miami Beach. They were photographed several times before even entering the restaurant. They didn't realize it, but Declan had followed them too, almost as closely as the paparazzi. Declan made his way to the bar and had a drink while he observed the two getting closer at dinner. Then he decided to make his move.

He came over with a drink in his hand and turned a chair around and sat in it backward. "Hey. I didn't know you were coming here, we could've all driven together."

"Hi, Declan," Claudia said.

"Hey man, what are you doing here?" Mark asked, gritting his teeth.

"Oh, I heard they make killer slow-roasted pork. You don't mind if I join you, do you?" Declan asked as turned the chair around and got comfortable.

Before they could answer, the waiter came over to help Declan. Declan wasn't shy about placing his order and asking for another drink. Mark gave him a look that said 'beat it,' but if Declan got the hint, he didn't take it.

"Sure, Declan, we're just talking about work," Claudia said.

"Oh, good, I thought I might be interrupting something," he said. "I wouldn't want to interrupt you if you're on a date or something."

"Well, actually, Declan..." Mark began, but Claudia interrupted.

"It's fine, Declan, you're not interrupting anything."

Mark was taken aback by this comment. Was she not attracted to him? He thought he had felt some spark between them. She *couldn't* be interested in Declan, he was such a jerk. What kind of woman would want him instead of Mark? With all of Mark's character flaws, he was still a better man than Declan could ever be. Mark would never make a woman do anything she didn't want to. *He* wasn't a monster. He's not like the characters he plays. Yet Claudia sat there, twirling her hair and laughing at Declan's un-amusing stories.

Declan shot Mark as look as if to say, "I won." Then he gave Mark a really mischievous smile. Mark had thought Declan would back off, but Mark's temporary acquisition of Claudia only made Declan want her more.

They all ate dinner in almost total silence.

"So, Claudia, how are those adorable kids of yours?" Declan asked.

"They're great, Declan. Thanks for asking," she said.

"I love kids, don't you, Mark?" he asked.

Mark just stared at him. Clearly, Declan shouldn't be around women, never mind kids. "Claudia, what are you doing this weekend?" Declan asked. "My friend has a really nice boat. I'd love to show you. I could take you out somewhere really nice – if you like," he said as he looked smugly at Mark, "I mean unless you have a boyfriend or something." Mark looked at Declan in horror at the thought of him taking Claudia to the scene of the crime.

Claudia looked at Mark, who wasn't being aggressive enough for her taste. "As it happens, I *don't* have plans for the weekend," she said, turning back to Declan.

"Really? Well, it's only a few days away. What do you say – you, me, and a romantic dinner in South Beach? I know exactly where to take you," Declan said.

"Yeah, that sounds great," she said, then remembered that she was on a date with Mark. She glanced over at Mark, who looked like a deer in headlights. He was livid, and you could tell. His face was red, and he had a vein popping out of each side of his neck. He ran his fingers through his hair and kept looking around to see if anyone was watching or listening. Declan loved it. He had a big smile on his face as he leaned back in his seat.

"Is that okay with you, Mark?" she asked. Now, there was no attachment between them, they hadn't even shared dessert, never mind anything else. What could Mark say? He'd look like an idiot if he tried to prevent it now.

He tried to recover. He looked at his watch, "No, that's fine, you two seem like you have a lot in common. Besides, I'm on the call sheet for five a.m., so I'm going to call it a night." Mark signaled to the waiter for the check.

Declan drained his glass. "That's right… those downtown

shots that had to be rescheduled because of your stint at rehab. You know, Mark, they haven't cast my sidekick yet in my next movie. I could call the director and put in a good word," he said with a wink. "Would you like that, Mark? You want me to make a phone call? It wouldn't hurt you to hitch your star to my wagon."

Mark just sat there, fuming, but trying not to show it. "Mark, Declan's doing you a huge favor," said Claudia. "That movie is getting a lot of buzz. It would be good for you to be attached to it…" She looked at Declan. "That's so nice of you to help someone like Mark out like that."

"Someone like me? What's that supposed to mean?"

"It's just that Declan's *established*. He can help you, Mark. He must really think you're talented to be pulling strings on your behalf."

"I've made it this far without his help."

Declan just smiled. "I *do* think you're talented, Mark," he said sarcastically. "You know the best part about your acting? You know when to be *quiet*." And at that moment, Mark realized Declan knew that he'd figured out what he had done to Britt, and Declan didn't *care*.

Claudia nodded in agreement. Mark couldn't believe Declan was buying his silence. Mark knew Declan could destroy his career. It wasn't about Claudia at this point. It was about Mark and Declan. Declan just smiled and nodded at Mark's powerlessness. He loved every moment of the discomfort he was causing Mark. They all chatted for a little, and then the check came. Mark paid for it and then looked at Claudia. "I'm exhausted; I think I'm going to just cut out on you guys. Declan, I trust that you'll walk Claudia to her car, so she gets home safely."

"Oh, sure, Mark. I'll make sure nothing bad happens to her," Declan said with a wink and a small laugh as he raised his glass to Mark and drank the contents.

"Goodnight, Claudia," Mark said.

"Goodnight, Mark," she said without even looking up.

"See you tomorrow, man," Declan said, moving over into Mark's chair. Mark totally ignored him. Declan was chuckling as he walked away.

Mark walked to his car and got in. He put the keys in the ignition and watched them swinging for a few seconds. He sat there, wondering how he lost control of that whole situation. He vowed to himself that he would steer clear of Declan and his path of destruction.

When he got home, Mark went straight to the kitchen. He was so mad at himself for not telling Declan where to go, embarrassed that he let Declan win. He didn't even attempt to fight for Claudia. He looked weak, and he knew it. He wasn't a pushover. Why did he allow that to happen? He wanted her, and he was so close to having her too.

He replayed the night's events in his mind, coming up with the right things to say. What good does that do? He opened his liquor cabinet and pulled out a bottle of Jack Daniels. He pulled a highball glass out of his cabinet, unscrewed the cap, and was about to pour it into his glass. But then he decided, why not just drink out of the bottle? Why not? No one was around. Who cares? At least he could control what he did in his own house.

He could control what he drank when he drank and how he drank. The one element he couldn't control was *why* he drank. And he didn't want to think about why. He just wanted to stop thinking about what Declan did to Britt, what he was doing to Mark, and what he was *going* to do to Claudia. He knew that they were going to spend the night together, and he just kept thinking it should've been him instead.

CHAPTER *Ten*

MARK HATED HIMSELF. He felt like he was in a teenage horror movie, and he let the prom queen leave with the killer. Mark walked into the living room with the bottle, and he held it up to the light and then paused. He got angry, so he turned around and went back into the kitchen to pour that bottle right down the sink. Standing over that sink, he thought how alone he was. Mark was asking himself his favorite question, "Why can't I find someone to love me?"

He grabbed the bottle of Jack Daniels he'd sworn he would pour down the sink and poured it down his throat instead. He slid down the kitchen cabinets to the floor with the bottle in his hand and just starting crying. No one cared. He didn't understand why no one loved him. Maybe he'd be better off dead. Then perhaps people would care. Drinking was supposed to help him forget how empty his life was, but it just seemed to make him angrier, and he didn't forget – in fact, his memories played back like one of his movies.

He kept drinking until that bottle was empty. It wasn't full, to begin with, but it was more than anyone should drink in one sitting. He passed out, and when he woke the next morning, he really had to pee. Unfortunately, he mistook a lovely potted plant next to the toilet for a urinal, which was odd since he didn't have one. He stumbled back to the sofa and went back to sleep.

He was startled by his cell phone and house phone ringing at the same time. He was late for work, and they'd been trying to get hold of him, to no avail. He finally picked up his phone, not realizing how late he was. He was always punctual. Mark was still a perfectionist on the set unless it came to mixing business with pleasure. That had changed as he got older and lonelier. Maybe he was no better than Claudia. He was only in his thirties, but he felt more aged from all the hard-living over the last few years. Life had turned out much different than he'd planned. Doesn't it always? Mark had desired to be married by now. He figured that was his only shot at being tamed. He *wanted* to be tamed. He didn't want to live this self-destructive lifestyle. He needed a strong woman, and he knew it – a woman who would put him before herself, his career before hers – a woman who would let him be a man.

Mark was out of control and had been for a while, and no one seemed concerned except Peter. But Peter was just worried that Mark was going to screw up his movie. How did this happen? He had never missed work before, and because of drinking and drama, no less.

He hated the idea of seeing Declan and Claudia on the set. He despised the thought of losing someone else he liked because of Declan. He wasn't much of a friend, so what kind of man would he be to any woman? He should be locked up, not getting involved with Claudia. Despite the fact she wasn't looking for anyone permanent, she definitely didn't deserve the kind of man Declan was. She wasn't marriage material, and she was self-absorbed. Mark knew she wasn't the kind of person to share the limelight with someone and put their career first, or change Mark's wild ways, yet it didn't soften the blow.

Mark got cleaned up quickly, and then he raced down to the set as fast as he could. He apologized profusely as Peter came over to his make-up chair.

"What happened, Mark? This isn't like you," Peter said.

"Sorry, I had a late night last night, and I slept through my alarm," Mark said.

"Will you excuse us?" Peter asked the make-up artist who was working on Mark. She nodded and walked away.

"Mark, I know you're drinking again. You can't let your friendship with Declan affect your work. We have a schedule, and we need to stick with it. I have the studio breathing down my neck because of weather delays; I don't need some out-of-control actor causing more delays. Look at Declan – I know he's hungover, he reeks of alcohol, yet here he is, on time and ready to work. He even *memorized* his lines..."

"I'm sorry, Peter. It won't happen again."

"It better not, Mark."

"It won't."

"Good," Peter said as he walked away. Mark just sat there glaring at Claudia and Declan laughing together as the costume designer put last-minute touches on Claudia's clothes. Mark got up and walked over to his mark on the set. His first scene was with Declan.

"Hey Mark, how was your night last night?" Declan asked smugly.

Mark just looked at him. He was still angry about what happened. How could he not be? Declan bought him off and made him look like a fool. Declan continued on, but Mark just wanted him to shut up.

Declan spoke so softly, he made sure no one could hear him except Mark. "Claudia is insatiable. She's a freak – even compared to the women *I've* been with. I knew she was going to pick me over you. It helps when you have your own production company," Declan said with a laugh. Mark just ignored him.

As the weeks went by, while Declan and Claudia managed to keep their relationship out of the media, Declan threw his relationship with Claudia right in Mark's face as much as he could. He acted so sweet, like bringing her coffee and buying her flowers. Had Declan not already harassed most of the women on the set, they might've thought he was terrific. But the female crew members just rolled their eyes when Claudia said how great Declan was. It was all an act, but that's why Declan gets the big bucks, isn't it?

Mark thought about Britt and how he could've stopped the whole thing if he had only been sober. He replayed every moment he spent with Natasha and Claudia back in his mind. He even had nightmares about what happened. Imagine the kind of nightmares Britt was having.

Nothing lasts forever, especially in a Hollywood fairy tale. Two months later, Declan and Claudia were fighting on the set, and they were very loud about it. Mark and everyone else tried to ignore it, but they were extraordinarily unprofessional by shouting in front of everyone instead of taking it back to their trailers. Mark wondered how people who haven't been together that long could get into such a heated argument.

Later that night, Mark heard a knock on his apartment door. He opened it, and before he could say anything, Claudia threw her arms around him and kissed him. He pulled her inside and shut the door. They kissed again.

"What about Declan?" he asked.

"This isn't about Declan. It's about you and me."

"I don't want any more meaningless relationships, Claudia."

"That's why I'm not with Declan. I'm ready for this, Mark. I'm sorry it took me so long to see that you were the one I should've picked."

They went into the bedroom, and Mark regretted it almost as soon as it was over. As they lay in bed, Mark smoked a cigarette and stared at the clock, deciding how to ask Claudia when she was going to leave. It was a relief when her cell phone rang.

She went over to her purse on a chair in Mark's room and pulled the phone out. The nanny had called her to tell her that one of her kids was sick. Claudia screamed at the nanny to take her to the emergency room and call if anything changed.

He waited for her to come back to the bed, "Is everything okay?" Mark asked as Claudia crawled back into bed and nuzzled into Mark's neck.

"Yeah, my daughter has a temperature of a hundred and three. The nanny is too stupid to figure out that she should take her to the emergency room. I swear I don't know what I pay these people for..."

"Are they in L.A.?"

"No, they're in my house in South Beach."

"They're *here*? Do you want me to take you to the hospital?"

"No. I'm here with you. I don't let my kids get in the way of my life."

"In the *way*?" Mark sat up and put his cigarette out on an ashtray on his nightstand.

"Yeah, I don't let them affect my *love* life," she said condescendingly as she sat up too, "No one gets between mama and her sexy time." Whew! Claudia was definitely a model parent. The magazines had it right. She did have it all! When you have money, you *can* have it all! And, better yet, you're not the one who has to take care of it!

Mark processed the words she was saying. He didn't understand how any woman could say such things about her children. Her words disgusted him. *Him!* He had already grown tired of her and her lack of affection for her children. How could she truly love someone if she couldn't even love the ones that came from her flesh?

"You know what?" he asked.

"What?" she asked as she touched his face lovingly.

"I think you need to leave and be with your family," Mark said as he got out of the bed and started getting dressed.

She threw the sheet off and shot out of bed. She shoved her arms into her shirt and yanked her jeans on. Then she sat on his bed and zipped her boots up, yelling at Mark the whole time. "Who the hell are you to tell me what I need, huh? You can't even take care of yourself. You think you'd be a better parent than me? You have no idea…"

"*Oh my God,* can you shut up and go?" Mark said as he put his hand to his head because she was giving him a headache.

Well, as you may have suspected, Claudia did not like being told to shut up. At least she left, not quietly, though. She was barking like her little dog the whole way to the front door.

CHAPTER *Eleven*

THE NEXT MORNING on the set, when Mark walked by Claudia and Declan, it was evident they were back together. Mark shook his head. It repulsed him that if Declan got too close to Claudia, he might smell Mark all over her. Mark thought about what a pig Claudia was to go back to Declan the very next day after she and Mark had sex. Mark didn't understand the head games she was playing. Maybe Claudia and Declan deserved each other.

There was more drama behind the scenes than in front of the camera. Claudia was still flirting with Mark even though it was clear that she was with Declan now. Mark was not responding to her come-ons.

One morning while making his coffee, Mark heard the thud of his morning paper against his apartment door. He opened the door, grabbed the paper, poured his coffee, and sat down. Pulling the newspaper out of the plastic wrap, he saw the headline, *"Declan O'Conner and Claudia James Fall in Love on Set of New Movie."*

Mark was appalled that this was front-page news. They were going out all over Miami and not trying to keep the relationship quiet anymore. He scanned the article, and the worst part was *they* were given a combined name, "Declaudia." Mark frowned. He was so angry after seeing and hearing the name all over the place that he decided to start referring to them as "De-clawed." That made him feel better. It even brought a little smile to his face, but he wished Declan was *neutered* instead of "De-clawed." Mark Taylor lost again! Enter more self-loathing here for our friend, Mark. What was wrong with him? Why couldn't he find someone to love him? Yes, he liked to drink and had a hard time stopping, but there was a lovable man in there somewhere. At that point, he decided he would find someone to love, even if it was just for the *night*.

Mark woke up naked in a panic, and in a strange bed. He sat up and looked around. He didn't recognize anything, but he could tell by the cheap, mismatched furniture that he was on the wrong side of the tracks. He pulled back the dusty blue-and-white checkered curtains and looked out the window. He'd seen a similar scene in neighborhoods he drove by – and he drove by them *quickly*. A car sat on its rims in the yard next door, more grass growing on the car than on the lawn itself. Appliances sat outside the houses, and dogs ran around unleashed, doing their business everywhere they could. How did he get there?

He then heard the shower running and got nervous about who was in it. The water sounded very loud to him. Women tended to be a little more attractive after he'd had five or six drinks.

Mark slithered out of bed and gathered his clothes from the night before. His head was throbbing, but he couldn't let that stop him. He had to get out of there! He got both legs in and started putting on his loafers. He was about to pull his shirt all the way down his torso when the water stopped. She was getting out of the shower. Mark said, "God, I swear if you make my head stop pounding, I will *never* drink again!" He heard the bathroom door handle turn and start opening. He tensed up. *What* was going to step out of the bathroom?

"Good morning," said his apparent lover, Emmy Lou, in a country drawl. He thought it was disturbing; this was the only *Emmy* he'd ever had his hands on. He was scared now. In front of him stood a woman who was a little bigger than his usual "type." She was about ninety pounds bigger than his usual – a hundred pounds bigger than his Hollywood girlfriends.

He convinced himself she must have a good *personality*. She wasn't beautiful, but not bad looking. Surely she *must* have redeeming qualities. She had most of her teeth, which was a bonus. She trotted over to the bed in her towel, which did not look sexy – in fact, Mark was feeling nauseous, and it wasn't from drinking. She hadn't even dried off, her hair was dripping everywhere. She looked as if she'd wanted to hurry up before Mark bailed like she knew he would. He couldn't remember anything about this woman. What could they have talked about? Maybe they didn't speak. Perhaps they just had sex all night. Mark gagged.

"So, I was thinking, maybe we could have dinner tonight," she said. "I get off at six."

That's something. She works. "Where do you work again?" Mark asked. He hoped it was at a homeless shelter or a school for special needs kids. Please let her have some redeemable humanity about her!

Again with that southern drawl, she said, "I work at *Wal-Mart,* silly."

Wal-Mart? Could this get any worse?

"Don't you remember? I'm the manager of the children's department. Don't you just love children? I can't wait to have a bunch," she said as she dropped the towel and started getting dressed.

Mark looked at her and almost dry heaved. This girl was a train wreck. Mark was horrified, yet he couldn't turn away.

Did he have sex with her last night? Seriously? There was not enough Jack Daniels in all of Miami that would make him sleep with *her*.

She giggled. "I can't believe you're up this early. We went to bed so late. I can't even believe you can walk! You're an animal, Mark Taylor."

Mark finished dressing in record time. He pulled his shirt down to his waist and grabbed his wallet and car keys off the dresser. "I would love to have dinner, but I'm really busy with work. I told you last night, right?"

"Oh, I understand, I was just thinking…"

"So, last night… you didn't take any pictures, did you?"

"Don't worry, Mark. I deleted everything off my phone last night," she said with a smile.

Mark sighed. "Oh, thank God." Then he smiled at her.

"There was no need to keep them since I posted them on Facebook. Plus, there were so many people at that honky-tonk anyway. Shoot, you should've seen yourself ridin' that bull. I knew I was going to take you home right then," she said.

Mark was horrified. He was *riding a bull?* At a *honky-tonk* bar? That did *not* sound like Mark Taylor. His head throbbed even harder. Surely he wasn't seen holding this girl in the bar. They must've hooked up in the parking lot, under the street lights, away from the crowd. Dear God, let it have been away from spectators.

Nope. The pictures were on all forms of social media. They were everywhere short of billboards and pizza boxes.

Mark said he had to go and apologized profusely to whoever this girl was. He practically ran outside, and then he realized his car wasn't there. Or… was it there and got stolen? His vehicle was worth more than the whole neighborhood! Why couldn't he remember? Whose idea was it for Mark to go to a *honky-tonk* bar?

He knocked on her door, and she came over quickly and smiled. "Couldn't stay away, huh?" she asked.

Mark just groaned, "Listen, I can't remember where my car is. Do you know where it is?"

She got serious and wasn't trying to be cute with a southern drawl anymore. "It's back at your apartment," she said with no accent.

Mark looked relieved and then didn't understand why it would be there.

"I'll give you a ride," she said. So Mark waited on the steps of her house until she came out with the keys to her car.

Mark hated not remembering the night's events. It was humiliating. Everything about it was humbling. Her car was disgusting. There were empty fast-food bags everywhere. What *was* that horrible odor? It smelled like a body was decomposing in the vehicle. He tried to account for his situation. He was at a strange bar, with a strange woman – he probably did weird things with her, and he had no recollection of any of the events that had taken place.

When she started the car, Mark had to start asking her questions. "Why did we come back here if we were at my apartment? I don't know why we would've left my place…"

She was getting irritated. "You need to be more careful, Mark."

Mark whipped his head towards her. "Excuse me? Who the hell are you to judge me? I slept with you last night. You should be *thanking* me."

She laughed, but she was angry. "Thanking you? What do you think you did to me that would make me grateful?" He started to give her directions. "I know where you live, Mark. Remember? I was there last night," she said.

Mark got really mad. "No! I *don't* remember. Why the hell did we end up at your place?"

"Because that's the way it was supposed to be," she said.

"What are you talking about?"

"You'll see," she said as they got closer to his building. Mark kept interrogating her, but she would not give him direct answers to his questions. Something was off. Nothing was making sense, and he was getting frustrated at her evasiveness. He made her drop him off about a block from his apartment building. He slammed the door and walked over to the next corner. How could he have spent the night with *her*? And what the hell happened? It felt like Mark was set up. Ah, maybe he was just paranoid.

CHAPTER *Twelve*

ON THE SET, the story was out. Declan was kind enough to brief anyone who hadn't already heard about the story. Declan was glad to show the pictures and videos. When Declan saw Mark walking towards his trailer, he almost skipped over to him. In front of everyone, he yelled, "So, Mark, how was your adventure with your big country girlfriend from the redneck bar? You sure looked like you were having fun riding that bull. And I didn't mean your date, I meant the actual *bull*. Yeehaw! I didn't know you liked 'em big, Mark. More cushion for the pushin' right?" Declan laughed with some of the crew members.

Mark just ignored them and walked to the tables provided by craft services to grab some breakfast. Two overweight female crew members went out of their way to say good morning with huge smiles. He gave them both phony smiles and took his plate to his trailer.

Mark sat down to eat, but there was a knock on the door. "Now what?" He was so annoyed, he didn't even bother getting up, he just yelled, "Come in," as he continued to chow down. It was Claudia. That made him stop eating for a minute.

"What now?" he asked as she sat down next to him.

"How are you doing?" she asked sympathetically. "I'm sorry, Declan's such an ass. I made a mistake."

Well, that sure made his ears perk up. "You did? And what was that mistake exactly?"

"Declan's a jerk, and you're not. Declan wouldn't be caught with a fat girl, and you don't care. You like people for who they are."

That wasn't *exactly* true. Mark wasn't thrilled with his associations of late. Being drunk and lonely is not a good combination. Not only do you wake up with a hangover, but sometimes you wake up with a husky redneck who took you home simply because she liked the way you rode a mechanical bull. And when you live in the public eye, with social media, there's no escaping every mistake you make.

"Yeah, about that, I…"

Claudia put her hand on his. "It doesn't matter, we both made a mistake. Maybe it's not too late to try again. I told Declan I don't want to see him anymore."

"Why?"

"I don't know. There's something about him I don't like. I woke up this morning and the way he was looking at me… I can't describe it. It was off. I know that sounds crazy. It wasn't like he was thinking I looked like an angel when I was sleeping. It was more like he could hurt me when I'm sleeping, and I wouldn't even see it coming."

"Declan *is* unstable. He's a bad person, Claudia. I can't tell you why. You have to trust me. You need to stay away from him. And, I'm sorry; you and I will never be together. You chose Declan, and I don't want to be with someone who would choose Declan over me. I'm not perfect, Claudia. But I'm not like Declan."

Declan had proven himself to be one of the most selfish, out-of-control, wicked predators that one could meet. Mark wondered what Claudia ever saw in him. It was clear that

Declan didn't really care about her or her kids. And Claudia had no idea what a monster he was.

"Please, just have dinner with me tonight," she pleaded.

Mark gave her a smile. "I don't think that's a good idea. I think I need to be alone right now. But thanks."

"Do you have feelings for that mechanical bull girl?"

"No! I just think I need to focus on my career right now."

No one says no to Claudia! She wasn't thrilled with Mark, and she told him so. But he thought adding her to his mess right now wasn't such a great idea. She didn't understand it, but Mark already had to deal with an angry woman – his publicist. He didn't need another angry woman around him right now. Claudia left in a huff, and Mark went home at the end of the day.

Mark stopped at a Japanese restaurant on the way back to his apartment and grabbed some sushi for dinner. He turned on the television and then walked back to the kitchen to take the food out of the bag and pour himself a Jack and Coke. He was standing at the counter with the glass touching his bottom lip when an ad came on the TV. *Do you or someone you love struggle with addiction? You are not alone; please contact a counselor in your area for free at (555) 725-HELP."*

Mark paused the ad and stared at the TV, long after the announcement had ended. He looked at the drink in his hand, poured it down the sink, and went over to the phone. He sighed and dialed the number. He sat down in the living room and talked to the counselor for a half hour. Mark didn't use his real name, but he did get some information about Alcoholics Anonymous meetings in the area. This was Miami; there were several meetings he could go to. There was one right down the road. Mark decided to go the next night, but he wouldn't tell anyone. What if he failed and started drinking again? No one could know. This *had* to work. He couldn't go on having blackouts and waking up not knowing where he was or what happened. Or worse – waking up knowing something terrible happened to someone, and he could've prevented it. And then this latest thing with Mark having no idea how he wound up on the wrong side of the tractor. What a mess.

Mark wasn't on the call sheet for the next day. Since he wasn't needed on the set, he went to his house to check on the progress of the renovation. He walked into the house from the side door of the garage and into the kitchen. Everything was coming together. It wouldn't be much longer now. Mark walked outside to his lanai and eyed a boat that was pulling away from his neighbor's house. Mark didn't know the people on the boat, but they waved at Mark. He smiled and waved back and then went back inside after looking at the view for a few minutes.

Mark still had a little time before his A.A. meeting started, so he went to the grocery store, and as he was checking out, he saw the cover of a tabloid magazine with his picture and the headline, "*Mark Taylor's Health Crisis.*"

Mark's shoulders sank as he unloaded the groceries from his cart unto the conveyor belt and then picked up the magazine. It had a picture of him passed out in a booth at the bar next to the mechanical bull while onlookers laughed and pointed. Mark realized that the girl's story didn't make sense. No way was she strong enough to carry him out of the bar, and Mark was in no condition to walk into her house, never mind have sex with her. He wanted to look at the photographs, but there were too many to flip through.

Mark tossed the magazine onto the belt along with his other purchases, and without looking up, the clerk said as she scanned it, "Can you believe this guy? He needs to go to rehab and get help before he kills himself!" Then she looked up and saw that it was *him*. She turned red. "I'm so sorry. I didn't know it was you. I'm so embarrassed."

"It's okay, I'm always embarrassed," he said matter-of-factly as he grabbed his bags, winked at the clerk, and left.

Mark went back to his apartment, and before he unloaded the groceries, he pulled the magazine out and studied the pictures. There was no way that the girl carried him home or drove his car. There had to be other people involved. Something sinister was going on. Mark did have a drinking problem, but this was something more significant. Someone was trying to destroy Mark and any credibility he had. But who? Who had something to gain from Mark's destruction? Declan, of course. Mark put the groceries away, made dinner, and then re-examined the pictures.

Later that night, Mark Taylor walked into A.A. and sat in the back. He hoped it would work. Mark hated who he was becoming. He felt like he was wearing his addiction on the outside and could see it every time he looked into the mirror.

They did their usual meeting protocol, which consists of reading their Preamble and opening the meeting with the Serenity Prayer.

God grant me the serenity to accept the things I cannot change, courage to change the things I can, and wisdom to know the difference.

Well, that seems like a prayer we all could use! He just sat there listening and hoped no one noticed. Needless to say, it's pretty hard to hide when you're Mark Taylor! You kind of stand out. When the speaker asked if there was anyone new, Mark stood up.

"Hi, my name is Mark, and I'm an alcoholic."

Everyone said, "Hi, Mark."

"It's been twenty-four hours since my last drink, and I am coming here now because I really want to stop drinking this time… and I don't want there to be the next time," he said.

The crowd cheered and clapped really loudly, and Mark felt overwhelmed. He looked around and got teary-eyed, and his lip quivered. He sat down, and the speaker came over and put his hand on Mark's shoulder. All of the people around

Mark patted him on the back. They had all been 24-hours-sober before and wanted to encourage him.

The speaker returned to the podium and asked if there were any other new people. If so, no one said anything. He welcomed Mark and assured him he would never be forced to say anything he didn't want to. He then opened up the floor to everyone else.

CHAPTER *Thirteen*

A FEW WEEKS PASSED. Mark was on day twenty-four without a drink. He was okay. He just decided he was going to go directly home after work every day, then to A.A., and then immediately back to his apartment. He wanted to remove all temptation from his life. That meant no nightclubs, no women, in other words, no trouble! Mark was feeling better. He was eating better, and he was maintaining his body by doing a rigorous workout in the gym. The others at A.A. warned him that he'd have to replace his drinking habit with something else. Working out helped. And that was okay because it was productive and not dangerous.

Mark didn't need another challenge, but not only did Declan and Claudia start seeing each other again, they got married at the courthouse in downtown Miami. Claudia had married a monster and had no idea. If he wasn't such a coward, he would've gone to the police. He would've spilled his guts about what Declan did. Mark chose his career over protecting people. He vowed to never keep silent about something like that again... um, *next time*.

The day after they married, Mark got to the set and was handed a new script. Some of his lines had been changed. He was flipping through them while he walked to his trailer when Declan came up to him. "Hey, you didn't come to the courthouse. I really wanted you there to be my best man," he said, laughing.

Mark stopped in his tracks and stared at Declan.

Declan shrugged. "Sorry, she wanted a *real* man. Let's face it; I can give her what you can't."

"What? Naked pictures of the girls you've assaulted?" Mark asked. That comment didn't make Declan happy. He pulled his fist back, but before he could make contact with Mark, Mark's fist was flying through the air and made a direct hit on Declan's chin. Declan flew backward and into some extras on the set.

"Hey, what are you doing?" Declan asked as he grabbed his chin with his right hand.

"That's not even *half* of what you deserve, you sick bastard," Mark yelled. His face was red and getting redder as Declan gained the sympathy of the extras, who didn't know what was going on but were taking Declan's side as they scrambled to help him up.

When he was finally on his feet, he held his chin. "Nice right hook," he said with a laugh. Peter ran over with a security guard, and he stood between Declan and Mark.

"What's going on? This isn't high school. I am trying to make a movie here," Peter yelled, glaring back and forth between Mark, who was shaking with rage, and Declan, who was smirking because he knew he was winning the crowd over. Claudia ran over to Declan and shot Mark a dirty look as she examined his chin. Again, the sympathy was directed at Declan. What was wrong with these people? Why couldn't they see the source of the problems around here was Declan – not Mark!

Claudia clicked her tongue and torpedoed a menacing look toward Mark. "You could've broken his jaw, Mark," she scolded him. "C'mon, let's put some ice on that," she said with her arm around Declan as they walked back to her trailer. Declan looked back and smiled at Mark. Mark wanted to kill him. He felt his blood pressure rise, and he was sweating from the encounter. Mark felt like he was going crazy.

"Mark, you need to come with me," Peter said as he gestured to a picnic table on the set. Mark just followed him like a wounded puppy. He had a flashback to high school when he was in trouble and going to the Principal's office. They sat down, and Peter exhaled. "Mark, there seems to be a problem with you and Declan. I'm confused. Does this involve Claudia?"

Huh? Claudia? Mark wished it were that simple. If it was just a woman – he had his pick. It was bigger than that, but Mark had to keep his mouth shut about it. Claudia thought it was about her too. Like her ego wasn't big enough already.

Mark didn't say anything.

"Of course it does... Mark, do yourself a huge favor and stay away from her. This isn't the first movie that I've directed her in. She is trouble with a capital 'T,' but then again, you seem to like a problem. And Declan – well, I warned you about him. They're married now; you've got to let her go."

Mark didn't say anything for a minute. He almost told Peter everything. Almost. But he looked around and decided he didn't want to give it all up. The truth always has a way of coming to light anyway. No way could people believe Declan was a decent person. Mark was sure he would show his true colors sooner or later. But sooner would be better.

"I'm sorry, Peter."

"Don't be sorry — be *better*."

"Okay," Mark said.

Peter walked away and left Mark to think about things. Mark knew he was right, but he couldn't shake it off. He had never been under someone's control before. Mark looked around. Everyone on that set thought it was just a love triangle. They all thought Mark was jealous, and it was entirely his fault. If they only knew what a sicko Declan was. If they only knew what Mark knew. Mark wondered how things might've been different if Declan wasn't there screwing everything up.

After sulking for a few minutes, Mark got up and walked over to his mark on the set. Peter came over and tapped him on the back. "All good, Mark?" he asked.

"Yeah, we're good, Peter."

"Good," he said. The actors rehearsed the screen and worked on blocking with Peter. When the shot was set up, the assistant director John yelled, "Picture is up" to inform everyone that the take was set to be recorded. Then he called, "Quiet on the set," and everyone stopped talking. Next, he said, "Roll sound."

The sound mixer yelled, "Speed."

Finally, John called out, "Roll camera."

The camera operator said, "Speed."

The clapper announced the scene and take and then clapped the board, and Peter yelled, "Action."

Declan stepped off his mark, which was right in front of Mark, and announced, "Now, I get to hit you!" This scene *was* a fight scene. Mark was prepared for Declan to "accidentally" punch him, but this was no accident. He made contact with Mark's gorgeous mug. Well, Mark wasn't about to let *that* go.

The two suddenly embraced in punching and being punched. Mark got in multiple shots while Declan looked like a scared child in a corner. Mark popped Declan's upper lip so hard that it immediately started bleeding. Declan didn't even notice. He was too busy trying to shield himself from Mark, who received training from a Golden Gloves champ for an episode of *The Trifecta*. Maybe Mark's not a good one to pick a fight with. Up to now, Declan's damage was psychological anyway. It took security a minute to break up the scuffle.

Claudia and Peter were yelling, but the two guys were busy scrapping and ignored them. Peter was going ballistic, yelling, "Cut, cut, cut!" But the guys didn't listen. Finally, two huge men from security came over and grabbed Mark and Declan and pulled them apart. It took them way too long to break up the fight. They were actually watching it until someone reminded them that they should intervene. Claudia went over to Mark and started yelling at him. Mark yelled back and called her some choice words. Claudia's character was supposed to come in and kiss Mark after he and Declan fought. But instead of kissing him, she punched Mark's left eye.

The cinematographer for the movie grinned as she captured all this anger between the cast. What awesome chaos! Peter went over and asked her to take a break.

Then Peter called the three stars back to Mark's trailer along with the security team and had a pow-wow. Basically, he threatened them and said that not one, but all three would go if they couldn't get along. Declan and Claudia knew it was an idle threat, and the only one replaced would most likely be Mark, who sat there with an icepack over his soon-to-be black eye. Most of his scenes hadn't been shot yet, and he hadn't proven himself as a box office draw. Besides, everyone thought it was a love triangle over Claudia. They had no idea what was going on in Declan's sick head. Mark was painted as a raging alcoholic. No denying Mark had an issue with alcohol, but he wasn't rotten to the core, like Declan. Looks can be deceiving. They finished the scene, and Mark was still angry enough to storm off the set when the day was over.

CHAPTER
Fourteen

LATER THAT NIGHT, Mark had a nightmare of that night on the boat. It wasn't just a replay of his memories. In his dream, he had seen what Declan did to Britt, and he stopped it. Declan was in jail, and everyone knew the truth about him.

Mark was so haunted by the decision not to go to the police over Declan's little hobby for fear of the backlash and because the public would question why Mark didn't do anything. Declan had ruined any chance Mark had of seeing Natasha again, and now he'd married Claudia. Mark knew it was wrong. He knew he should've gone to the police. His decision may have been right for his *career* – but it was clearly not right for his *conscience.* Who knew what Declan would do to Claudia? Maybe it would be okay because she had an entourage. Perhaps she'd be okay because she was rarely alone. Besides, marriage was good for both of their images right now.

Even with all the drama on the set, Mark was still not drinking. He made a commitment to eat better and maintain the extra muscle he had put on for the movie. In Mark's quest for personal improvement, he started going to a sunset yoga class on South Beach.

He had gone a few times and met a woman attending the same classes. Her name was Reagan, and she was new in town. She was cute, and they seemed to have a similar sense of humor. She'd moved to Miami to host her own morning radio talk show. Mark thought it wouldn't hurt to befriend her. Of course, he always has ulterior motives. In the back of his mind, he knew she would be an excellent person to have on his side.

Mark offered to take her around and see the sights, mainly his bedroom, but he decided to be a gentleman and take it easy on her. He wanted to make sure that she thought he was a nice guy. Besides, he was in A.A., and his sponsor, Carl, told him not to start a new relationship until he'd been sober for a year. And not just a meaningful relationship, Mark was told *no sex* either… for a *year*! Maybe the *average* person could pull that off. But Mark Taylor? Seriously?

His sponsor also encouraged Mark to get a plant. Carl said if Mark could keep a plant alive for a year, then he could maintain a relationship. Mark kills plants, and when Mark thought about not having sex for a year – the very thought of that *almost* killed Mark! A plant was not the kind of company that Mark longed for. Mark was a sex symbol. Imagine looking at that perfectly chiseled jaw in the mirror every morning and going to bed alone at night!

Mark knew befriending this new woman would be advantageous, given her high-profile job in the media. He needed to establish himself as a good guy with someone who mattered. She could be an essential ally. After a few more classes, he asked her to come over to his apartment the next Friday so he could make her dinner. She accepted, and when Mark heard her radio show, she told everyone that she had a date with him and her producer, Josh, warned her about Mark on the air. Josh wanted her to know that Mark was a player and was very wild. She reminded her listeners that they shouldn't believe everything they hear, and she was willing to give him a chance. Mark was encouraged by a new shot at redemption. Well, he thought it was a new shot...

The day after they made a date, Mark woke up with terrible stomach pains and not to get too graphic, he was having problems in the *bathroom*. Did he have food poisoning? Did he eat a mad cow? Maybe it was an ulcer? He *had* been under an inordinate amount of stress dealing with Declan.

After a few hours of abnormal trips to the bathroom, when he looked into the toilet, he saw you-know-what... but he also saw little *worms*! They were alive... and they were coming out of his ass! He panicked. Who do you call about ass worms?

He went straight to the Emergency Room. They ran a bunch of tests on him and discovered he had an abnormally high parasitic count. They sent him home with a prescription for a heavy antibiotic and a phone number for a local Infectious Disease doctor.

He was seen the next day. It's really great when you're a celebrity. You get pretty girls, movie roles, and the best tables in town. And, most importantly, you can get right into a doctor who isn't accepting new patients when you have worms coming out of your ass.

The doctor asked him if he had been out of the country recently. He had not. But, when the doc asked if he ate sushi recently, Mark told him he ate it every week. The doctor informed him that he had seen a dramatic rise in the number of parasitic infections from raw food consumption. He warned Mark to cut back since there was no way to determine precisely how he had contracted this parasite.

After a few very uncomfortable tests, the doctor gave Mark a few little containers in which to collect his stool samples for the next three days. They were to be collected and stored in the refrigerator until they were analyzed. He wanted to make sure that he took the proper course of treatment for

Mark. He also gave Mark a heavy pro-biotic to help clean out his intestinal tract. Mark looked at the clear containers that had "Mark Taylor" written on the side. Usually, Mark likes to see his name written, but not in this case.

A few days and stool samples later, Mark was feeling better. Medicine appeared to be helping. He was finally *alone* in the bathroom! He cleaned up his apartment and went grocery shopping for his date with Reagan.

It was hot, and he was sweating when he returned to his apartment. Now sometimes Mark is sweating at the end of his dates, but never before. So, when she arrived early, he apologized for his appearance. He asked her if she minded if he took a shower. She didn't. Then he did something that men never do, he handed her the remote control and told her he'd be right out of the shower. He told her to help herself to a drink in the fridge. He stepped into the shower and started to soap every part he thought she may be touching later.

As Mark soaped up his hair, he thought about what a great thing it was to have her there. She would surely tell the world how fantastic Mark was. She would negate everything people ever said about Mark. She might even care about him. She might be "the one," Mark thought as he started scratching the shampoo into his hair. He started visualizing how the date would go, and then he thought about her… and where she was and what she was doing.

Shit! His eyes opened wide, and he feverishly rinsed his hair out. Shit! He hoped to God that she hadn't gone into the fridge yet. He smacked the water handle off before his hair was even thoroughly rinsed and ran out in his towel to the other room, where he saw her, bent over into the fridge. She had a clear container in her hand, and Mark heard her say, "Shit?"

She screamed and then threw it on the ground and ran over to the sink, scrubbing her hands until her hands and wrists were red and scratched. She ran out the door, and

Mark chased her down the hall to the elevator, trying to explain to her why he had three coils of shit in plastic containers in his *Meat Keeper*. She wouldn't even listen. He got to her right before the doors closed, and she called him a sick freak. Mark sighed while clenching his towel and dripping all over the cream marble floors. He walked back to his apartment as an elderly couple eyed him, wondering what he did *this time*.

Mark woke up the next morning and turned on Reagan's radio show to hear her discussing fecophilia with a psychiatrist. He was trying to give the warning signs of a fecophiliac. Turns out, keeping poop in your fridge is a big red flag unless you have a medical reason for doing so. Mark tried to call into the radio show and explain himself, but she wouldn't take his call. Great. There was no way to "worm" his way out of this one. Needless to say, Mark looked bad again, or should I say *still*? Now Reagan never talked about her date with Mark on the air. In fact, she never mentioned him at all. So, Mark quit going to beach yoga!

CHAPTER *Fifteen*

MARK WAS four months into A.A., and everything was going really well. He was doing the program and sailing right through it. His sponsor was old school and believed Mark should try and work through the steps quickly so he could really get control over his addiction.

He had changed his lifestyle. There was no more going out with friends. Who were his friends anyway? Other people who drank were not a good influence now, and they would never be. He was eating better, sleeping better, and working out every day. Mark read books and went for walks. Everything was normal. It was the way it should always have been. Clean living and clear thinking looked good on Mark. It felt good, too.

I'm sure you know that part of the twelve steps is making amends to everyone you've hurt along the way. With Mark, that was a very long list. No big surprise – many people didn't want to pick up the phone when Mark Taylor called. To the women in his past – at least the ones he *remembered* – Mark sent a lot of flowers with notes on them. But one, in particular, stood apart in his mind: Megan, the woman from

Phillip's architectural firm. She saved his life and Mark had never forgotten about her.

Mark went to the florist in person and picked out the biggest and most expensive bouquet for her. Surely she would forgive him; he'd never met her in person and was embarrassed to. He even hand wrote the card and gave it to the florist.

Megan, I'm sorry that I didn't apologize to you sooner. I know you're the one who found me and stayed with me until the ambulance arrived. I credit you with saving my life! I was in a bad place, but now I'm in recovery and doing well. So I hope you forgive me because I'm not who I used to be.

– *Mark Taylor*

Mark wasn't expecting a thank you card, but he assumed that she got those flowers. When they came into the office, the delivery guy gave them to the receptionist, and she was going to give them to Megan when she returned from lunch. Phillip saw them sitting on the counter at the receptionist's desk while he was reading his mail. "Nice flowers, who are they from?"

"Mark Taylor," she said, and that piqued his interest. "They're for *Megan*!" She knew that would annoy Phillip. He looked up from the mail and moved closer to her desk.

She was right, he *was* annoyed. "Why did he send *her* flowers?" he asked as he ripped the card from the bouquet.

"I don't know – *I don't* read other people's cards!" she said as Phillip yanked the card out of the envelope. He read it and let out an irritated sigh.

"I'm taking these to Megan's office," he said, holding up the card, "and you're not going to tell her they're from Mark Taylor." He slipped the card into the inside pocket of his suit coat.

"Oh, I promise I won't tell *Megan*," she said with a little smile. As Phillip walked away with the considerable vase, the receptionist went over to the other secretaries and started whispering. Phillip carried those flowers right into Megan's office and plopped them on her desk like he bought them for her. Too bad, Phillip couldn't blame addiction for *his* bad behavior. He's just an ass.

Mark didn't hear back from any of the people that he apologized to, except for Regina. She called him.

"Hi Mark, it's Regina."

"Hey, Regina. I'm so glad to hear from you."

"I got your flowers. They're beautiful. Thank you."

"You're welcome. Listen, it wasn't you, I liked you. I was just in a bad place and let my drinking control my life. So, I just really wanted to say I'm sorry. I wasn't in any condition to have a relationship. I hope you will forgive the way I treated you. You didn't deserve that."

"Yeah, sure. I understand. You're an alcoholic."

"Yeah, well, we say we're in 'recovery.' But yeah, I wasn't the same person I am now. I just wanted to say I was sorry. Thank you for calling me and letting me say that to you."

"Uh, you said that you're not the same person, but now you're ready to have a relationship?"

Mark got uncomfortable. "Uh, actually, I'm not supposed to get involved with anyone for a year. I just have to make sure that I'm stable enough to maintain a normal relationship. You understand that I..."

"But when you can have a relationship, I mean, would you want to get together again?"

"Well, I hadn't really thought about it. I'm just trying to stay on the right road, you know? I can't really be with someone who drinks anymore."

"I would totally quit drinking," she said sincerely.

"Right. I'm sure you would, I just... maybe in a year or two. But I'm sure you'll be involved with someone by then, Regina. I have to go, but take care," Mark said and hung up. He'd discovered a lot of deal-breakers with women – desperation was one of them. He was tired of women throwing themselves at him. Would there ever be a woman who didn't offer Mark Taylor a challenge? Maybe he was growing after all!

Mark was eating well, sleeping well, and staying out of trouble. His body was in top form, and work was excellent. Mark had received a lot of kudos on the set for doing his own stunts. When Peter played back the dailies, which is the daily playback of the day's footage, he would tell Mark that he was a natural. Life was good! And then the story broke...

CHAPTER Sixteen

MARK GOT a text from someone on the movie set, telling him to turn on the local news. "Two of the stars of a movie being filmed in Miami are under investigation tonight for assault of an unnamed woman in Miami. Declan O'Conner and Mark Taylor..." the voice trailed off. Mark was horrified. *He* was being investigated? How come he didn't know, and it was being reported as if it was news? Just then, someone started really pounding on his door. Funny how the "news" will run a story and then fact-check later so they can break a story before their competitors. Who cares about being accurate?

A man with a badge stood there. "Mark Taylor, I'm Detective Ken Dixon. I need to ask you some questions regarding Britt Kennedy. May we come in?"

"Sure, come on in." Mark could hardly control his voice.

"This is my partner, Detective John Wallace."

They both sat on the sofa and started asking Mark questions about that night on the boat. The detectives told Mark that he could be charged as an accessory if he didn't cooperate, but he was ready to reveal what Declan did. They seemed like they believed what Mark was saying. Apparently, they were investigating Declan and only *questioning* Mark about what he knew. Mark told them about the cell phone and suggested that Declan might have uploaded the pictures to his laptop. He said he'd seen the images himself, and then they asked why he didn't come forward, and he didn't really have a good answer. What do you suppose he should've said? That he was only thinking about his career and nothing else – that would've been the truth, but it would've made him look like a jerk – which he was.

The next day, the police got a warrant to search the house Declan was staying in. He'd deleted the photos from his phone, which was restored to its factory settings, but he didn't wipe his hard drive. The pictures were retrieved from the laptop, even though they were hidden. Declan also neglected to conceal the unmarked pill bottle in the medicine cabinet. There was enough evidence to convict Declan. No doubt, he was going to jail.

Mark wasn't being investigated, yet he was found guilty in the court of public opinion. Maybe if he had come forward, he would've been a hero, but now he was raked over the coals. Some people on media shows were even questioning if Mark set *Declan* up for the fall.

What would Declan have to do to prove how bad he was to the masses? How could the public be so ignorant and believe the lies that the media told them? They painted Declan as the victim, and Mark, the culprit. As usual, the media had it backward.

Declan was arrested and remained in prison with no chance of bail because the judge deemed him a flight risk. Declan was going to sit in jail until his trial. Mark wondered what was going to happen. Then Mark got a text from Peter. Because of Declan's mess, the studio had suspended the production for a few days while they scrambled to figure out a solution. Declan was not going to finish the movie, and the cast and crew would just be on stand-by until the studio found a replacement.

The next day, Mark got weird looks in restaurants and stores. He decided now would be a good time to start drinking again. His sponsor called him several times, and Mark just ignored his calls.

Mark drove himself to a liquor store and sat in the parking lot for a few minutes, contemplating his next move. He clutched the inside door handle, and he tried so hard not to use it, but he caved.

In the liquor store, he saw another tabloid with a picture of Declan and Mark on the front page with the caption, "PREDATORS!" Mark couldn't believe it. *He'd* been cleared by the police. But the tabloids were reporting he was involved in the filming and picture- taking of Declan's victims. Yup, this was the *perfect* time to start drinking again.

When he got home, he drank until he didn't feel bad anymore. Actually, he felt pretty good. He felt like himself again. The only thing missing was a woman. Oh well, he was in no shape to entertain tonight anyway. Mark was very, very angry. Rightly so. He was in a mess.

Later that night, Mark got a text from the assistant director. Declan was going to jail indefinitely and would have to be replaced. Mark wondered what jerk was going to be cast as *Don O'Malley*.

Mark woke up the next morning and went down to the kitchen to start his coffee. He went out and grabbed the paper, and on the front page was a headline that read, *"Declan O'Conner Paid Me to Drug Mark Taylor."* Mark ripped the paper from the plastic wrap and started reading the article. That girl from the honky-tonk bar gave an interview confessing that Declan gave her a drug to knock Mark out, and she had accomplices carry him into her house. She said that she voluntarily undressed Mark after they had placed him in her bed.

It had been a setup. Mark *knew* it, and this girl came forward to defend Mark. She said that she met Declan through one of his fan pages, and he contacted her and paid her to drug Mark and then post those pictures all over social media. She said that Declan had a "special kind of hatred" of Mark to do something like this. The police questioned her, but charges would not be brought against her in exchange for her cooperation in Declan's case.

Well, that was it. That proved Mark was innocent. And that was when the tide started to turn. Mark received a call that he was needed on set as soon as possible. He was so happy that he ran out of the house without his cell phone, so he missed an urgent text from his manager. When Mark arrived at the set, he opened the back window and waved at the people lining the streets with signs that read, *We Love You, Mark!* And *Mark Taylor is innocent.* Was the public starting to change its opinion? It looked like it. People on the set acted nicer, too.

While Mark was walking to his trailer, Peter joined him. "Mark."

"Good morning, Peter."

Peter put his arm around Mark and said, "We need to talk." They got to his trailer, and Peter shut the door and gestured for Mark to sit down at the table. Peter stood across from him, resting his hands on the back of a chair. "Look, this thing with Declan is a PR *nightmare.* The studio is freaking out. They don't want his name associated with anything right now – since the police have pictures. He obviously did it, so how quickly do you think you learn some new lines?" Peter asked with an apprehensive smile.

"I can learn 'em quickly. Some of my scenes got re-written?"

"Look, Mark. I know you've been attending A.A.; I know you're trying to get your act together."

"How do you know I was in A.A.? I thought it was

supposed to be *anonymous*?" Mark got upset that someone would give that information out.

"My sponsor's in that group, and I told him I was worried about you," Peter said as he pulled a 10-year sobriety coin from his front pocket and flipped it on to the table. Mark picked up the coin and inspected it. Now was *not* the time for Mark to confess that he had fallen off the wagon the night before.

"I hope you get one of these someday," Peter said as Mark returned the coin to Peter, who immediately put it back in his pocket. Peter was in recovery? Mark had no idea. He seemed like he had it all together. Could Peter be a mess inside like Mark? "So, Mark, how would you feel about playing *Don O'Malley*?"

Mark smiled. "I'm replacing *Declan*?" He pointed to himself. "You want *me* to play *Don O'Malley*?"

"Yup. It was the studio's idea. We're behind schedule because of this mess with Declan. We have to re-shoot everything. Of course, we'll have to recast your part, but it's doable." Mark smiled. "Now listen, I assured the studio that you're getting help with your drinking. Please, no more bad publicity. It's both of our heads if you screw this up…"

Peter looked at his watch. "I have some shots I need to set up. You're good, right? You can learn this pretty fast?" He put his index finger on the script on the table.

"Yeah. I memorized the whole script anyway. But, yeah, I'll get to work right now," Mark stood up and shook Peter's hand. "Thanks, Peter. Thanks for believing in me."

"I never liked Declan. This role is a game-changer for you, Mark. It's *your* time."

CHAPTER Seventeen

MARK WAS IN A DAZE. Things were turning around. He was starring as the lead. This would be the movie that would transition him from TV star to action hero. This was the big break he needed. It didn't happen the way Mark thought it would. But it happened, and Mark was determined to make the most of it.

Mark memorized all of Declan's lines, and they re-shot some scenes with Mark as the new lead. Mark acted obnoxious to stay in character as Don O'Malley. He wanted to play it correctly. They recast Mark's old role with a newcomer named Oliver. But he and Mark got along well. Mark was surprised at how much better everyone treated him. He wondered if it was because his name had been cleared or because he was the star now. He tried to stay grounded because he couldn't let drinking screw up his big chance.

Jack Daniels and Claudia James were the two things that made Mark's life difficult for the remainder of the production. Mark managed to quit drinking but was embarrassed to rejoin A.A. Why Mark thought he was the only one who had tried to stop drinking and felt like a failure is beyond me. But at least now he realized that he couldn't go back to living the way he did. He wouldn't have gotten his big break in the starring role if it weren't for A.A. And as far as Claudia goes, Mark wasn't biting. He now held the power position, and he wasn't about to jump into something he knew wasn't going to end well.

As the production was winding down, someone was growing very fond of Mark. Sophia Rae, a supporting actress, came knocking on his trailer door.

Mark yelled, "Come in," and glanced up from a book he was reading. When he saw it was her, he put the book down. Mark wore glasses, and no one knew about it. He was a little embarrassed, and he tossed them as soon as she came in.

"Hi," she said as she stood over him, next to the sofa.

He perked up. "Hi. I thought you were Claudia."

"Did I disappoint you?" she asked.

"Not at all. Have a seat," he said as he patted the seat next to him on the couch. She sat down, and they smiled at each other for a moment while thinking of what to say or do next.

"I just wanted to tell you that I never liked Declan and I think you make a much better Don O'Malley."

"Thanks!"

"Sure. Did you want to have dinner with me sometime, maybe?" she asked.

"Definitely. Just let me know when," he said with a smile. There was another knock at the door.

A woman with a headset and a clipboard stood there. "Sophia, they're ready for you."

She got up and looked at Mark. "I guess I'll see you out there."

Sophia left his trailer at the same Claudia was coming out of her own. Claudia didn't want Mark. She only wanted to play games with him. But she sure didn't want anyone else to have him either. So when she looked back and saw Sophia leaving his trailer, Claudia made it her mission to make Mark want only her. Public perception was the only thing that mattered to Claudia, and if Mark was going to be a huge star after this, then she wanted to be with him. Besides, she had to sever any ties with Declan, and what better way to move on than with the next best thing?

When they wrapped for the day, Claudia did the same thing Declan had done to herself and Mark – she followed Sophia and Mark to a restaurant. She had one of the other members of the cast go with her to make it less noticeable. But Mark knew what she was doing since she was the ultimate opportunist. The whole thing with Declan had hurt her image, but being with the new star of the movie would boost her celebrity status, and she knew it.

After Mark and Sophia had a few glasses of iced tea, Claudia told her co-star to stay at the bar, she would be right back. Claudia made her way to their table and rudely sat right down in the middle of their conversation. Mark was really irritated.

"Hi, guys!" Claudia said as she put her cocktail napkin down and set her drink on top of it. Mark and Sophia just looked at her. Claudia put her big handbag next to Mark's leg, and he looked at it and then back at Claudia.

"What do you want, Claudia? We spent enough time together on the set today," Mark said as he swallowed his last sip of tea. The ice clanked together as he slammed the cup down. He was annoyed that Claudia was there at all. He knew just what she wanted, and he refused to waste another second on her.

Sophia grabbed her purse and stood up, "I'll give you two a minute."

"Thank you," Claudia said to her.

"No, sit down, Sophia. Explain yourself, Claudia," Mark said. He crossed his arms as Sophia sat back down.

"I don't want to interrupt you if you're on a date," she said, leaning toward Mark with a flirtatious smile.

He smiled and leaned into her. "As a matter of fact…"

Claudia perked up, and Mark looked at Sophia, "we *are* on a date. Why don't you go see what Declan's doing? Oh, I forgot, he's in *jail*. You sure know how to pick 'em."

While Sophia watched with wide eyes, Claudia yanked her purse from under the table and held it against her chest. Then she glared at Mark and said, "At least I'm not an alcoholic!"

Mark smiled at her sympathetically and said thoughtfully, "You're just not ready to admit it yet. I hope you do soon since you're almost forty. Your time is almost up in Hollywood. And when that happens, you're *really* going to be hitting the bottle… *hard*."

Claudia stood up, her mouth open. She was stunned. Even though Claudia knew her time was almost up, she couldn't believe someone would say that to *her*. She turned to Sophia and said, "He's *selfish* in bed."

"Not when I care about the person," Mark said to her back as she walked away.

Sophia watched as Claudia, and their co-star left the restaurant, squawking the whole time. Sophia looked at Mark and asked, "So is it true? Are you selfish in bed?"

"No! I'm selfish *everywhere*," he said with a big smile.

CHAPTER *Eighteen*

MARK REFRAINED from drinking through the remaining months of the production. He and Sophia weren't serious, but they liked being with each other. She was a good influence. At least she didn't drink or do drugs.

One of the last scenes to be shot was a crucial one. Mark had to fire a gun at a bad guy while riding a motorcycle. This was the scene they had to reschedule because of Mark's time in rehab. It was being filmed on location on the Brickell Avenue Bridge, which is U.S. 1 in Miami. It was just down the road from Mark's apartment. It's the main artery in downtown Miami, and the locals weren't happy about the bridge being closed. They *had* to finish the shot.

Unfortunately, on the only day, the traffic could be rerouted, it was raining. Peter was informed about the weather reports and knew he had a limited window to get the shot he needed, so Mark and the rest of the cast and crew got ready to start filming. They did a few dry runs, and it looked good. The stunt crew made sure that Mark was outfitted with enough protective gear to sustain an average incident.

Unfortunately, by the time the lighting and blocking were

set up correctly for the take, rain had made the ground slick. In the shot, the actors and stunt drivers were to drive in the opposite direction of normal traffic flow. However, the transition on the bridge from concrete to asphalt was never safe for people to drive on the wrong side of the road. When Mark hit the gas and then braked on his mark, the tire treads held the water, and the bike couldn't stop. It hydroplaned, and Mark dumped the bike to the left. The weight of the motorcycle snapped his leg instantly. And Mark broke both of his arms and three ribs on his left side, trying to brace the impact. Luckily, he was going slowly. It could have been a lot worse – he wasn't dead. But he wasn't going to be walking out of a hospital anytime soon.

Everyone ran immediately to Mark's aid, but it didn't look right. While Mark was lifted on a gurney into the ambulance, Peter reviewed the footage. John, the assistant director, came over to Peter.

"You know he's not going to be able to come back?" John asked.

Peter looked at the crash a few times, inciting oohs and aahs from the crew. Most of the women turned away, unable to watch. "I think we can use some of this footage." You could actually see Mark's bones breaking in the playback. He looked like a rag doll when his arms hit the pavement.

Industrial fans were used to completely dry the location, so the same thing didn't happen again. Peter and John had the stuntman for the second male lead fill in for Mark.

After a few days, Peter took some of the cast and crew to see Mark in the hospital. Mark looked ridiculous. He was in traction and had road rash on his chin. At least his head wasn't bandaged. The good news was, unlike every relationship he'd ever had, every break he had in his bones was a clean one. The bones would heal properly without grafts or pins. But he was warned by the hospital staff that he would have a tough road ahead.

"Hey, Evel Knievel, we came by to cheer you up!" Peter said. Some of the cast and crew carried balloons and plants and put them all around Mark.

"I don't think Evel ever dumped his bike because of a puddle," Mark said.

"No, but he was in similar traction... a few times," Peter said as he gently touched one of the wires. Everyone laughed. Mark was on a heavy morphine drip, so it was difficult having a conversation with him. Besides, Mark was physically exhausted. Everything hurt, even while he was on pain medication. He was rendered totally useless. He couldn't even feed himself!

"So, what do you think... you want to keep doing your own stunts or what?" Peter asked with a laugh.

"Maybe. Let's see how bad off I am after this," Mark said slowly.

The visit was short. After everyone left, Sophia stayed behind and kept Mark company. That only lasted a few days. She was flying back to L.A. to shoot a mini-series. Mark was told he'd be in the hospital for at least a month. Peter told the hospital not to rush. The movie studio was nervous that Mark was going to sue. Talk about biting the hand that feeds you! Mark wouldn't be stupid enough to do that.

Mark missed the wrap party for *Don O'Malley*, but Peter came to visit and showed him a video of the cast and crew wishing him a speedy recovery and saying goodbye. Peter also showed Mark the playback of his crash on his iPad. The scene would turn out fine with the stunt man filling in. It was not the memory Mark would've wanted to take from his first starring role, but that's life.

The hospital staff was very attentive and concerned about Mark. They checked on him frequently and made sure he had everything he needed. The nurses found Mark very charming and flirtatious, and they responded in kind. Aside from the staff, Mark didn't have much interaction with people.

Mark didn't have many visitors. His parents flew down but only stayed a couple of days. His father was busy, and his mother didn't want to be alone in Mark's place. It made him realize that he didn't really have any friends. Funny, isn't it? The rich and famous seem like they have everything. I wonder how many of them would trade their lives just to be healthy.

Mark had to cancel the next project he was scheduled for. He would face several months of rehabilitation in Miami. He wasn't going anywhere, and he wasn't happy about it. It was supposed to be the next big movie. Mark was secretly hoping it would flop without him. He worried about how the accident would affect his future. It wasn't his fault, but still…

In the hospital, Mark grew accustomed to people preparing his meals and taking care of him. He realized that he was going to have to hire someone to do simple things for him. Things like making dinner or going to the grocery store. Fortunately, before he was released, the movie studio was gracious enough to provide a chef, driver, and personal assistant. They wanted to ensure that Mark got all the help he needed to ensure a speedy recovery.

His agent called as soon as he got home with excellent news. The studio wanted to sign Mark for another movie right away. Obviously, it was with an ulterior motive. Of course, I'm not implying that Mark's not a great actor and didn't deserve it. However, the timing was more than questionable. But Mark was only too happy to put a very messy John Hancock on the line immediately to star in another action film and continue his career as soon as his body would allow.

While Mark recovered at home, he got a few calls from his agent about offers that had come in while he was on the mend. *Don O'Malley* was in post-production and would be released in a few months. The studio was happy, and it looked like Mark's career was going to be okay. As long as he could maintain a low profile, he would be fine. And between the hospital and intensive physical therapy, keeping a low profile would be easy. It felt good to be home, and every day he received letters from fans wishing him well.

CHAPTER *Nineteen*

A FEW MONTHS after Mark finished his rehabilitation, *Don O'Malley* came out. It was a huge hit. After a few weeks of talk shows, premieres, and traveling with his co-stars all over the world to promote the film, things started to settle down. There was a lot of buzz around Mark's accident and Peter leaving some of the footage of it in the movie. Mark was everywhere, but he was alone.

Claudia decided now that Mark was on top that she would try again. The whole time they were traveling and doing foreign talk shows together, she was building him up, and he noticed. But every time he'd hear a knock on his hotel door, he'd tell her to go away. He didn't want to go down that road again. Finally, though, Claudia's persistence paid off. Mark agreed to have dinner with her when they returned to Miami, where she also owned a home.

They went to Miami Beach and had dinner at Wet Willie's, then went to a nightclub. Mark was doing everything he could to not drink anymore, but she made it very difficult. Especially since she was just like Mark – a binge drinker. They are tough to control and even harder to stop. Mark tolerated a night here and there with her, but it was difficult not to fall right back into his old patterns. Fortunately, she was leaving to go back to L.A., so Mark would be safe this time.

Mark himself was headed to New Zealand in two weeks to shoot an epic adventure about the Middle Ages. He had a lot of preparations to make before shooting began. He had to grow his hair out a little, put on some weight, and learn how to use a sword. He was looking forward to it. It would be a new experience, and he would be away from all the bad influences around him.

But for now, it was the start of football season again, and Mark was still *alone*. This would be the test. Mark was an insane football fan. Would he be able to watch football without drinking? That was something he couldn't remember ever doing.

He had, though. He'd been a football fan since he was a child. There was a time when he'd been content just having a Coke and potato chips during game time. How he longed to return to days of simplicity, the days before he tasted his first sip of alcohol. Maybe he could've stopped himself if he had only known then how it would drain every real emotion from him. How there wouldn't be a day when he would wake up without that craving to put a drink to his mouth. But oh, that wicked, detestable feeling when it actually ran down and burned the back of his throat. He wanted it and hated wanting it at the same time.

Clemson was playing a Florida team on this beautiful September day. He decided to go it alone and not invite anyone over. He didn't know his neighbors very well, and the only friends he had in Miami were still drinking and doing drugs. Carl warned Mark not to go to a bar and watch the game. That wasn't even an option in Mark's mind. Or was it? What could possibly happen? Mark knew he was better off not drinking.

Every time his team missed the ball, fumbled or threw an

interception, Mark went insane. He cussed, threw things, yelled at the television, and shook his fists.

He grabbed the keys to his car and proceeded to that sports bar at the marina down the road from his house.

He pulled into the lot and threw the car into 'park' before turning the ignition off. Then he leaped to the outside bar and started looking for a television with his game on.

The bartender came over and placed a napkin down in front of him as he sat down. He noticed it was Mark Taylor. "Hey, how's it going, man? I'm a big fan."

"Thanks."

"Hey, what can I get for you?" he asked Mark.

Mark didn't waste a breath. "Rum and Coke," he said. He started rubbing his fingers together, anticipating the drink in his hand, and there it was less than a minute later. He rolled the liquid around his tongue and let it hit his cheeks. He closed his eyes to take in every sensory moment. He smiled to himself and said to the bartender, "I'll take another one, please," as he placed the glass down gently and stared at the empty bottom and licked his lips slowly. Why did he fall back into this wicked deception of thinking he could stop at one drink?

"Coming right up," the bartender said as he poured another drink and slid the glass in front of him.

Mark's team was losing badly, and there were people in the bar wearing the jerseys of the opposing team. Mark was greatly outnumbered, but that didn't stop him. He cussed at the refs, using some colorful names. Every call they made was wrong! Then an old man on the stool next to him said, "Look, buddy, it's just a game. If you're looking for happiness at the bottom of that glass, you're never going to find it."

Mark stood up. "Who the hell are you? You don't know me."

"Hey, take it easy, son. I'm just trying to enjoy the game, okay? You need to calm down."

Mark didn't understand the source of the anger was his feeling like a failure again. It actually had very little to do with the game.

"You know what? You don't need to tell me to calm down, grandpa, okay?"

The bartender looked around at the agitated customers rooting for the winning team. Then he came over to Mark. "You need to chill, man."

Mark got really irritated at that. "Just give me my check. You know what? Never mind, just keep the change," Mark said as he threw a fifty across the counter.

Mark got into his car and drove to another bar further down the road. It was a little dumpy outdoor biker bar where he certainly didn't belong.

He went up to the bar, where some of the patrons recognized him. Even though the game was on, they were more interested in sharing motorcycle accident stories while they bought Mark drinks until he couldn't stand. The bartender called him a cab, and Mark went home and fell asleep on the sofa. He had to return the next day to pick up his car, but at least he got back safely and remembered where his car was.

CHAPTER *Twenty*

MARK'S HOUSE was finally completed! He didn't have time to get settled in, but at least he could return to his own home when he came back from New Zealand.

Mark did a walk-through with Phillip and was delighted. Everything was perfect. He was alone, but other than that, it was what he'd always dreamed of. Phillip and Mark stepped out the back sliding glass doors and looked at the water. There was a yacht coming close to the house, and the people on the boat yelled, "It's Don O'Malley," and Mark smiled and waved. Phillip told Mark that he was glad Mark was happy with the end product. Phillip shook Mark's hand and then let himself out.

It was late when Mark packed up the last boxes in his apartment. The movers would arrive the next morning to move everything. He looked out the window one last time. That view always looked different. Yeah, it was still the ocean, but sometimes it was sideways, and occasionally it was swirling. In the day, it looked like a new start, and at night it looked like diamonds with the promise of a better tomorrow that never came.

Mark exhaled and grabbed his laptop and walked out the door. He turned around and looked at the apartment one more time and smiled. On his way to the elevator for the last time, a sense of relief came over him. He'd never bring another woman up to this place for a loveless night with morning regrets and awkward goodbyes. He was happy. A fresh start is always a good thing. He made his way down to the parking garage and climbed into his Mercedes feeling excited about the next chapter in his life. He drove to his new house and wondered what kind of adventures he'd have there.

The next morning, Mark started moving his few pieces of furniture he had around the house. He couldn't arrange it to his liking. With every move, his focus kept going to the window, facing the neighbor's yard. Mark cocked his head sideways. How come he'd never noticed their yard before? No wonder he got such a deal on this house. He opened his front door to take it all in.

The neighbor had plants everywhere. It was like a bad sci-fi movie from the '50s. They looked like they were just potted plants, but maybe they were plotting to take over the world… or at least Mark's yard! *Plant people!* Leaves were draped over everything. Why did this guy need to plant so many trees and bushes? What was buried under them? Mark's imagination was getting carried away.

After eating some cereal, he changed into running clothes and jogged around the new neighborhood. His new neighbors, the "plant people," came over to greet him as he jogged back to his front door.

"Howdy, neighbor," the man said as he extended his hand. "Name's Ted." Mark shook his hand.

The woman took off her garden gloves and handed Mark a plant. "Hi, I'm Margaret."

"Oh, a *plant.* How unexpected," Mark said in a phony tone, but he shook her hand.

"We are just so excited to have a movie star living next door. If you ever need anything, please don't hesitate to ask us," Margaret said.

Mark looked at their yard, "Thank you. I will keep that in mind if I can find a path to your door," he said with a laugh.

Margaret didn't laugh. She was a little offended at his comment. "Well, Margo loves plants!" Ted told Mark, trying to sidetrack Mark's rude comment.

"No kidding," Mark said as he lifted the pot up a few inches. "Thanks for the plant. It was nice meeting you, folks." And he went inside.

Mark took off to New Zealand for six months and promptly got into more trouble. He again got involved with the starring actress, who was a complete psychopath, probably because she hadn't eaten a simple carb in twenty years. She smoked and drank like a fiend, not a good match for Mark's addictive personality. Not only that, she liked to slap Mark around when she drank. Literally, she physically assaulted him on more than one occasion. I guess it's true – love hurts! But, this wasn't love. Mark's a bright guy, but he sure had a hard time learning a lesson. He was locking himself in his trailer, showing up late on the set, and not memorizing his lines. Kind of reminds you of someone else, doesn't it?

The tabloids were filled with stories about the volatile relationship between Mark and his leading lady. She could drink Mark under the table, and she proved it more than once. Hard to believe too. She was just a little thing. She shouldn't have been able to pack that much liquor away. She was definitely not the woman Mark needed at that time in his life. When the movie wrapped up, so did their love affair. Actually, there wasn't any love involved. Just two lonely, unhappy, addictive personalities. That doesn't ever end well.

When Mark returned to Miami, he felt alone again, and he couldn't stand it. He barely dropped his luggage in his bedroom before changing into fresh clothes and heading to South Beach to fill the emptiness inside. The intention was just to get drunk and take a beautiful, empty soul home. Sounds easy enough, right?

CHAPTER
Twenty-One

NOTHING IS EVER that easy for Mark. He remembered drinking at the bar and dancing with someone, but that's the last thing he remembered before...

He was alone in his car when he looked in the rearview mirror and saw the blue lights. They were blurry, as blurry as his speedometer. How the hell did this happen? *Damn!* How did this happen? Mark was just trying to get drunk and screwed. Well, Mark was really going get screwed now!

This was Mark's first official offense, which generally wouldn't mean jail time, but Mark was driving at a genuinely excessive speed. This was turning into one expensive night. Besides drinks at the bar, and the fine he'd just earned by going over 50 MPH in a residential area, now we can add the loss of his license, attorney fees, and court costs to his little adventure. What he *did* get for free was a ride to jail and more lousy publicity proving that his drinking was out of control, contrary to what he kept telling himself.

But hey, in the end, he *is* Mark Taylor. He's an international star. He'll get off lightly. At least those were the thoughts running through his head. Mark knew dozens of celebrities who had gotten out of worse. But that was in *California*. How hard would they throw the book at him in Florida? He was banking on the fact that *everyone* loves celebrities.

Mark blinked long and hard. He was hoping it would all go away when he opened his eyes. Of course, it didn't. He was trying to process what was going on. It felt like one of his movies. There was Mark Taylor, drunk and handcuffed. Not his first time, of course, but the first time like *this*.

Mark was no stranger to breaking the law. He'd had his share of speeding tickets and driving while under the influence, but he was going to *jail* this time, not getting a ride home in the back of a cruiser so no one would know. *Everybody* would know about this.

The cops didn't waste any time. They booked him right away. Mark's picture was going to make the paper, and it was a terrible mug shot – worse than a driver's license photo!

When they threw him in the "drunk tank," as they referred to it, Mark quickly made enemies of some men who were larger, stronger, and scarier than he would ever be. This sobered Mark up pretty quickly. And he had no way to put up his dukes, either. They kept him in handcuffs even after they booked him. They threw him around and treated him like a common criminal. Surprise! He *was* a criminal! He'd never viewed himself that way. Who was he violating with his drinking? And now there he was, in the same cell with pedophiles, rapists, burglars, and killers!

How could this injustice be happening to Mark Taylor? He's hot! And famous! And well-liked. Sure, he's an alcoholic, but he's still a star – granted, a *falling* star. He was going to have to stay sober to have any hope for a future living that involved acting.

How did his friend Jack get him in such a mess? In the jail cell, some of the prisoners resented that Mark was in there with them. They felt it was their duty to intimidate Mark and make him uncomfortable. One large, sweaty, bald man, who was a big fan of denim, kept coming into Mark's personal space and rubbing up against his side. Mark tried to get away, but where could he go? He was still handcuffed, and the small cell was getting smaller by the moment. Some of the men made comments to Mark that would make any man uncomfortable, but especially a man who has all the comforts of someone rich and famous.

Simple things were now a luxury, like pissing without an audience. Mark wasn't Houdini, how would he even take a piss with handcuffs on? No one else was Houdini either because that cell smelled like a crap hole. He pushed his way through to the front of the cell and started yelling, "Guard! Guard!" It must have been ten minutes before someone came over – good thing someone wasn't getting stabbed or fondled in the cell.

"What do you want, prisoner?"

"Prisoner?" he scoffed, and the guard rolled his eyes. "Look, man, I really have to piss, please just let me use the bathroom out there," Mark pleaded as he gestured with his head to the freedom outside the cell while he did the pee-pee dance.

"We don't give preferential treatment, prisoner," the guard said.

"C'mon, if you don't let me go, I'm going to be pissing out of a catheter for the rest of my life."

The guard didn't have to, but he let Mark out, un-cuffed him and let him use the bathroom for non-criminals. That really angered the other prisoners in the cell when Mark got back. The guard slapped the cuffs back on Mark and put him back in. A few minutes later, a guard yelled that the prisoners were going to be transferred to jail. Mark was confused. Why the hell was he in the same cell with *these* people?

Mark started yelling to the sympathetic guard, "Guard? Guard?"

The same guard came back over and told Mark to shut up.

"Listen, I want my phone call. Why can't I call my attorney and get out of here?"

"Be patient, man. It's a full moon. We have a larger crowd than normal," the guard said.

A few hours later, after Mark had sobered up, he called his attorney. After spending the night in jail, he was transferred to the courthouse for his preliminary hearing.

Mark's attorney seemed like he didn't want to be there. Defense attorneys are supposed to love court, but the judge presiding, Danielle Martinez, had no tolerance for anyone – *especially* celebrities – breaking the law. As Mark was escorted into the courtroom by a policeman, his attorney, Trevor Russell, sat down at the table and pulled out a file. Mark's handcuffs were removed, and he rubbed his wrists, then sat next to his lawyer.

The judge came in, and everyone stood up. She sat down and put her glasses on. "Oh, looky here, we have ourselves a real-live celebrity," she said to her bailiff, who snickered as he handed her the court docket. She opened the file. "Well, Mr. Taylor, it seems that you've been arrested for drinking and driving. At least it's not for assaulting paparazzi this time. I'll never understand why you rich people don't have a taxi take you home. This is Miami, Mr. Taylor. We even have mass transit here," she said over the bailiff's chuckle.

"Your honor, Mr. Taylor would like to seek treatment in a rehab facility," Trevor stated.

"Really? Is this a publicity stunt, or do you want real help for your drinking problem?"

"Your honor, if I may, my client…"

She started looking through her calendar and didn't look back up as she lectured. "Let me guess, he's learned his lesson and won't do it again. Well, Mr. Taylor, you have a few months to get serious and clean up your act. I'm scheduling your trial for September 27th." The judge then looked up and gave Mark a stern look. "You'd better take this seriously, Mr. Taylor, or you're going to wind up dead. Or worse, you're going to kill some innocent bystander."

Wow. She thinks it'd be better if I were dead than if I hurt someone else. That was an ugly thought.

She glared at Mark as he left the courtroom. "Next case," she said. Maybe he really would take it seriously.

Mark's attorney walked with Mark out to his car. "Stay out of trouble, Mark. No drinking – and I'm serious. That judge hates celebrities; you'd better behave yourself until after the trial."

"Hey, I'll stop drinking until this blows over, okay?" Mark said as he got into the passenger side of Trevor's silver Infiniti.

Trevor rolled his eyes as he got into the driver's seat and threw his briefcase into the back. "We need to get you into rehab quickly; the court looks favorably on someone like you voluntarily going to rehab. I know the administrator at a local rehab; we can get you in right away. What's your schedule like?"

"I'm supposed to be in Canada in March."

"Then we need to get you in right away. You can go to 'Serenity Gardens' here in Miami. It's not really strict, they have alternative methods."

"Fine. It's only for thirty days," Mark smirked.

"I don't think you understand how serious this is. Your blood alcohol content was twice the legal limit. And the police had to set up a roadblock to stop you. I doubt I can even get your charges reduced. For now, all you lost was your license. You're looking at real jail time here, Mark. You need to straighten out your act."

Mark looked at Trevor. He didn't believe it. Real jail time? He didn't even hurt anyone. Besides, he was a celebrity. He deserved preferential treatment. He was used to it. Who could he buy to make it all go away? That's what wealthy people do – they just make problems disappear. Poof. Mark didn't realize there would be no easy resolution for him this time.

CHAPTER
Twenty-Two

IT WAS A SAD SIGHT, seeing his half-million-dollar car being lowered from the tow-truck onto his brick driveway when it came back from the impound yard. He had no idea when he would be able to drive it again.

Mark packed his bags and was chauffeured to 'Serenity Gardens' in Miami. It was the place where the locals went to do their rehab. Mark was let out at the back entrance for high-profile clients – which was pointless because his publicist had told everyone he was going. The paparazzi and fans were all lined up at the gates getting pictures of Mark in the limo. He put down the window and waved. Just so you know, when celebrities are serious about getting clean, no one knows about it. No one holds a press conference when it's for *real*. And getting clean is no joke, even though it's been made into entertainment by our media. Aren't we so amused by drunk and overdosed celebrities and drunk stars of reality TV? Maybe it makes us all feel better if we think that they have so much more than us, yet they're just as screwed up as we are.

The driver opened the door, but Mark's bags on the luggage cart and pulled away. Mark stood there for a minute, ignoring the attendant who came to collect his bags and escort him to his room. "Welcome, Mr. Taylor," the attendant said with a smile. Mark didn't even bother responding. He didn't want to be there. And he certainly didn't feel welcome when he was being forced to stay there just to reduce his sentencing. And for a whole month, no less. He devised a plan. He was an actor after all; he'd only do and say whatever they wanted so they'd sign off that he'd completed the program.

Mark's stay was unsuccessful. He resented every minute of every day. To make matters worse, the place didn't have that pleasant spa-like atmosphere that people like him are used to in a rehab facility. This was clearly not like L.A. where people go to get a nice massage and do yoga while listening to new age music. This place was a dump, from its gray exterior to its white walls and brass beds. It looked as though it had been abandoned in the mid-eighties, and someone just took Mark back in a time machine to this facility.

Their practices were also more than questionable. They made every one of the residents wear robes like monks. It was creepy and cult-like. The staff wore regular clothes to further separate and humiliate the residents.

The food was as good as the fashion. Mark wasn't going to get any help there, even if he wanted it. So, thirty days in the hole, with nothing to show. At least rehab would be checked off his little list for the judge. It looked like he gave a concerted effort.

When Mark did get out, he sent for a driver to pick him up. He would need one for at least eleven months, assuming he wasn't put in jail after his trial.

Every time Mark turned on the television, he saw "news" anchors bantering about "Mark Taylor being in trouble again" and laughing about it. What about the real problems in the world? They made jokes at Mark's expense instead of concentrating on real news, like all the corruption in Washington D.C., or a missing plane in the Pacific Ocean. What about all the starving people in the world or the trouble with public schools in America? No, the news programs would instead cover stories about people who are addicts and then make fun of them... *Mark Taylor, just another famous drunk.*

Where were the stories about people in recovery? Where were the stories about people making it out of addiction and helping others? The media loves stories about stars in rehab, maybe like bullies; it takes the heat off the "news" anchors and their lack of ability to find a real story. Who's controlling these people and deciding what trash to report? It's a dog and pony show, and Mark is just one of the many victims – like Don Henley's song, "Dirty Laundry."

It's funny, too, there are a lot of news anchors in rehab, but they go in there very *quietly* – again, a deliberate sleight of hand on their part. One has to wonder what these people are doing in their own screwed-up lives that drives them to enjoy destroying other people – people they don't even *know*. Wouldn't it be nice to peer into their secret lives and see what self-destructive behaviors they have? Wouldn't it be nice to see *their* dirty laundry on TV? They're merely puppets practicing deception and lies. And sadly, our society can't get enough. Why would anyone want to read tabloid magazines? Never mind watching the entertainment channels and shows, "real" news isn't reporting real news anymore. *Journalism is dead.*

Embarrassed by his negative attention from the media, and their comments about his failure to stay sober, Mark thought he'd go back to A.A., but he chose a different one. He was too late for the meetings that day, so he promised himself he would go the next day. He took a limo service to buy some groceries. As he walked towards the exit, he passed some plants on sale. Remembering what his former sponsor had said about keeping a plant alive for a year, he stopped to look. He liked one in particular and went back to pay for it. It was big and leafy. When he came home with the groceries and new plant, he looked around the house for a prominent place to put it.

He walked all over the house with it. He even tried rearranging his furniture for his new friend's comfort. He finally found a place he liked on a table near the kitchen counter. That way, he'd see it every day. He figured it would be hard to kill when he'd see it every time he got water for himself.

The next morning Mark awoke refreshed and happy to be in his own home. He got out of bed and stretched and then went into the kitchen to brew some coffee. While the coffee was dripping too slowly into the pot, Mark got bored and started looking at his plant. He stuck his fingers into the soil and realized that it was too dry. He couldn't let this plant die! He ran over to the sink and filled a coffee mug up with water and quickly dumped it into the pot.

He sighed with relief. "I saved you! It's just the two of us, so we need to look out for each other. Hmm. I probably should give you a name, shouldn't I?" While he examined the plant, the coffee pot started beeping. He filled the mug that saved his friend's life and then added some cream and sugar. As he stirred, he dripped some coffee on his Led Zeppelin t-shirt. Then he had an epiphany. He smiled, "I'm going to call you Robert Plant. I think that's a good name for you." He walked outside and got the paper. Then, still astonished by his brilliance, he sat down and drank a couple cups of coffee while reading the news.

CHAPTER Twenty-Three

MARK HAD BEEN clean for almost two months when he was slated to write a love song for his upcoming movie, *You're the One*. It was no secret that Mark was a songwriter and could sing. The highest-rated episode of *The Trifecta* was when Mark's character got serious and sang his marriage proposal to his girlfriend on the show. Mark had composed the tune and written the lyrics. It even made the Billboard charts for a few months.

However, it's hard to write about being in love when you're not... even harder when you can't have a relationship even though you want one. So for two weeks, Mark sat in front of his baby grand and just tinkered with the keys and zoned out.

His eyes roamed around the room that used to spin. He lay down on the floor and looked up at the ceiling. He started fires in the fireplace and listened to his iPod. He watched television and sang lyrics that he made up while he was cooking his meals. Nothing gave him any clues. Mark would be singing the song to one of the characters in the movie. So the song had to be completed in pre-production where normally it would be done afterward. He *had* to get it done.

So he wrote about the only thing he had any attachment to. He wrote about the only thing that made him feel like he had any power or control. Ironically, he wrote about the only thing that took all of his power away and made him lose control. Finally, after two weeks of the worst writer's block ever, he was able to write about the one thing he knew better than anything else.

He sat down at the piano with blank sheets of music paper and started writing feverishly. The ink was flowing now, and he knew the song would be a hit. The best part? No one would know it was about his love affair with booze, set to a catchy little tune. He thought how stupid it was that inevitably, people would use it as their wedding song. How touching it would be when two lovers gazed into each other's eyes to a song about getting wasted. Oh well. People don't really pay attention to song lyrics nowadays anyway. No matter, no one's writing meaningful songs anymore – just ones about "bitches and hoes." Their mothers must be so proud.

Mark knew he had a winner. When he played it for the film's composer, he applauded. There was no doubt that it was going to work.

Mark was scheduled to record the single for the movie soundtrack at a music studio in Miami. After the session was completed, Mark felt good. Filming wasn't set to begin for a couple of months, so Mark had some time to get into a routine in his house.

Stability wasn't something Mark had ever really had. His mind went back to his childhood. He thought about all the decisions he had made, even way back then. He thought about the first time he drank alcohol. He was thirteen and at a party in the middle of nowhere. He went with a bunch of older kids, and they had to ride ATVs to even get there. He thought about all the times he'd put his life in other people's' hands. How he entrusted people with events his life and they exploited him. Why did he trust anyone who hadn't proven themselves to him?

Mark was a regular attendee at A.A. and started to form relationships with some of the other regulars. He got a sponsor from the group. His name was Fred, and he picked Mark up for the meetings and dropped him off afterward. It gave Mark more time to talk about recovery without other people around.

He confided in Fred that sometimes he felt overwhelmed. Fred encouraged Mark and admitted he had been there. And said that sometimes he still had bad days. Fred reminded him of the Serenity Prayer. And to say it slowly.

Some of the guys in the group sometimes met for coffee and talk. Since Fred didn't attend these sessions, another man brought Mark, so he didn't have to take a car service to A.A. His name was Hank. Another chance to talk one-on-one with someone who had worked the program. Hank suggested some books that would help Mark's recovery. He told Mark to enjoy the little things in life and reminded Mark to laugh. If Mark couldn't learn to have a good time without drinking, he'd never stop. It was good to be around someone who knew what Mark was going through. Mark was glad he was going. He knew it was where he needed to be. Progress is a beautiful thing.

One night at the regular meeting, Mark sat down with the usual guys from the coffee group. When it was time for people to speak and share their stories, a woman that Mark had never noticed piqued his interest. There was something familiar about her. She was a short Hispanic woman with sunglasses and a baseball cap. Mark was fixated on her. That voice, it was so familiar to him. Almost haunting, even.

"Hi, my name is Danielle, and I'm an alcoholic. My sobriety date is July 27, 1995. That's when my husband walked out on me because I was drinking and driving with our baby in the car. My dad was an alcoholic, and I knew if I didn't stop, I would wind up like him. He accidentally killed himself. I made a choice to live. If you work this program, it will change your life." She sat down.

Mark's eyes widened as he realized – my God that was the judge who would be presiding over his trial. When the meeting was over, Mark tried to avoid her by going to the back to grab some coffee. She wasn't about to let him avoid her.

"Mr. Taylor?"

"Oh, hi," he said as he took a sip out of his Styrofoam cup.

"You look like you're avoiding me."

"I have my trial coming up. I thought it would be inappropriate to talk to you."

"You're probably right. Are you serious about this?" she asked as she looked around the room and then back at him.

He took another sip of his coffee. "I'm a joke in a late-night monologue now. I wake up sometimes, not knowing what I did the night before. I can't live like this anymore. I never thought I'd be an alcoholic."

She smiled. "No one ever thinks they're going to be an alcoholic. The good news is, you don't *have* to be one. That's what we're here for. You made the decision to come here on your own. You *know* you need to be here."

Mark looked down. "I never thought I'd have to get help. I wanted to quit on my own."

"Are you embarrassed that you're in A.A.? Because I think waking up with a stranger, naked on a lawn, or seeing scandalous pictures of yourself all over TV would be more embarrassing."

Mark smiled. "Yeah, I was trying not to think about all that. I've let a lot of things happen that I'm not proud of."

"We all have made mistakes. The key is learning from them. Put that past where it belongs… *behind* you."

"Did you reunite with your husband and daughter?" Mark asked.

She pulled out her phone and showed him a picture of her family. "We've been married twenty years, and this little girl never saw me drink," she said as she pointed to the girl on the phone. "Mark, I hope you can overcome this disease so you can be a role model and show people that alcohol doesn't have to control your life. Show it who's boss, Mark."

She stepped towards him and patted his chest, "Get some new friends, keep coming to these meetings and then one day find a woman who doesn't drink, and you'll be fine."

Mark exhaled, "Okay."

"Well then, I will see you next time," she said with a smile as she walked away.

CHAPTER
Twenty-Four

TIME HAD GONE BY SO QUICKLY. Before Mark knew it, September 27th was upon him. That was the date of Mark's trial. He was so nervous! He could get jail time. Mark got dressed and had his driver take him to court, where the media anxiously waited to snap pictures of Mark Taylor getting out of his limo. They were practically frothing at the mouth for more opportunities to humiliate him. Mark and his attorney made their way past the flashes and headed into the courtroom.

They went straight to the left side of the court and sat down. Trevor started unpacking his files, pens, and paper. Mark looked around the courtroom and wondered when he would see his home again.

As Judge Martinez finished her coffee and doughnut in her chambers, the bailiff knocked on her door and asked if the prosecuting attorney could come in before the trial began. She wiped her face with a napkin and told him to show her in.

Theresa Jackson came in, and the judge pointed to a chair in front of her desk. Theresa sat down as the judge looked at her watch.

"I'm sorry for the short notice, your honor, but I have a favor to ask you."

"Please, we need to begin. What is it?"

"My daughter applied for a scholarship to your alma mater. I wouldn't ask, but I know you sit on the board. I was wondering if there was any way that you could put in a good word," she asked with a tentative little smile.

The judge put her hand up. "Say no more, Theresa."

Theresa stood up. "Thank you so much, Judge Martinez," and she started walking out of the judge's chambers.

Before she could reach the door, the judge called out, "Hold it!" Putting her glasses on, Judge Martinez looked into the open file on her desk. Theresa walked back to the desk.

"Are you still intending to prosecute Mark Taylor?"

"I want *jail time,* your honor."

"It would be nice to see the charges reduced to Reckless Driving. How about a driver's class and some community service, Theresa?"

Theresa sighed really dramatically. "You *hate* celebrities. I don't understand."

"I wonder, Theresa, what's more important... your daughter getting a scholarship or Mark Taylor getting jail time? You think about it, and I'll see you in my courtroom."

Theresa crossed her arms and groaned. She exited the judge's chambers, wondering why the judge was going soft on a celebrity when she detested them so.

A few minutes later, as Mark was asking his attorney about the possible outcomes of the trial, Theresa came into the courtroom and gave both Mark and his attorney dirty looks.

"What's her problem?" Mark asked.

"She's trying to intimidate you. Just ignore her."

When the judge came in, Mark stood, along with everyone else, and smiled a little bit at her. The bailiff told everyone to take a seat. He read the docket information to the judge and named the parties involved. The judge looked at Theresa and said, "Is there anything that has changed since I set a date for this trial, Ms. Jackson?"

Theresa exhaled very loudly. She looked at Mark then back at the judge. "Your honor, we'd like to reduce the charges against Mr. Taylor to Reckless Driving. The State recommends a Defensive Driver's class and 500 hours of community service with time served."

Trevor stood up, almost giddy. "Your honor, we think this is fair." He looked at the prosecutor and said, "Thank you, Theresa." But she just snarled at him. This was *not* fair, and everyone in that courtroom knew it!

"Good," said Judge Martinez. "Mr. Taylor, Christmas came early for you this year. I hope I never see you in my courtroom again." She smiled and banged the gavel.

Trevor and Mark both thanked the judge and exited the courtroom. Mark was a free man! He wanted to jump for joy, but the media was disappointed with the outcome. They'd rather have photographed him in an orange jumpsuit and chains. How about an exclusive of Mark picking up trash along the highway? That would've been better. Oh well, it was just a matter of time before he screwed up again. Mark wouldn't stay out of trouble for long.

Mark was still without a license for nine more months. But he did everything else he was supposed to, including his community service. Because of Mark's history, the judge recommended Mark serve at a battered women's shelter in downtown Miami. It would be suitable for Mark to see what victims go through.

For months, Mark went and painted houses, helped people move, did laundry – whatever they needed. He got to know many of the victims and hear their stories… a lot of stories. Some of the women were beaten so severely, they wound up in the hospital. Some came from families that had a history of abuse through several generations and thought it was normal. How do you break a cycle like that?

Mark was at the shelter one day when a young woman came in with a baby. She had two black eyes, and her baby's arm was in a cast. She told one of the counselors that her husband had beaten them both while he was drunk and didn't even remember doing it. Mark saw a lot of bad stuff there. Something was stirring inside of him. Something he wasn't familiar with: compassion.

Mark was invited to all the talk shows to discuss his recent trial. His first public appearance this time was *The Tonight Show*.

When Mark came on stage, he felt at ease right away. He had been on with Jay Leno before, and even though he had been the punch line of many of his jokes, Jay liked him and went easy on him. They showed the footage of Mark's accident on the set of *Don O'Malley*. There was a loud chorus of oohs and aahs from the audience as Mark turned away from the video. He said that he still couldn't even watch it. By a twist of fate, on this night, Claudia James was the second guest on the couch. Mark hadn't seen her for about a year. She asked him if they could have dinner and catch up. He was very hesitant, given their history, but he caved, as he always did with beautiful women.

They went out to a very secluded mom and pop restaurant in Burbank to avoid the paparazzi. The waiter came over to take their drink order. Mark ordered seltzer water. "Do you mind if I drink?" she asked him. He did, but he told her it didn't bother him. A few minutes later, when the drinks came, she wasted no time getting that burn down her esophagus. Mark knew this wasn't a good idea. He knew he shouldn't even entertain the idea of being with Claudia again. They ordered their meals and laughed all the way through dessert.

As they walked outside, she asked if he wanted to come

back to her hotel. Against his better judgment, he had already decided *before dinner* that he was going home with her.

When they got to her room, they kissed the whole way in, and it progressed quickly from there. They headed for the bedroom, and by the time they got there, she was barely dressed. She went into the bathroom and stayed so long that Mark got out of bed and opened the door.

"What are you doing?" he asked.

"I just wanted to do a few lines first," she said, like it was no big deal.

Mark got very angry and pointed to the bedroom, "You leave me lying in your bed while you're snorting coke?" Mark stormed out of the bathroom and started to get dressed.

She came out after him wiping her nose with her index finger. "What's the big deal? You used to be just like me. I just wanted to take the edge off."

"If you can't have sex with me without getting high, then we shouldn't be having sex, Claudia."

This angered her. "What are you – my father?"

He laughed in anger as he grabbed his coat. He was going to be kind and just walk out, but she just couldn't let him go. She grabbed his arm. "Don't leave." And then she said those words that he *hated* to hear. "I don't want to be alone."

"I don't either, but I *sure as hell* don't want to be with you." He pulled his arm away and left.

He was driven back to the airport and had an unusually hard time saying no to a real drink when the flight attendant came by. He just looked out the window for the whole flight, wondering. Was Ms. Right out there somewhere?

CHAPTER Twenty-Five

A FEW WEEKS LATER, Mark's single from the *You're the One* soundtrack debuted at number one in the Top 40 music chart. That was good news on this day – the *only* good news. Every media outlet carried the story that Declan had been released from jail, and he didn't do it quietly. He was telling the press that Mark had set him up, and somehow there was no evidence to refute Declan now. The District Attorney was forced to drop all the charges against him because the evidence went missing. Mark went down to the police station and asked to speak to the two detectives who had interviewed him. Only one of them was there, Ken Dixon. He came out to the front desk as soon as he heard Mark Taylor was waiting for him.

"What the hell happened? You *had* him. How could he go free now?" Mark yelled.

Detective Dixon went over to him, put his arm out, and pointed to a room off the waiting area. "Come with me." He shut the door.

"I don't understand this. You guys *lost* the evidence?" Mark said in disgust.

Ken sat down. "We didn't lose the evidence," he said. "Why don't you have a seat, Mr. Taylor?"

"He held a press conference saying I sabotaged him so I could be a movie star. Do you believe that?" Mark asked, pacing the room.

"Sit down, Mark. I'm going to tell you the ugly truth."

Mark sat down. "I mean, what's the deal? Even if you guys lost the evidence, the phone carrier has a copy of those pictures. And what about his laptop? Aren't those pictures saved on his mother ship?"

"Motherboard."

"Whatever! I didn't set Declan up. How is this spinning this back to me?"

Ken Dixon remained calm. He put his hands on the table, looked down, and said, "Look, do you know how much Declan O'Conner is worth?"

"What does that have to do with anything?"

Ken looked at Mark and said quietly, "He's worth five hundred million. It's like this: when you're worth that kind of money, the evidence tends to *disappear*."

Mark looked down. "So, no one *lost* the evidence?"

"Of course not. Do you know how hard it is to check those things in and out of evidence? There's a huge trail of paperwork."

"The phone company is in on it too, then?"

"'Fraid so. Sorry, Mark. You were just in the wrong place at the wrong time."

"This could ruin my career. Can't you hold a press conference and say that you *had* evidence against Declan?"

"I've been instructed to stay as far away from this as possible. I'm sorry, I really am. You're just another casualty of powerful people."

"What about justice for Britt? And there were others. What about the *victims*?"

"I hope to God Declan gets what's coming to him," Dixon said sympathetically as he got up from the table.

"Isn't there anything you can do?"

"Hey, I've got a family. You have no idea who you're dealing with. Just let it *go,*" Dixon said, and he left the room abruptly.

Declan took the opportunity to make the rounds on talk shows with Claudia holding his hand. They made it all about a love triangle, and people bought it. Declan won over the media. The tide turned once again in Declan's favor.

Robert Plant was slumped over, all floppy and weak. Poor Robert. He was so neglected! Mark went over and tenderly touched his limp little arms. "I'm sorry I left you, Robert. Look what I did to you! And you're the only one who understands me." Mark thought about how pathetic *that* was.

Of course, it's not like he responded, but Mark vowed he would never leave Robert alone again. Mark fled to the sink and returned immediately to Robert with a watering can, and he filled Robert's pot until he was full. He looked so lifeless. Even his color was off.

The loneliness he'd felt before he wrote the song came back, with a vengeance. He looked at Robert, and then he looked around at the empty house. It had been vacant for a while, and Mark longed for some company even if it was just for a few hours. He went into his bedroom and contemplated his next move. Sex or booze? He did *not* want to feel alone anymore.

He changed into some designer clothes, fixed his hair, checked his wallet for a condom, and grabbed the keys to his car.

He drove to a trendy bar in downtown Miami and had the valet take his car. He went right to the front of the line, and the bouncer let him right in. Everyone in the club was *someone*. And they were all beautiful. I love the term Oscar Wilde liked to use

"Beautiful idiots." It seems way more appropriate now than it could ever have been in Victorian times. Mark went up to the bar and tried to decide what he was going to choose, women or booze. The bartender came up to him. "What can I get for you?"

"I'm not sure yet. I need a minute to decide," Mark answered. Mark looked down at his smartphone. He scrolled through the names until he got to his sponsor. He didn't want to drink. But he needed something, something to satiate his appetite. Just then, a lovely young thing came up to him and started to make conversation.

"I loved your last movie, Mark," she said with a wiggle.

"Oh, thanks," he said, looking around to see if there was anyone hotter that he could take a crack at.

"Do you know that scene where you took your wife into the bedroom after you rescued her from her kidnapper?" she asked.

"Yup. I know that scene," he said.

"If you take me home right now, we could re-enact that scene."

He looked at her and smiled. He grabbed her hand, and without even asking her name, they went back to her house. They had a wild night. She was no saint, that's for sure. But then again, neither was he. He left in the middle of the night, and by the time he got back home, he felt hollow, empty. He regretted even leaving his house. He felt guilty. Why should he? He was an adult. What was the big deal? It drove him crazy. Why did he have to be so analytical about every stupid thing?

His throat was parched, so he went into the kitchen, and something caught his eye. Robert was slumped over. He was dead! How could he be dead? He was alive and perky just a few hours before. Oh no! He had sex, and it *killed* poor Robert! He smacked his head. He was guilty, all right — guilty of involuntary plant-slaughter because he slept with some random bimbo.

The next morning after he'd had his coffee, Mark put forth a serious effort to revive Robert. He even went to the home improvement store to talk to one of their plant experts. Robert *had* to live! He bought some fertilizer and an automatic watering container. He would do whatever it took.

It was just him and Robert. At least they had each other. That wasn't very comforting, he *was* just a plant. It's not like he talked back. On the other hand, maybe that was a good thing. Mark really didn't want to hear what anyone thought of him, even Robert.

CHAPTER
Twenty-Six

A FEW MONTHS PASSED, and the media kept running stories about Declan's charity work, feeding starving children in Africa, and rescuing pilot whales off the coast of Florida. Declan loved photo ops for the press. He took narcissism to a whole new level. As soon as the news left these functions, so did Declan. But it didn't matter. It was already out there. Look how fantastic Declan was! Yeah right.

Meanwhile, Mark went back to his old lifestyle, and who could blame him? Ever felt like the whole world was against you? Imagine being in the spotlight, with a nemesis whom everyone loved and put on a pedestal.

College football season was starting again. Mark spent the first half of the night watching college football in the bar at the marina near his house in Miami, called Flamingos. You remember the one he got kicked out of last year?

Clemson was losing – by *a lot*. Leave it to Mark to mix Jack Daniels and football. This has never been a winning combination. Mark acted like he was wearing the uniform. The bartender cut him off before halftime because Mark was hammered and stammering, yelling things that would make a sailor blush. Oh, Mark, when will you learn?

As the game ended, he watched the opposing team charge the field victoriously. That should've been a win for his team! He took it as hard as anyone in the locker room, except his body was taking a far worse beating than the scoreboard. He was escorted out of the bar by the scruff of his neck like a bad puppy. Then Mark made a fateful decision to put his keys in the ignition. The bartender had already called him a cab, but Mark is Mark, and no one is going to control him… at least that's what he thought.

Unfortunately for Mark, there was a rookie cop in the marina parking lot just waiting to bust someone, and on this night, it was Mark. As the policeman led him to the cruiser, Mark saw a boat pulling away from the dock. Looking closely, Mark noticed that the boat's name was *Sobriety*. This struck Mark as funny, and he started laughing hysterically as the cop pushed his head down into the backseat and slammed the door. The policeman called a buddy of his down the road as Mark passed out.

The other cop came to the marina as "backup."

"What do you have, rookie?" he said as he walked over to the rookie, seated behind the wheel.

"Mark Taylor," said the rookie, motioning with his head to the backseat.

"Oh, too bad, I thought he was on the wagon."

"Guess not. What should I do with him?"

"You have his keys?"

"Yeah, the bartender brought them out," the rookie said as he held the keys up with the Mercedes logo twinkling like a star.

The other cop smiled. "Are those the keys to the McLaren over there?"

"I think so. No other Mercedes here."

"Well, then you should drive him home," said the second cop as he grabbed the keys from the rookie. "We are here to protect and serve." The cop locked his patrol car, got into Mark's McLaren, and followed the rookie to Mark's house.

They walked Mark inside and laid him on his sofa. They put his car keys on the kitchen counter and locked the door from the inside. Of course, Mark didn't know any of this, so he kind of freaked out when he woke up the next day and didn't know how he'd gotten home. The last thing he remembered was that Clemson lost their game. To this day, Mark doesn't know how he got home safely that night. He glanced over at poor Robert, who looked like he was shrugging in disappointment at Mark. You're in bad shape when you feel like your *plant* is convicting you.

When he woke up the following day, he had a massive hangover. He decided to make coffee, which he desperately needed. But he didn't have any left. He drove to the grocery store, and as he walked by the other shops in the strip mall, he noticed a pet store. He didn't know what compelled him to go in, but he did, and it would change his life forever.

As he walked in, the clerk perked up. *Mark Taylor* was in her store! He went to the adoption counter and saw that there were animals from a nearby shelter. He started putting his fingers in the cages, and the dogs came up, tails wagging and tongues hanging. They were all so cute. He didn't know which one to pick. The clerk came over and started talking to him about the dogs.

There was a German shepherd that seemed to like him. Mark started asking questions and found out the dog had come from a house where there were too many dogs. They were all malnourished. This dog's name was Jasper, but she said he was young enough that Mark could re-name him with no problem. Jasper liked Mark. Mark smiled at Jasper. "This is the one," he said as the clerk unlocked his cage and let him go to Mark. A little while later, Mark and Jasper were driving back to Mark's house – *without* coffee.

Mark got to the house and showed Jasper where he was

putting his food and water. He gave him a tour of the house as if Jasper was a prospective buyer like the dog had a clue what he was talking about. Mark then showed him the back yard. Jasper didn't comment on the water view. But he did enjoy whizzing on the tree in the side yard.

After a few days went by, Mark changed the dog's name to Angus. They spent days together jogging, going to the beach, and just hanging out in the yard. Mark loved throwing the ball, and Angus loved retrieving it. They watched TV together every night and slept in the same bed. Mark was the happiest he'd been in a while. Angus was brilliant, too. He had figured out how to get out of the house by smacking the kitchen handle with his paws. Mark was eating well, working out, and abstaining from both alcohol and sex. He did Tai Chi in the mornings and then worked with a relaxation therapist in the evenings. Life was getting better. Even Robert had perked up.

A couple months into his new life of sobriety and his best friend, Angus, Mark started training for a lead role in an action movie. He was working out at his house with his personal trainer when a news bulletin came on the TV. He didn't stop working out, he didn't even lift his head, but he did hear what the news anchor was saying. "Breaking news out of Hollywood. Declan O'Conner was found dead in his home this morning of an apparent drug overdose. The actor, best known for his role in…" her voice trailed off.

Mark looked up at the television and said, "Declan," and shook his head. He immediately thought of Claudia. He didn't know if he should call her. Mark didn't want to jeopardize his new life. He didn't want to go back to what was comfortable, what was *wrong*.

Mark's trainer looked at him, "That guy was such a mess. Those girls… he did all those things, didn't he?"

"Well, there's no evidence… *apparently*," Mark said, looking away.

"Why are celebrities so whacked?" There was a pause, and then the trainer blurted out, "Oh, no offense, man. Sorry."

Mark laughed. "It's okay, but if you don't mind, I'd like to make some phone calls."

"Okay, man. I completely understand. Just call me, and we'll set up your next session." The trainer showed himself out, and Mark just sat at his kitchen table for a really long time. Angus came up to him and lay at his feet. Mark reached out for a few strokes but didn't feel like petting him right then.

Later that night, Mark was about to fix dinner when Claudia called. She was in Miami filming a commercial. He didn't sense any remorse on her part for not being in L.A. with Declan when it happened. She asked if Mark would come to her hotel for dinner. He told her he would meet her there in a little while.

I know you're probably thinking Mark was crazy for even contemplating "entertaining" Claudia. There's an explanation for that. There's something about Mark that you don't know. Something very dark from his past. But I can't tell you yet because Mark has buried it so deeply that it won't come to light until he gets the help he needs. It's hard to understand, but victims tend to fall back into patterns, and they don't know why. It's what they know, even if they know it's wrong. Sometimes they do the same to other people; sometimes, they drink to dull the pain as in Mark's case.

He went into his bedroom and started going through his closet feverishly. He wanted to look good. Then he felt guilty. What did he think was going to happen? Claudia's *husband* just died. Truthfully, Mark was glad he was dead. At least he wouldn't hurt anyone anymore. Mark only wished the truth would come out. Mark would never be able to clear his name now.

Angus came into the bedroom, jumped on the bed, and let out a whine.

"I'm just going to dinner, boy," Mark said as he scratched Angus' neck.

The dog sat up and tilted his head and barked.

"I promise, I'm coming back right after dinner."

Angus barked twice as if to say, "Yeah, right!" But Mark meant it. He was just going to dinner. He was just going to give her a shoulder to cry on, that's all. Nothing was going to happen. Mark thought about the last time he saw Claudia and left her in that hotel room in L.A.

Life was stable now and he didn't want Claudia screwing him up. Claudia was safe in that Mark knew exactly what to expect from her.

Mark put on jeans with a white t-shirt and a navy blazer. He slipped on brown loafers and put gel in his hair. He dabbed on a little cologne. Then he thought about it and washed it off. He took Angus out for a walk and then returned him to his favorite resting spot in the living room near the fireplace. Mark gave him one last pat and reassured him that he would be back shortly. He didn't even acknowledge Robert as he walked out the door.

CHAPTER
Twenty-Seven

HE MET her in the restaurant downstairs at a secluded table in the back. She smiled and waved him over. She looked like she was handling her grief exceptionally well. She stood up as he came to the table. He tried to kiss her cheek, but she pulled him in for a hug that felt a little too intimate for someone who needed to be consoled. She was wearing perfume. He thought it strange for someone in mourning.

"So good to see you," she said as they sat down.

"You look good," he said.

"Thanks, you too," she said with a smile.

"So, how are you holding up?"

"I'm okay. I don't know if you knew, I had just filed for divorce."

"No, I hadn't heard that."

"Declan was not what you would call a 'good' step-dad," Mark remembered all the times he'd called Claudia's kids ugly names.

The waitress came over and took their order and then came back with their drinks. Claudia gulped a glass of wine down. "I noticed you ordered San Pellegrino," she said.

"Yeah, I'm not drinking anymore."

"Well, this whole thing with Declan has got me considering making some changes," she confessed.

"We never really liked each other after I found the pictures on his phone."

"He considered you a friend," she said quietly, "despite what happened."

"Declan never *considered* anyone."

Claudia raised her eyebrows.

"Sorry," Mark said. "I didn't like the way Declan treated anyone, but I *really* didn't like the way he treated you."

Claudia smiled. "You were always a nice guy."

He took a sip of his drink. "Huh, I guess that depends on who you ask." Much to Mark's surprise, this night was not about two people grieving. It turned more into two people discussing what might have been. They sat there for hours, just talking.

Claudia looked at her watch, "Well, I'm going back to my room."

He looked around at the empty room, "Yeah, it's getting late."

"Do you want to come up to my room for bottled *water*?"

He smiled at her, "I don't think that's a good idea. But thanks."

She got up from the table and hugged him, whispered in his ear, "Room 615," and slid her key card into his front right pocket. Then she walked away without saying anything else.

He stood there for a minute and looked around. Then he threw some cash on the table and made his way up the elevator.

He pressed the button several times. He leaned forward and started tapping his hands on the elevator doors. "What am I doing? What am I doing? It's been six months since I got laid. I have pressure building… that's what I'm doing. *This is wrong*." The elevator dinged, and he said, "I'll worry about it tomorrow." He stepped out and found her room. He looked around and slid the key into the slot and opened the door.

He called out to her, "Claudia?"

"I'm in the bedroom," she said.

He walked in. She was wearing a bathrobe.

"I wasn't sure you'd show up," she said.

"This," he pointed to her and then to himself, "doesn't mean anything," he said.

She smiled. "It never does."

Afterward, he waited until she fell asleep, and then he got dressed and left. He just wanted to get home to Angus.

Of course, there had to be fans in the hallway to catch him sneaking out of her room. One of them even filmed him leaving, which wasn't a big deal, until the next day when those same people saw that it was Claudia's room. It's hard to understand how people who consider themselves "fans" would deliberately hurt the celebrities they claim to love. They contacted a tabloid magazine and sold them the story and pictures. Hey, it was a quick $500, right? Who's it hurting? If celebrities didn't want the attention, they shouldn't be famous, right? I'm glad I don't live under a microscope. Aren't you?

No surprise, when Mark got home, Angus was angry, and Robert was dying *again*. Now his dog *and* plant were both reacting to his bad behavior.

It took two weeks for the autopsy results, which showed that Declan "accidentally" overdosed on a mixture of drugs. I don't know how they make that determination. It's not like the coroner was with Declan when he did it. Maybe Declan knew what he knew doing, and it wasn't an accident at all. Mark wondered himself about it being accidental.

Claudia flew out to L.A. for the funeral. She would have to face Declan's friends and family for the first time since the tabloids had run the story and picture of Mark leaving Claudia's room with the title, "Claudia and Mark Taylor Spend Night 'Grieving' in Hotel Room Together."

Claudia didn't get a good response from people at the funeral. Mark didn't even bother to go. Why would he? He hated Declan and also called him a predator to anyone who would listen. Claudia was left to receive the brunt of rude comments and poor treatment from people. They didn't hide their feelings and let her know that she had no right to sleep with Mark. Declan's mom called Claudia a whore during the eulogy in front of everyone! She went on quite a rant saying that Claudia was the reason Declan was dead. Even with all the information that came out about Declan, no one wanted to admit what an evil person he was.

Mark got a call from his publicist. She was trying to do damage control. This whole situation with Claudia was hurting his likability with the public. The stories didn't stop coming either. At least Mark had Angus by his side. Mark flipped on the TV, and Angus jumped on the couch and put his head on Mark's lap. Somehow that dog always knew when Mark needed him. Mark petted him and started watching a late-night talk show. They were doing the opening monologue…

"Senator Mitchell Rider passed away this week, but don't worry, Mark Taylor's going to sleep with his wife to help her through the grieving process. If this is the sober version of this guy, someone give him a drink!" The crowd started laughing. Mark changed the channel. He was the butt of all the jokes on late-night television. People make mistakes all the time, but when you're rich and famous, everyone finds out about them.

CHAPTER *Twenty-Eight*

A COUPLE OF WEEKS LATER, Claudia was back in Miami and dropped by, with no warning, to see Mark. She got all dolled up and rang the doorbell. She was holding her little Yorkie while it did what it did best, yapped incessantly. Angus started barking too. He probably thought Claudia brought him a chew toy. Mark saw that it was her through the glass on the door. He sighed and then restrained Angus, who was ready to take that Yorkie down! Mark held him by his collar and then opened the door.

"What a cute dog..." She stuck her hand out to pet Angus, and he showed her all of his teeth with a nasty growl. "Argh!" she said as she quickly pulled back her hand and her living dog toy. "What a *mean* dog!"

That's always the wrong thing to say about man's best friend. Mark got angry. Angus, too, because he wouldn't stop barking at Claudia and her precious ball of fur. "Go lie down, Angus!" Mark ordered him. Angus whined and then went to his bed by the fireplace, put his head down, and curled up, but he didn't take his eyes off Claudia or her appetizer and occasionally threw out a bark and snarl to remind her that he was there. "What are you doing here, Claudia?"

She didn't wait to be invited; she just stepped into his house. "I came here to be with you," she said, putting her hands on Mark's chest. Angus picked his head up and barked.

He took her hands off him. "I think we are better off as friends. I have a lot of stuff going on right now, okay? I just don't have time to get involved with anyone right now."

She kissed him. He just stood there, imagining his publicist yelling at him if she could see him. "I think you'd better go, Claudia."

"What about the last night we spent together? Didn't it mean anything to you?"

"It was just *sex*, Claudia. I was trying to console you." Only Mark could give someone sympathy sex. Mark couldn't figure out why she was so infuriated.

"I thought we had something, Mark. I wanted to make this work."

"Make *what* work? You know what, Claudia? I'm really tired of all your head games. It was just sex, okay? You're the one that said it never means anything."

"Please just give me another chance," she pleaded. She was almost tearing up. "Please, Mark. I really want us to be together." Her dog let out a long snarl and showed its pathetic little teeth.

Mark looked at her skeptically. "What's going on?"

"It's this whole Declan thing. The papers are all saying that I'm an aging starlet who acts like a whore."

Mark found that amusing. "Finally, the media's got it right," he said as he pushed her outside and slammed the door in her face. He locked the door and sat back on the sofa to watch TV. Angus whimpered, and Mark called him over to the couch. He jumped up on the couch and put his head on Mark's leg and started whacking the arm of the couch with his happy tail. Mark smiled. Life was good. What more did he need? He had his best friend, he was ready to start his new project, and he had not had a drink for three months. He'd denied Claudia James. Everything was good. No, everything was great. He felt happy. That was a feeling he hadn't had for a long time. And Declan was gone. Even if Mark did get the brunt of the bad publicity from that, at least it was over. Everything was looking up.

But Claudia didn't leave. She came back to the door a few minutes later with an envelope. At least she left her little mutt in the car this time. Mark was really irritated now because Angus had to move so Mark could get off the sofa to open the door. He flung the door open. "What now, Claudia?"

"I wanted to see if you wanted me anymore, but you don't, so I just wanted to give you this. I found it in Declan's things, and I thought you may want to give it to that Detective that you were working with," she said.

Mark opened the envelope. It was full of pictures, and there was a journal. Mark pulled it out and started flipping through the pages. He looked at Claudia, who had tears rolling down her face.

"He kept a diary of the things he did to those girls," she said.

Mark took Claudia in his arms and hugged her, "I'm so sorry, Claudia." He pulled away. "Do you want to take a ride?" She nodded. They got into Mark's car, and he held her hand. "You know, if you had just told me this from the start, you would've gotten a better response." She smiled and they drove down to the police station and handed the journal to Detective Dixon.

The police had to authenticate Declan's handwriting and round up his accomplices, but at least someone would be brought to justice, even if it wasn't Declan. At last, the story would break and clear Mark's name. Declan would finally be implicated. Claudia rode back to Mark's house with him, and she walked him to the door. "Do you think I could come in?"

Mark looked inside his house and turned back to her. "I

don't think we should prolong the inevitable. But I do want to thank you for what you did. I know you didn't have to."

"Despite what you think about me... about us, I do care about you, Mark. I know you're a good person."

"I may have done a lot of stupid things in my life, but I would never hurt a woman like Declan did, Claudia. Too bad we both care more about our careers than anything else. Who knows what might've happened?"

"Bye, Mark."

Mark shut the door and walked to the sofa. Now, did Mark even want to love Claudia? Who knows! But, Mark certainly knows how to add drama to a situation. He wished the best for Claudia. But they both knew the best thing for both of them were other people!

That night, Mark fell asleep on the couch with Angus, who was snoring and slobbering on Mark's leg. Mark woke up and decided to go to bed. He made sure the upper lock on the door was locked, so Angus didn't let himself out, and then Mark went into his bedroom. He turned down his sheets, and Angus lay at his feet.

Mark went right to sleep, and he had a dream. He was walking the beach with a brunette whom he seemed very smitten with. They went to eat at a restaurant and spent a long time talking. He saw himself smiling. There was something oddly familiar about that face; Mark was convinced that he had seen her before. She seemed so real.

Mark woke up and saw a head on the extra pillow. Mark raised his head, and so did Angus, letting out a whimper. It was only Angus, not the woman from his dream. "Too bad," Mark said as he turned over and went back to sleep.

CHAPTER
Twenty-Nine

A FEW DAYS after Claudia and Mark turned over the envelope to Detective Dixon, the police held a press conference exposing the evidence. They told the shocking things Declan and his accomplices did, and they painted Mark as the hero of the story. They said Claudia found the evidence in their house in L.A. and that she came forward with the evidence.

Mark enjoyed the positive press he got in the media after they discovered he was the good guy. Maybe the lesser of two evils, but he sure wasn't fighting the good publicity. He headed for Texas to shoot a movie and took Angus with him. They would be away from Miami for five months. Ted promised to take good care of Robert while Mark was gone. Unfortunately, that five months turned into five months of drinking, going home with strange women and getting into bar fights alongside his co-star, who was a lot like Mark.

By the time Mark and Angus returned to Florida, Mark was a mess. He succumbed very quickly to the lifestyle he'd sworn off not so long ago. He was cracking under the pressure of being a hero, pulled in every direction. If depression had made him drink before, now he drank from everything going well. Mark was in serious trouble. He no longer had negative emotions to blame his drinking on.

Mark arrived home after his movie wrapped, and began the first night back by drinking and drinking some more. In fact, he drank so much he fell into a drunken slumber and didn't realize he had left the top lock on the back door unlocked. That wouldn't have been a big deal, but since Angus had figured out how to open the door by twisting his paws around the rectangular handle, it would soon prove to be a life-changing mistake. A minute later, a loud screech and a loud scream came from the street outside.

Mark's neighbor, Ted, ran out to see if everything was all right. But it wasn't. He saw Angus' lifeless body in front of the wheels of a black Cadillac Escalade and a woman leaning over his body, crying. Ted put his arms around her while she sobbed and explained that the dog came out of nowhere and gave her no time to stop. Ted knew it wasn't her fault, and he knew if Mark wasn't with Angus, he was passed out.

Ted came to Mark's open door with Angus' body wrapped in a blanket. He kept calling Mark, and after several minutes he woke up. By that time, Ted had to put the dog down on the floor because he was so heavy. Mark tried to understand what was happening, but all he heard was Ted saying he was sorry.

"She didn't have enough time to stop," Ted said. Mark fell to his knees and started petting his dog frantically, screaming, "Wake up, Angus. Wake up, damn it!" Mark pulled back his hand and looked at his fingerprints coming through the blood on his hand and started crying. Mark looked up to God and screamed, "Why did you kill my dog? How could you kill my dog?" Then he slumped over Angus' body and sobbed.

Ted was left in the awkward position of deciding what to do. Mark wasn't in any condition to make decisions at that moment. Ted asked Mark if he wanted him to take care of it.

Mark nodded. Ted took Angus to his veterinarian and had him properly disposed of. Mark wasn't even sober enough to say a proper goodbye. How could he live with the guilt of knowing that his drinking was the reason Angus had died?

Ted came back the next day to speak with Mark. He'd decided he was going to lay it on the line and tell Mark what he didn't want to hear. Ted was expecting a fight or some resistance. He got neither.

Mark wasn't handling Angus' death well. He was sickened by what happened and wracked with guilt. You can replace things – even friends. But an animal just loves you, no matter what.

Ted didn't do what most people would've done. Ted wasn't there to judge him. He was sincerely worried about Mark and the direction his life was headed. Ted knew the next course of action had to be rehab, but not if Mark didn't want it. The only way Mark was going to get better was if he wanted it this time. Angus' death might be the catalyst that would get him there.

Mark wasn't used to breaking down in front of people – especially another man. But Ted acted kind, like a father-figure. Mark realized why it all made sense – Ted must be in recovery and not revealing it to Mark. Ted asked Mark to trust him, and then he made a call to The Naples Recovery Center. How did Ted know that this place would be different? Mark figured he'd been through it himself. Ted volunteered to drive Mark to Naples.

Mark was quiet for most of the ride, reflecting on his life and all the mistakes he'd made. When they reached Naples, Mark started looking out the window at the town that he would call home for the next two months. As they drove down a little road, he saw the street sign. Recovery Road. Mark laughed. "Did you see the name of that road?"

"This isn't the first time I've been down this road, Mark," said Ted.

"I didn't realize you had a problem," Mark said.

"We'll talk about it when you get out," remarked Ted.

"Thanks for not passing judgment on me. I guess now I understand why. It takes one to know one," Mark said as he looked out the window at his new home.

Mark was nervous. He didn't want to go to rehab again just to fail again, but he blamed himself, and rightly so, for Angus' death. Would he be able to stop drinking? Would this time do it? What would be so different about this place? At least he knew someone who'd been through it, and it seemed to work for Ted. Look at how well-adjusted Ted was. Mark knew his life was about to change. He would have to remove all the alcohol in his home. He would also have to figure out what his trigger point was. If being alone drove him to drink, he'd have to find a new circle of friends who could have fun without drinking. If he couldn't go to a bar or nightclub because he'd backslide, he would have to stay home.

Ted parked the car and walked Mark into the intake office. After Ted took care of the paperwork, he left. They made Mark turn over his phone and keys and then brought Mark into the medical services area. They ran some physical and mental tests on him and then sat him down to discuss treatment options. He answered a lot of intimate questions, and it made him take a personal inventory of all of his screw-ups. They created the best course of action, which included a tobacco program to help him quit smoking too. Statistically, people in recovery have a better chance if they are treated for all their addictions at once.

At least this place was like an apartment complex and not a prison-like the other rehabs Mark had been in. Mark was allowed to roam the campus and go down to Fifth Avenue and eat his lunches and dinners at real restaurants. They did make it mandatory for the residents to eat breakfast in their apartments because their days started so early. It was also easier to keep tabs on people when they were in their studios.

The facility would send monitors out after the residents to make sure they were not down the road drinking or meeting someone to give them drugs. Sadly, many of the people in rehab have their recovery sabotaged by "friends" and family members who come and drop off their vice of choice while they're off the rehab's property. Nice.

As Ted was leaving, he promised to take care of Robert again while he was gone. But Ted was taking care of more than that. While Mark was checking into his room and unpacking, Ted walked into Mark's house and poured every bottle of liquor down his kitchen sink. Ted's wife took all the pictures Mark had of Angus – which were few – and had them framed. They put the pictures on the fireplace mantel. Ted hoped they would be a constant reminder of how important it was for Mark to stay sober.

CHAPTER *Thirty*

AFTER A COUPLE OF HOURS, a counselor walked Mark to his two-story apartment. She said, "You're 207," as she unlocked the door and gave Mark the keys, and he smiled softly. It was surprisingly luxurious, like his first apartment after he had gotten successful.

The door opened right into the kitchen. It had dark espresso contemporary cabinetry and white-and-gray Carrera marble.

It led to the dining area with its matching table and chairs. On the walls hung beach scenes so blue you could almost smell the ocean air. Across the room stood a marble fireplace that matched the kitchen. There wasn't much of a view, though. The window showed the brick wall of an opposing apartment. There was no celebrity status at this rehab – average people were housed with celebrities.

The counselor showed Mark to the main bedroom, and he noticed there were two beds in it. He looked at the counselor. "You're going to have someone else bunk with you," she said with a hesitant smile.

"Oh, I didn't realize that," Mark said, disappointed.

"It's okay. We pre-screen everyone. Most of the residents

here form life-long friendships with their roommates," she said.

Mark raised an eyebrow in disbelief. He walked into the attached bathroom. It reminded him of some of the best hotels he'd stayed in. More Carrera marble waited, surrounding a soaking tub with a beautiful chandelier hanging over it. The walls and shower were coated in more marbled decadence. It was precisely what he needed, and a stark contrast to what he'd been subjected to at the rehabs in Miami. The whole apartment smelled of lavender. Mark made a mental note of the use of color and scents. They certainly knew how to make people feel at ease in an already tense situation.

The counselor showed him the upstairs bedroom and bathroom. That made Mark unhappy. "More people are coming?" he asked.

"Yeah. We can house sixty residents, and we are almost at capacity right now." She looked at the beds. "And I got word that we have another group coming by the end of the week. So, these beds will be filled in the next few days."

Again, Mark wasn't happy. He was a celebrity, dammit! This wasn't like the spa rehabs in L.A., where it's like a vacation. God only knew who he was going to stuck with.

At least this place gave him freedom. He could walk around and meet people. There was a gym and a pool the residents could use, and the local grocery store hand-delivered anything the residents wanted.

After Mark had unpacked his bag and reviewed his schedule, he thought he'd walk down to the coffee shop at the facility. He had free time before his first scheduled relaxation session. It might not be wise to drink a large cup of caffeine before relaxation therapy, but he decided to chance it anyway. The coffee shop was open to the public, so you didn't know who was a customer, or who was staying there. He bought a coffee and started talking with the people there. One was an employee, and he found out the other two were residents.

Mark enjoyed talking to the people in the shop so much that he was almost late for his appointment. He looked at the clock and ran out the back door, which led right into the relaxation office. Mavis Foley, who was a volunteer, led Mark to the back room of an office and had him lie down on a bed. He looked at the large television and heart rate monitor. She slipped a finger cuff on him to monitor his pulse and gave him headphones. She explained what relaxation therapy entailed, and she started the massaging bed. The monitor began showing pictures of nature alternating with ambient colors, while tranquil music and the smell of lavender filled the room.

"This probably isn't going to work for me, he said. "I just had a huge coffee, and I usually need a drink to fall asleep." His heart rate was 100 beats per minute. He felt nervous like he was on a spaceship, and an alien was conducting weird experiments on him. He thought about how different this place was different from Serenity Gardens.

"Why don't we try it for a couple of minutes, and if it doesn't work, we'll try again tomorrow, okay?"

He was willing. He wanted it to work. "Okay," he said.

Mavis sat down and started monitoring his heart rate at the computer. He closed his eyes, and after a minute or two, his heart rate fell to 60 beats per minute. He was totally relaxed. His thoughts were clear, and about ten minutes into the session, he was in REM sleep. His eyes twitched, and he snorted a couple of times.

Mavis made notes and chuckled. Then she waited by the monitor for Mark to wake up.

When he did, he was startled. The pillow held a puddle of drool, and he could tell he'd fallen into a pretty deep sleep, pretty fast. "Did I snore?" he asked.

"Just a little. It felt good, didn't it?"

"Yeah, that's quite a setup," he said, motioning to the equipment.

She looked at her watch, "You have a group activity. Are you ready?"

"Sure."

He followed her to a vast room filled with chairs and sofas. He sat down as people started to fill the room. There were some women there giving him the eye, but he purposely avoided eye contact with them. A counselor named Dane came in and sat on a table. He had some papers in his hand. He looked around the room and welcomed everyone.

He started reading questions from the papers in his hand to inspire conversation and sharing. He looked around for volunteers to share their feelings. That wasn't going to be Mark. He wasn't into the whole sharing aspect. In fact, Mark didn't want to be there, but you had to attend at least one group therapy session a day. Mark was afraid someone would write about their time in rehab with Mark Taylor. He wasn't about to offer material for a book.

No need. Dane was saying enough, talking about the thousands of people who had walked through the doors over the years. His field of expertise hit close to home for Mark. He was the resident counsel to celebrities. I'm talking A-listers here. Of the who's who of the red carpet, many had chosen Dane to help them get clean. Dane had a solid reputation, and he had been through it all.

It wasn't enough that Mark was there. Dane wanted him to digest what he was saying. Typically, counselors don't make it a point to pick people out of a crowd, but as he got off the table and stood up, he looked directly at Mark Taylor.

"For those of you who are famous – you, the actors, artists, comedians, musicians – not only are you mobbed by fans. You're stalked by the paparazzi when you try doing normal things the rest of us take for granted. You have the world watching what you'll do next. Hopefully, something embarrassing. But, for you, I have more bad news; there is a direct correlation between those who are highly creative and those who suffer from depression and addiction." Mark squinted at him. He looked around the room and saw that all eyes were on him while Dane was making his point. Mark inched down in his chair, slightly… even subconsciously.

Dane continued. "Why? Some of you must be asking yourselves this question. How could someone who brings so much joy to other people be so depressed? Why can't they just be *happy*? The answer isn't always black and white, you see? That's why we have to talk and get to know each other here. There is a dark side in each one of us. That's the side that we need to bring to the light. We need to figure out what makes us do the things we do. And when that happens, we can stop doing them and get you all on the road to recovery – for good!"

Dane went on for a little while, but he was no longer focused on Mark, and Mark tuned a lot of it out. He'd heard plenty to keep his mind busy as he walked over to his next class. Mark had known a lot of people over the years who were depressed. Mark started counting how many people he knew who had committed suicide or attempted it. There was a lot. Too many. How come Mark never noticed before? He was so wrapped up in his own life, in his own darkness that he had never realized.

He thought about Dominic and wished that he had gotten the help that he needed. Sure, Dominic had been in and out of rehab in L.A., but it never made a difference. It had to make a difference for Mark. He didn't want to end up in a slideshow of dead stars at the next televised awards show.

CHAPTER
Thirty-One

THE NEXT MORNING, Mark awoke to the sound of someone stirring in his room. He sat up with a start and rubbed his eyes, but settled down when he realized it was Scott, one of the volunteers. Scott put a set of Louis Vuitton luggage on the bed, so Mark knew it had to be someone wealthy. Or someone with lots of debt!

"Sorry, I was trying to be quiet," Scott said.

"What's going on?" Mark asked.

"You're getting a roommate today," Scott said with a smile.

"Great," Mark said sarcastically as he stretched and got out of bed.

"Oh, I wouldn't worry about your roommate; you guys have *a lot* in common."

Mark was annoyed, "What, we're both *alcoholics*?"

"No! You're both *famous*!" Scott said, and he walked out in a hurry.

Mark followed him through the living room to the kitchen, but he was gone. Mark was really curious about who his new roommate was going to be. He went over to the coffee pot and turned it on, yawning. No sleeping late on a

Sunday around here. Mark looked around at the empty apartment and realized how badly he needed a sober friend. It was way too quiet. Mark remembered the counselor telling him that people here make friendships that last a lifetime. Mark could use a friend for life.

After he ate breakfast, read the paper, and took a short walk around the campus, Mark was ready to start his day. After a few hours, he was in his free time and decided to grab a cup of coffee at the coffee shop downstairs.

A huge man with a navy baseball cap and Minnesota Twins t-shirt walked in. It was Billy Hernandez, an outfielder and big-time home run hitter from the team.

Mark recognized him right away. Billy knew Mark, too. "Hey, man. *Don O'Malley* is one of my favorite movies," Billy said.

"Thanks," Mark said with a smile.

Billy went up to the counter and ordered his coffee, then took a seat next to Mark.

"So, how's the action in Naples?" he asked Mark.

"It's slow," Mark said.

"Well, I'd say that's a good thing since we're both in rehab." Billy laughed.

Mark looked at him, startled. How did he know Mark was in rehab? No one was supposed to know. Billy saw the concerned look on Mark's face.

"Oh, it's okay, man, I just checked in. I'm your new roommate," Billy said.

"Oh. Good."

"So, you think it's helping you?" Billy asked as he carefully sipped his hot coffee.

"I've only been here a day," Mark said.

"I didn't even hear you were in rehab, and I watch a lot of television."

"Well, it was kept pretty quiet," Mark said. "It wasn't court-ordered this time..."

"Oh, for real? So, it's serious this time!" Billy said. "That's good, I hope it sticks, man. The Twins said I had to get clean after the regular season so I could start spring training with a clean slate."

"Is this your first time?"

"Yeah, the Twins keep threatening they'll trade me to the Yankees!"

Mark laughed. "You're from Boston, aren't you?"

"Yeah, that's why they say it – to piss me off. I always wanted to wear the Red Sox uniform. I was a Red Sox player every Halloween when I was a kid."

"You don't have that Boston accent," Mark said.

"No, I'm from the Western Mass. I'm glad I don't have an accent, people in the south are wicked nasty, they call me a 'Yankee' every chance they get." Billy took a sip of his coffee. "So, where are you from?"

"Charleston."

"So you're from South Carolina?" he asked with a chuckle. "Where's your confederate flag?"

"Hey now, don't stereotype me just because of where I'm *from,*" Mark said in the southern drawl he'd worked hard to eliminate.

"Does your family still fly the confederate flag in their yard?" Billy asked.

"Uh…" Mark hesitated because they did!

"That's what I thought. That's why we call Southerners *racist,*" Billy said.

Mark got serious. "It's not about race. It's about southern *pride.*"

"Please, man. I've heard that all my life from southerners. And the Civil War was just about states' rights, not slavery, right?"

"That's right. You Yankees always come down to the South and tell us how much better everything is up north – then stay up there! That's why we call you 'Massholes!'"

"I guess we'll never have world peace when we can't even get along with other Americans," Billy said.

Mark put his hand up. "Nothing personal – we just don't like Yankees." He lowered his hand and picked up his coffee.

"Uh oh, I forgot the South is supposed to rise again! You know what? I hope you *marry* a Yankee," Billy said with a laugh.

Mark laughed. "I'd *never* marry a Yankee."

They talked for a few minutes more, then went to a group session, which was about to start. Mark had already decided that he wasn't going to participate. But Billy opened up and told the group he had always been a drinker but had tamed down over the years. Lately, his problem had been with drugs he had gotten from the latest surgery for an old knee injury. All the years of playing in the MLB had finally caught up with him, and he thought his career was over. It was harder to quit this time when he thought his baseball career was over. It dulled the pain of losing a job that he loved. The problem was, he was going to lose his wife too if he didn't kick it now.

The counselors said that it's actually harder for married couples when one is in rehab, and almost impossible if the one in rehab is married to someone who is still using. When they get out of rehab and go back to the spouse who's still using, their chances of falling back into addiction are really high. Fortunately for Billy, his wife didn't drink or use drugs, and she was happy he was in rehab.

Mark was glad he didn't have to worry about a spouse. He had enough to focus on without trying to make someone else happy at the same time. Mark wasn't happy himself, how could he make someone else feel that way?

It was time for Mark's one-on-one session with a therapist. He wasn't thrilled. He knew he'd have to open up and deal with everything he'd been so bad at suppressing all these years.

Mark walked into the office of Dr. Beverly Winthrop. She was in her fifties and about forty pounds overweight, which was accentuated by her five-foot frame. She had red hair and glasses and wore black from head to toe with a pink scarf around her neck. She welcomed Mark with a warm smile and gestured to an empty chair.

Mark looked around the office. It was painted an aqua blue that reminded him bitterly of Key West. She had pictures all around her office of what he assumed were family members. There was a clock that he noticed was ticking exceptionally loudly. He bet himself that he would be able to count the ticks of the clock for most of their meeting. There wasn't much furniture. Just a chair and a sofa.

She looked at Mark, knowing she only would have a short window to uncover what was destroying him. Would he open up to her?

Mark looked at the chair and then at the sofa. He didn't know where to go.

"You can pick the chair or the sofa, wherever you're more comfortable," she said with a gentle smile.

Mark sat down on the chair, and they exchanged polite nods. She put her notepad on her lap. "Is there anything that you'd like to discuss?" she asked.

"Not really," he said as he continued to look around. He noticed her stupid poster of a kitten trying to climb a branch that read, *"You can do it!"* and he laughed.

"You like my poster?" she asked with a smile as she looked at the poster. She seemed pleased with it.

"Not really. I'm a dog person."

She wrote something down.

Mark tried to see what she'd written. "Are you writing down that I'm a *dog person*? I thought you were supposed to write down things of importance… like why I drink or where do I see myself going with recovery," he said sarcastically.

"Is something bothering you, Mr. Taylor?" she asked.

"No!" Man, this was annoying.

"Okay… but it seems like something has you… I don't know, *on edge* a little?" she shrugged her shoulders.

"Yeah, now that you mention it, the stupid instrumental music around here doesn't relax me; it makes me want to drink."

"The music?"

"I *hate* it. It makes me angry."

She chuckled. "Our relaxation soundtrack makes you angry?"

"Yup."

"Do you think something else is making you angry, and you're transferring your anger to our... music?"

"Nope, your music just *sucks*."

They didn't make much progress on the first day. In fact, Dr. Winthrop didn't even write anything else down. She just kept trying to talk to Mark, trying to crack his tough exterior. He was very bitter. He wanted to be at work... or *anywhere* but there.

They finished their session, and Mark went back to his room and started reading a script his agent had sent him. There was a message on the apartment answering machine from his publicist telling him he was on the cover of several tabloids, but she reassured him that it was great for his career, and all of the A-list stars were checking into rehabs to bolster their careers. He just rolled his eyes. That seemed pretty ridiculous. At least *he* was taking it seriously, perhaps the only one in Hollywood who was.

CHAPTER
Thirty-Two

THE NEXT MORNING, a new and unexpected roommate came into the apartment like he was John Wayne busting through saloon doors. Mark and Billy stopped eating their breakfast, annoyed at the intrusion. Who was this guy and how could he have the audacity to barge into the place like he owned it?

It was apparent he hadn't been told that his new roommates were Mark Taylor and Billy Hernandez.

"Wow! I cannot believe I'm in rehab with celebrities! This is great!" His name was Jared, and he did not hide his excitement at all. He did nothing but smile at the stars who sat staring at him with their spoons halfway to their mouths.

Mark had already made up his mind; this fool wasn't going to be worth his time. Jared threw his cheap, mismatched suitcases on the counter, which of course annoyed Mark, and walked over to the breakfast table.

He shook both Mark's and Billy's hands vigorously. "I'm Jared Decker. I'm a *huge* fan. *Don O'Malley* is like my favorite movie of all time." Billy waited for Jared to say he was *his* fan, but he never did. He spent five minutes talking about himself and rambling on about his whole life story while Mark and

Billy tried to get a word in – without any success. He just kept on talking about himself. Mark and Billy looked at each other. Jared asked the guys where his room was, and Mark pointed as he said, "Up the stairs."

Jared scooped up his bags and made his way up the stairs and said he was going to unpack his stuff. "Best court-ordered rehab stay ever!" Jared said as he climbed the stairs.

Mark and Billy just nodded politely as he left. "He's quite a character," Billy said.

"You have to wonder what's going through his mind – getting placed with us. He's not serious about being here."

Billy laughed. "I would guess that he thinks he'll make life-long friendships with us."

"He talks too much," Mark said with total distrust and apprehension.

"He'll be fine," Billy said, trying to give Jared the benefit of the doubt.

"He's nothing like us," Mark said as he looked upstairs. "He likes attention, and when it comes to me getting sober – I don't like the idea of having someone like him around."

Billy noticed the time and realized they had a group session to attend. He called up the stairs for Jared so they could all walk down together. Jared trotted down the stairs a little too excitedly for the meeting and gave them a huge smile. "Imagine me, being in rehab with you guys – this is awesome!" he said with a big dopey grin, and Mark and Billy gave him a look that instilled reality in him.

"Oh, I mean – it's not awesome that we all have addiction issues, it's awesome that I'm with two celebrities! The counselors told me I'm probably going to form life-long friendships with my roommates, and you guys are famous – so I'll be friends with *famous* people! *That's* what I meant by this being awesome."

He didn't stop with that stupid smile.

Billy laughed at how annoyed Mark was by Jared's ignorant comments. He patted Jared on the back and said, "C'mon, we need to get down there so we can get a good seat."

"Can I sit next to you guys? We are roomies now, and we'll be spending the next... how long do you guys have left?" Jared asked. Mark just shook his head at Billy, and they started walking down to the group meeting room, without answering Jared's questions. Mark realized it was going to feel like a lot longer than eight weeks with this guy in their apartment.

After the group session – where Mark was much quieter than usual – the three of them walked back to their room and got a snack from the kitchen. Mark said he was tired of everyone trying to beat him over the head with a "God stick." He didn't mind anything else, but the religiosity of the whole thing annoyed him. "God" this and "God" that. Blah, blah, blah. Mark and Billy sat down in the living room and turned the TV on to watch some college basketball. Suddenly, an ad came on from an attorney's office. "If you are a boy or have a male child between the ages 8-13 who took medicine for ADD or ADHD and developed female breasts, we can help get you money today. Please call our number now!"

Mark looked at Billy and said, "Poor kids. They're boys with no attention span that developed breasts, now they'll *never* pay attention!"

Billy laughed and said, "I'd never leave the house." Jared just looked at Mark with no reaction, which made Mark and Billy look at each other a few times. Then Jared scurried over to the space open between Mark and Billy, which wasn't much space at all. Mark sighed as he begrudgingly moved over for Jared. Then Jared got a look of panic on his face. He jumped up again and grabbed the newspaper off the coffee table, and said with squinted eyes, *"I gotta take a deuce."* To that, Billy laughed out loud at Jared's lack of class. Mark was appalled – which is funny for someone who woke up naked on his lawn more than once.

"Who would I have to pay to get this guy moved into someone else's room?" Mark asked Billy.

"Good luck, man. I heard they're at full capacity this week."

"I can't believe this." Mark looked up at the ceiling as if it were God. "I'm sorry for whatever I've done to deserve this."

Billy laughed. "Oh, so you're praying to God now, huh?"

"Don't start," Mark said.

Jared came out of the bathroom. "Whew. I thought I was going to have to change my shorts. I hate that," Jared said innocently, like that was a normal conversation with strangers – or anyone, for that matter.

Mark was disgusted. Billy loved it. He liked Mark, but he enjoyed the fact that Jared was irritating him so much. Mark was supposed to be so relaxed and laid back. That part of his Jimmy Buffet-style reputation was not accurate. Mark looked at the TV and then back at Jared, who had a big, dumb smile on his face. Jared grinned at him as if he was Mark's puppy. He longed for Mark to interact with him – just to throw him the ball if you will. Of course, Mark *didn't*. He didn't want to encourage him. He just wanted him to shut up and go away.

CHAPTER
Thirty-Three

JARED TOOK it upon himself as Billy sat there and watched, amused by the whole thing. "I've seen *Don O'Malley* like five-hundred times!"

Mark tried to be polite, "That's about four hundred and ninety-nine more times than me."

"You know that scene where you're riding a motorcycle on the bridge? It looked like you really got hurt bad when you dumped your motorcycle," he said, waiting longingly for a response.

"Yeah, I got hurt," Mark said, and then he turned his attention back to the TV as to dissuade him from any more conversation. If things were only that easy!

"Was that the scene that you tore your meniscus in? That's when you got addicted to Vicodin, wasn't it?" Mark broke multiple bones, but he didn't want to encourage any more conversation between him and Jared. Besides, Mark *never* took Vicodin!

Mark looked at Billy briefly, who was trying hard not to laugh. "You really shouldn't believe everything you read about celebrities, okay?"

"I heard that you and Claudia James hooked up on that

movie. She's hot! Is she really as slutty in person as she seems?" he asked excitedly.

Mark gave him a really fake smile. "Even *more* so," he said, thinking that would shut Jared up, but it only made him ask more questions.

Billy could see Mark was getting really annoyed, and Billy's ego was hurt that Jared wasn't talking about him or how many home runs he hit last year. So Billy decided to interject his baseball stats into the conversation.

"Jared, did you know that I hit more home runs last year than anyone else in the majors?" he said.

"Oh, I *hate* baseball," Jared said and turned his attention back to Mark. Now Mark was nodding in amusement, and Billy was annoyed. He didn't understand how anyone could not be a baseball fan.

Mark looked at his watch. "Oh, look at the time. Hey, Billy, weren't we going to go to that place?" he asked.

"Oh, right, that thing were we going to do," Billy agreed, and they both got up from the couch.

"Can I come?" Jared asked.

"Um, we had plans to go out to dinner. Sorry, we only made reservations for two," Mark said with fake sympathy.

"But you two are big-time celebrities. You don't think you could get me in?"

"Sorry, man. We are going to a really exclusive restaurant. They're very strict," Billy said as he and Mark headed out for the restaurant.

While they were walking to the restaurant on Fifth Avenue, they saw an attractive brunette getting into a black Bugatti. She took off with an alarming screech. "Did you see that?" Billy asked.

"I think I'm in love," Mark said, "and the girl wasn't bad either." They both laughed.

They walked into an Italian restaurant with no reservations and were seated in the back. On the way to the back of the restaurant, many people said hi and asked for autographs. Several women asked to buy the guys drinks, but of course, they refused.

A few minutes after sitting down, Jared popped his little head around the corner of the dining area. "There you guys are!" he said. Mark and Billy rolled their eyes. "I told the hostess I was with you, and she said to come on back!"

Jared picked up a smartphone from a neighboring table. "I'm with Mark Taylor; can I borrow this for a minute?" He didn't wait for the woman's response, he just snagged her phone, walked over to the guys' table and said, "Smile," and he took a selfie with Mark and Billy. Jared was the only one smiling. He went back over to the woman and entered his number into her contact list, and then sent the pic to his phone. "Now, you can contact me any time you want," he told her. Then he returned to the guys and said, "Can you believe I followed you, and now I'm eating dinner with you guys?"

"No, I honestly can't," Mark said. He was embarrassed to be seen with this guy.

"This is great. Maybe I'll, like, make the newspaper, and everyone will know that we are hanging out together," Jared said.

"Actually, Mark and I are hanging out, you're more like stalking," Billy said.

"Stalking? We live together. You guys are like my best friends now."

"Best friends? We've known you for three hours," Mark said quietly, trying not to make a scene.

"What's your problem, Mark? I thought we were clicking," Jared said defensively.

"You *did*? We have nothing in common," Mark said, completely dumbfounded.

Jared got up out of his chair, "Fine, if you want me to leave, then just say so."

"Okay, we don't want you here!" Mark said.

"Why not?" Jared whined. "Why can't I just hang out with you guys?" By now, people were looking at them and not in a good way. Certainly not the way they were used to getting attention.

"Look, man, just keep your voice down," Billy snapped as he looked around. He was mortified at all the attention they were getting.

Mark said, "We are having a serious conversation, man, and we don't know you well enough to include you in it. It's nothing personal. We want you here, but Billy is uncomfortable with some *male* problems he's having..." Billy was so surprised he spat his drink out, then wiped his mouth and gave Mark a dirty look. "You understand that, right? It's embarrassing, especially when you're a big, macho baseball player. You get it, right? No hard feelings? And, please... let's keep this on the down-low," Mark said as he put his index finger to his lips. Billy shook his head.

Jared looked at Billy and said, "Sorry, man. I didn't know you couldn't, like, get it up or whatever." But like a child, Jared did not use his "inside voice."

That brought the crowd's attention back to their table. Billy sat there and shook his head 'no' at the group. People started laughing.

"I've heard that long-term steroid use can do that to a guy," Jared said.

Well, *that* did it. You can make up stories about erectile dysfunction, but DO NOT accuse Billy Hernandez of using steroids. He shoved his chair back from the table and stood up, towering over Jared. He grabbed Jared by the scruff of the shirt and tossed him back and forth like a rag doll. The crowd gasped. "No one says that Billy Hernandez uses steroids. Every home run last year was 'roid-free, do you understand me?"

He looked around and saw that the crowd was nervous

that he was going to pound Jared and ruin their dinner. "And furthermore, my wife and I have sex all the time. There's nothing wrong with me, man. I'm still like a twenty-year-old in the sack," he said as he tossed Jared across the room. By this time, everyone was staring, and some people were recording the whole thing with their phones. Billy looked around, "Sorry, everyone. You can all go back to eating your meals, okay? Our friend here is leaving."

Jared didn't take his eyes off Billy as he backed out of the restaurant. Mark gave Billy a look and followed Jared outside. The patrons went back to their dinners, with occasional glances at Billy, who sat by himself waiting for Mark's return.

Outside, Mark yelled to Jared, who was now quite a few steps ahead. "Hey, Jared."

Jared turned around and put his hands up. "I don't want any more trouble with you guys," he said. He was obviously shaken up by the whole ordeal.

"I'm sorry about that, Jared. That was my fault. I was trying to be funny. Listen – we're all tense because we're trying to be serious about recovery, and we didn't really want another roommate. So, sorry. Billy's a good guy, we're just all struggling, okay?"

Jared managed to choke out one word, "Okay," and then he headed back to their apartment.

Mark told him they would be home later and went back into the restaurant. As he walked by the hostess stand, he said, "Billy and I don't want any other crazy fans bothering us, okay?" Mark certainly wasn't about to tell her that Jared was their roommate from *rehab.*

"Sorry, Mr. Taylor," the hostess said, and Mark walked back to the table and sat down. He placed his napkin on his lap and sipped his tea.

"Well, I think you sufficiently scared him, Billy," Mark said.

"Thanks to your handiwork, Mark," Billy said.

"Yeah, sorry, man."

They ate their dinner and went back to their apartment, expecting to find Jared there, doing something annoying. Instead, they found a counselor there helping him carry his bags out and making way for a new resident to come in. They didn't say any goodbyes. Mark and Billy just looked at each other and watched the whole thing unfold.

CHAPTER
Thirty-Four

A FEW MINUTES LATER, into their apartment walked a short, good-looking New Yorker named Nick Trevino. He was from Long Island. He was a twenty-eight-year-old, with wealthy parents, who hadn't worked an honest day in his whole life.

He had moved down to Florida a few years ago because he couldn't hack it when his parents retired to Naples. They were, in fact, just down the road, but they had had enough of his antics, like getting so intoxicated at his parents' country club that the guards had to drive him home in a golf cart regularly. That might've been funny at the frat house, but not when your parents live in a multi-million dollar house in Naples, and your father was a well-respected attorney. There was nothing funny about it, especially when the neighbors watched everything you did and reported it to all the other neighbors.

This was the last shot for Nick. His parents not only threatened to cut him off financially but totally disown him for the embarrassment to the family name. Even worse than his bad behavior was the fact that his brother Tim was perfect in every way. Tim was only a social drinker, and he was a hard worker. He graduated magna cum laude from Stanford and took over the family's law practice when their dad retired. It's bad enough when you have problems, but when it seems that your sibling is perfect, your problems only get magnified. Nick was an embarrassment to the family. Sad too, because he really wasn't a bad guy – when he was sober.

Nick stuck his hand out and introduced himself. Mark took his hand and gave it a firm shake. "How's it going, man?" Mark asked.

"I hope you guys are going to go easier on me. Jared's not a fan," Nick stated with an uneasy smile.

"How well do you know, Jared?" Billy asked.

"I was his roommate, but he got moved into your room because of 'personality conflicts,'" he said, making air quotes with his fingers.

"And what did you think of him personally?" Mark asked.

"He's obnoxious. He's the only one in rehab that made me want to drink – not the kind of guy I need around me at this point in my life," Nick said.

Billy shook his hand, "I think you're going to be fine, Nick." The three of them sat down.

"So, how much time do you guys have left?" Nick asked.

"We're in for sixty days. We just got here," Mark said.

"Me too. Do you think we'll get cured?" Nick asked the both of them.

"Man, I don't think an alcoholic is ever *cured*," Billy said. "I still think about drinking," he said as he looked around, "and look where I'm at!"

The three laughed. Mark spoke up. "I know I'll never be *cured* of wanting to drink, but I look at the mistakes I've made and the things it's cost me, and I know I don't ever want to let it control my life anymore. I may never work again, you know? I may have blown my whole career."

Nick paused, eyeing Mark. "Have you ever thought about doing Broadway?"

"Broadway? And be near all those Yankees?" Mark and Billy laughed. Nick wondered what joke he was missing out on.

"Mark is from South Carolina," Billy stated.

"Still bitter about the war, huh?" Nick asked sincerely, not realizing that Mark and his whole family despised people from the North.

Billy laughed.

Mark was slightly offended, "Hey, I lived in New York when I was on *One Time to Exist.* It just never felt like home to me."

"Oh, that's right, I forgot you were on a *soap opera,*" Nick said in a sing-song tone, making fun of Mark. "What's it like to be the fantasy of every bored housewife in America?"

"Well, I was never *alone*. But I wasn't happy. That's when I really started drinking," Mark said.

"I'd be drinking too if I had to be on a soap opera," Billy said with a devious smile.

"New York is indeed a city that never sleeps," Mark said, "and for me, if I'm not in bed, I'm getting in trouble."

"Man, you get in trouble *in bed* too!" Billy stated, referring to all the tabloid stories about Mark.

"Did you ever go to see a Yankees game?" Nick asked.

"No, I've never been much of a baseball fan," Mark confessed. "No offense, man," he said as he motioned to Billy.

"That's all right. I've never been a fan of *soap operas,*" Billy said with a smirk. Mark gave him a dirty look.

"You haven't lived until you've gone to Yankee Stadium and had a hot dog and a beer," Nick said enthusiastically.

"Well, you won't be doing that anymore," Billy said. Nick didn't know what he meant, and then he realized that no, he would *not* be doing that anymore – at least not with a beer in his hand. Oh well. He always caused trouble when he was drinking there anyway – especially when the Yankees were losing. And he was especially rowdy when they were playing the Red Sox, no matter who was winning.

Nick had already decided he was going to like Mark and Billy, even though Billy confessed that he'd always wanted to play for the Red Sox. They spent the next few hours talking over poker and pretzels and then went to bed.

When they awoke the next morning, Nick was in the kitchen cooking breakfast. It smelled delicious. Bacon and hazelnut coffee wafted through the air. Mark and Billy were in a zombie trance until they got into the kitchen and helped themselves to the java. Nick dished out the portions and gave the guys their plates. They were thrilled. Neither of them enjoyed cooking. Nick admitted that he wanted to be a chef but had no formal training.

The guys sat down and marveled at the elaborate breakfast he'd made for them. They told Nick he should have his own restaurant. Mark went to the front door of the apartment and grabbed the morning newspaper. He opened it up to the social pages and read some of the articles.

"Anything interesting?" Billy asked.

Mark looked up at him and then threw the paper down. "No, you know these small towns, there's nothing ever going on in the paper," Mark said, but Billy seemed to think he was hiding something.

Billy picked up the paper and started reading the article that Mark had shut just a minute earlier. His eyes opened wide, and he looked at Mark, who was staring out the window facing the brick wall.

"Hey, I never noticed how many bricks were out there before," Mark said as he got out of his chair and walked towards the window.

Billy continued reading, out loud, pointing out key points such as the altercation with a fellow patron and the false information that Billy had erectile dysfunction as a result of years of steroid use. "Man, I never used steroids, and now everyone's going to think I can't get it up. I earned my home run record, and now my career's going to be reduced to monologue jokes on late-night shows."

"I'm really sorry," Mark said.

"You should be. You owe me, big time," Billy told Mark as he threw the paper down.

"Wow. You guys had quite the night before I got here," Nick said.

"And I thought I only got into trouble when I drank," Mark said.

"Yeah, I guess you're a jerk when you're *sober,* too," Billy said.

The three new friends walked down to group together and went over to the snack table to grab some more coffee. The room was starting to fill up with other residents. Billy grabbed a doughnut and a napkin along with a massive cup of coffee. But he accidentally dropped his napkin, and before he could pick it up one of the residents grabbed it and said, "Let me get that, I have no problem *getting it up*… for you." A burst of laughter came from the crowd.

"Thanks for that, Mark," he said as he sat down. Everyone took their seats.

CHAPTER
Thirty-Five

THE COUNSELOR TOOK out his notepad to read the agenda for the meeting. "Does anyone have anything they'd like to share with the group before we move into today's topic?" he asked.

Billy spoke up. "I just want to say that it's been tough getting used to rehab, but I want to thank you all for your support and encouragement. Even though it's been difficult, for the first time, I feel like I want to stay clean."

"I hope you can *keep it up*," said a voice giggling from the back of the room. Well, that spurred a roar of laughter from some of the other residents.

"Can I also say that there is no truth in that article in the newspaper? I don't have a problem with steroids or E.D., okay? So I'd appreciate it if you'd all just forget about that. That is a rumor that is based on nothing. My wife and I have crazy, mad sex all the time."

One of the female residents sitting with her arms crossed piped up. "I didn't believe that article for a second, Billy," she said.

"Thank you, Marsha," Billy said, relieved.

"It must've been *hard* for you to read it though," she said, drawing chuckles from the immature residents. Not realizing she was joking, Billy nodded his head in agreement. She continued, "I knew something was *up* when I read that trash." That got more laughs, and Billy kept nodding like an idiot. Even Mark was snickering, cluing Billy in on the joke. "I'd say there's a *good stiff chance* that someone else is going to write another rude article about you!"

"Okay, that's enough, everyone," the counselor said with a little smirk. "We're here to build each other up and encourage each other. So let's get started." He looked around. "Does anyone have any struggles or accomplishments they'd like to report? I see we have some new faces, so for those of you who have just arrived – don't feel pressured to add to the discussion until you're comfortable."

Nick spoke up. "I am going on three days, and that's the longest I've gone without a drink." Everyone applauded. "I just want to thank the others in this group for their encouragement. It really is one day at a time, but for the first time, I feel like I'm going to make it!" Nick sighed with relief and looked at the members of the group.

It was a very emotional session. Like Mark, the others didn't think their drinking was hurting anyone. But of course, it was. It made them unreliable and vulnerable to their own risk-taking behavior. It destroyed their families and cost them money – there wasn't one redeeming factor about alcohol or drugs. Well, maybe in the short term, it gave them a temporary fix, made them feel a little better, and made them feel like reality wasn't so bad. But as good as they were when they got drunk or high, they weren't as good as anyone else who wasn't drunk or high.

That's the funny thing about substance abuse; it makes users feel invincible. Ironic, isn't it? They feel stronger, yet they are so much weaker, physically, and mentally. It's not like the '80s when marijuana was the worst thing people were doing. You just didn't hear about heavier drugs like cocaine infiltrating the small suburban areas the way meth and heroin do now. And Mark met plenty in people in rehab who had only tried those one time, and they were hooked! Once! At least it took Mark a while to ease into his drinking.

What were these people missing that drove them to use drugs and alcohol the way they did? Was it something in their past that they couldn't deal with? Was it because that was the way their families deal with their problems? Mark knew that every one of his friends in rehab had to figure out what it was that drove them to do what they did, or they would never kick their habits.

When the session ended, Mark headed over to the group for nicotine addiction. It had been four days since his last cigarette. He was doing really well. That's the longest he'd been without a cigarette since he started smoking at fifteen, and if possible, it was his hardest addiction to quit. He had smoked pot several times, but he didn't really get anything from it. Not like alcohol. He liked what he got from drinking.

Mark walked across the campus to the next building. When he entered the room, there was a guy in his sixties standing in the front of the group. Mark sat down in an empty chair. After the session was over, Mark headed back to the main meeting room. There was a guest speaker who had come to talk to the group.

When the room filled up, the man started speaking. He introduced himself as Tyler, and he said he had been sober for thirteen years. He was a stand-up comedian. He was there to entertain, but also to tell them how hard the journey was and how he still struggled not to drink. He said that for him, the temptation never completely left him even though he lost his wife and kids over it. Sometimes it takes someone losing everything to make things right.

About a week into his stay, Mark walked into Beverly's office. He looked at the chair and then at the couch and smiled as he sat down in the chair.

"You look well today, Mark," she said with a smile.

"You know what? I feel well."

"So, you're sleeping better?"

"Much. That relaxation therapy really works. And I'm getting used to the smell of lavender."

"This is the first time I've seen you looking rested."

"I love relaxation therapy. I haven't slept that well in a long time – I mean without a drink."

"I'm so glad you're doing well."

"I think…" he said slowly.

"Yes?"

"I think I'm going to make it this time," Mark said with a smile. "I feel good."

"I'm glad to hear you say that. But the real challenge comes outside these four walls, Mark."

"I made a decision. No offense, but I don't want to come back!"

"No offense, I hope you never do!"

Mark and the doc laughed and continued their session. She shared a little about her past. How her mother was an alcoholic, and you didn't talk about alcoholism in the '70s. She shared more about herself than Mark expected, leading up to her own battle with addiction. She and Mark hugged after this session, and then Mark went down to his apartment and took a nap.

The guys were starting to get into their routine. The next day, when it was time for Mark to go to another one-on-one session with Dr. Winthrop, he sighed. He dreaded talking about stuff from the past. What good does it do? No one likes to rehash mistakes from their past. How is that therapeutic?

Mark was edgy. Some days are better than others. That's why people in recovery say, "one day at a time."

Mark walked into Dr. Winthrop's office. With sunken shoulders, he dragged himself across the room and again sat in the chair for what felt like more interrogation. Mark felt like if he got on the couch, he'd really spill his guts. The chair felt safer for some reason.

Dr. Winthrop gave him a sympathetic smile. He folded his arms; he had already decided he wasn't going to talk to her today. He was so tired of the people in rehab and all of them expressing their "feelings" about everything.

"Have you had a chance to think about why you drink?" she asked.

"Do you think you're really going to unlock the key to my drinking problem? Like, there's some magical answer, and when you uncover it, I'll have an epiphany and be cured of my drinking problem forever?"

"That seems negative to me. You don't seem open to the idea of even being able to stop drinking."

"As you know, I've been through this before."

"Do you think you'd be here if you knew why you drank?"

He snickered. "Do you think I'd be here if I didn't have to be?"

"You don't think you have a problem, Mark?"

"I think I have several."

"Are your parents' drinkers?" The doctor started to jot down notes.

"Social," he said.

"What about your brother?"

"Yeah, he drinks a lot. So?"

"You have alcoholism in your family?"

"Doesn't everyone?" he asked. It seemed evident to him.

The rest of the session was filled with questions that Mark felt were too personal. He just wasn't ready to talk to her, even with all of her prodding. She just looked at him and continued the line of questions with no success. She didn't take many notes with his one-word answers. Maybe tomorrow would be better. You just can't force these things.

Later that night, the guys ate dinner, went to their A.A. meeting, and then went back to their room and started up their nightly poker game. Mark was so glad that the guys were roommates and got along so well.

CHAPTER
Thirty-Six

THE NEXT DAY, Mark started to lighten up in group therapy. He had always avoided forming relationships at all costs. He didn't want to be social with other people like him. It would be too easy to fall back into the same patterns. I mean, if not for Angus, Mark would still be doing the same old thing. Mark realized that he might be forming real friendships with people who cared. Maybe that would make the difference this time.

There were some new people in this group session. The counselor, Dane, opened up the group, not saying a word, but just standing beside a whiteboard. Then he turned to the crowd of newbies. "Welcome, everyone. Let's get right into it. Some of you want to be here, some of you were court-ordered, and for others of you, this is a last-ditch effort to keep your families or your jobs. You've heard the names; we've all been called them. So, someone… give me a name. We're all addicts; let's just call it like it is."

Everyone started yelling out names that they'd been called or they'd called others: junkie, alky, drunk, crack head, meth head, smacker, addict, crack whore, coke head, wife beater, etc.

Dane looked at the faces on the members of the group and smacked the whiteboard. That got their attention. "*Don't* be these things anymore! Start being who you want to be, not who people think you are! In fact, right now, you are to say – you are in *recovery*. I don't want to hear that you're an alcoholic or crack head. The first thing that needs to change is the way you perceive yourself. No need to call yourself names. There are plenty of other people around you who will be glad to do that. Quitting is the easy part. Staying clean – that's your *real* challenge. Now, I'm not going to stand here and lie and say it's easy. It's not, and you all know it. I bet half of you have already tried rehab. And I'm not going to promise that you'll repair all the damage you did when you were using. Some people may never forgive you for the things you've done, and that's something you'll have to live with. But you *can* do it. I promise you now if you stay clean, your life *will* get better… it can't get worse. Look around – *you're in rehab.* I've been in your shoes, and so has everyone else in this building. We can help you because *we* got help. Recovery is possible. Until you start looking at this as a disease, you won't be able to see that light at the end of the tunnel, and no, it's not a train. That light is hope, my friends. I am standing here as a man who has been in recovery for fifteen years. Has it always been easy? Of course not, but then again, no great achievements ever are. Think about what your life will be like when you walk out those doors breaking free from the chains of addiction. What could you do? You – you, my friends – will be *unstoppable*."

Mark got choked up. Could he kick this disease? Could he be the man he wanted to be? He'd have to have a support system of people around him if he was going to make it. He couldn't be around the old friends he had. He would have to make a clean break. Mark zoned out as the therapist continued talking. He thought about his arrests and his stomach being pumped. He thought about how painful this addiction was, both physically and mentally. He didn't want to wind up like Declan. And he knew if he didn't learn to live without drinking, he wouldn't be living at all.

After two weeks of Mark and Beverly dancing back and forth about his drinking and drug use, something started to change in Mark. Maybe it was that the other people there were really trying to get clean. Perhaps it was just the fact that the people who encouraged him to live life on the edge weren't there. He didn't know what it was, but he began to let his guard down. It was a rainy day; heavy rain, too. Mark sat down in the chair and looked out the window. The doctor sat down in her regular chair and offered him a smile.

"What a rainy day!" she said, making small talk.

"Yeah," he answered as he looked at her cat poster and then turned his attention back to her.

"How are you feeling today, Mark?"

"Great. Glad to be here, Dr. Winthrop," he said sarcastically.

"You still aren't open to trying to get something useful out of your sessions with me?"

"Nope."

"It's been two weeks, why don't you call me Beverly? It may make you feel like we're more casual... you know, just two friends talking."

"I never talk to my friends about deep things. It was mostly about women and getting work."

"Sounds like you need new friends. How is the roommate situation working out?" she asked.

"It's good. Billy and Nick are great. It's hard to believe we've only known each other for a couple of weeks."

"People tend to form deeper relationships when they have mutual goals. It sounds like you hadn't had a good support system around you when it came to trying to not drink."

"No. Sobriety is not a popular stand in my circles," Mark said, looking down at his hands clasped in his lap.

"Tell me about your childhood."

"Again?"

"Well, you never really got in-depth with it."

"I had a very normal childhood."

"What was normal about it?"

"You know, I came from a normal family; two parents, a brother, a dog, a white picket fence, and a flag hanging in the yard – normal."

"Go on."

"With what? That's it."

"Were you a good student?"

"Yeah. I mean, I got decent grades, but I got distracted."

"Distracted how?"

"When I fell in love the first time, it really messed me up."

"Do you think that's why people label you as a womanizer?"

He just sat there for a minute. He didn't really want to talk anymore. He looked at the sofa.

"Do you mind if I lie down?" he asked.

She tried to hide her enthusiasm at his move to the couch. People tend to feel more informal and squeal like little truth-telling pigs when they're relaxed. "Please, make yourself comfortable." Her eyes followed him to the sofa.

"I think that's from when I was a dancer," he said.

"What kind of dancing?" she asked as she jotted down a note.

"I was in a male revue in college." He turned away.

"You mean you took your clothes off?"

He looked at her again. "Yeah, I danced under the name 'Dr. Feel Good' because I was in pre-med. So?"

"*So?* You're used to women looking at you as a sex object."

"Yeah, well, isn't that what men want?"

"I don't know, Mark. I'm not a man. You tell me – is that the way *you* want to be looked at?"

He looked at the clock.

"Is there somewhere you'd rather be?" she asked.

"*Anywhere* but here," he said with a half-hearted smile.

"You don't like it when I ask you these personal questions, do you?"

He laughed. "Who would? I mean… most famous people love talking about themselves, but I don't really see the good in re-living a bunch of bad memories."

Mark wasn't used to speaking with a woman, especially one who was intruding on his personal thoughts. Not many people knew about the things he'd been through. Really, only the people who were there when they happened. He was listening to her and answering her questions, but he didn't want to tell her. He knew it was in the strictest confidence, but he really didn't want to say them to her. Was it just a matter of time before it came out? Well, it never had to go beyond the two of them. Maybe he'd feel better if he just told her. How would she react?

She kept pressing him. "You said you were in love. Was it a meaningful relationship?"

"It was for me. I don't start relationships with bad intentions."

"How long were you with her?"

"It was a really long time."

"How long, exactly?" she prodded.

"A year."

"Do you feel like you could have a relationship like that again with the right person?"

"I could never have a relationship like that again."

"Now, Mark, don't sell yourself short…"

He interrupted. "You don't understand."

"You're afraid to have your heartbroken. I get it."

"No. It wasn't like that. I loved her. But it wasn't right that we were together."

Just at that moment, someone knocked on the door. It was

Dr. Winthrop's next patient. She frowned and shook her head. She finally felt like he was opening up, and now she would have to wait until tomorrow to get to the bottom of this. She stood up, and her shoulders drooped. Mark smiled as he stood up.

"Sorry, Doc, I guess I'll be a puzzle for another day!"

"Bye, Mark," she said as she walked him out and greeted her next patient.

CHAPTER
Thirty-Seven

THE NEXT DAY at group therapy, Mark stood up in a sea of vaguely familiar faces and said the words he was finally ready to speak. "I came here to rehab because my best friend died because of my drinking." Everyone looked at him with sadness. Mark was stable until he made eye contact with a couple of people, and then he broke down, explaining what happened to Angus. It was a story that not even Billy and Nick had heard.

Mark felt better after he confessed to a bunch of strangers that his drinking made him lose everything. But nothing meant anything except Angus. Mark only thought about how out-of-control he was to lose his best friend that way. Another resident made the comment that Angus unknowingly gave his life for Mark's. Angus' death was the only thing that seemed to get through to Mark. He just couldn't retake that kind of pain. He didn't want to be controlled by alcohol anymore.

When the guys went back to the apartment, they ordered some food from the local grocery store to be delivered. Billy ate a lot. A lot! Mark wasn't used to sharing food. He hadn't had roommates since college, and they certainly didn't eat like a Major League Baseball player!

The next night, the guys were getting into their nightly poker game when they heard a knock on their door. It was a new roommate. His name was Derek, and he was pretty laid back. He was a deacon in his church, but his regular job was as an accountant. Many accountants had darkened the doorways there over the years. He was a quiet guy until you got to know him. He was about 5'8" and balding. He had a huge stomach, which was strange because he had little chicken legs and a small face. He looked like he was standing in front of a funhouse mirror, but he had a great sense of humor.

After living together for a few days, the guys gave him the nickname Deacon. It really amused Mark that someone so active in the church had a drinking problem – especially a Southern Baptist. He knew religious folks were far from perfect, but he was surprised that someone churchy was in rehab. Although Billy seemed somewhat serious about his faith too. It seemed strange that people who had a supposed relationship with God would have any problems – particularly with addiction. And Deacon played cards, also. Another major sinner enters Room 207!

The guys sat down, and Deacon dealt. Billy had a good hand right off the bat; you could tell because he had the worst poker face at the table.

"So, Deacon," Mark said, "you're Southern Baptist, and you drink and play cards? You must be the most fun Southern Baptist in *history*."

"There's a lot of Southern Baptists that drink and play cards," Deacon said.

"Not out in the open, though," Mark said.

Deacon got defensive. "No, they don't *brag* about it."

Mark laughed. "Because they know they're going to hell for doing it! I love it! You church folks love to condemn everyone else for what you do behind closed doors. That's exactly why *I* don't go to church."

"Hey, Mark, knock it off," Billy said as he changed the order of cards in his hand. "If anyone's going to hell here, it's *you*. What's all this talk about hell anyway? You said you don't even believe hell exists,"

"I believe we're living in hell *now*," Mark said.

"Rehab is not that bad!" Nick said. They all laughed.

"Not *rehab*," Mark said. "I mean – like earth. *This* is hell. There's nothing after this."

"I'm not a religious man, and even I don't believe that, Mark," Nick said as he threw down his chips in the pot.

"So, what – you think when you die, that's it?" Deacon asked. "There's no afterlife? I hate to tell you, my friend, if that's what you think you are in for a rude awakening. Good thing you live in Florida, so you'll be used to the heat!"

"How are you some expert on something that you don't even have any evidence of?" Mark asked.

"Evidence?" Billy asked.

"Yeah, like where's your God? Why can't I see him?" Mark asked as he looked around the room.

"You can't see the wind, but you know it's there," Billy said.

"I just don't buy it. I think when you die, that's it. Lights out," Mark said as he folded.

"Let's say you're right, and when we die, it's lights out and nothingness… no afterlife. Then I've lived my life in futility for this *Jesus* character. That's okay, I've still tried to be a better person while I was on earth," Deacon said.

"Says the guy in *rehab*!" Mark laughed.

"But what if I'm right?" Deacon went on. "What if we're judged by our sins? Then I'm in trouble and can't save myself. That's why we need Jesus."

Mark rolled his eyes as Deacon gathered the pile of chips

to his part of the table and re-dealt the cards. "It sounds like a big, steaming pile of bull..."

Then came a knock at the door. It was their food delivery from the grocer down the street. The guys took a break from the game, tipped the delivery guy, and attacked the paper bags filled with goodies.

Mark took a container of key lime pie out of the bag and opened it. He pulled out a knife from the drawer and cut it into four huge pieces. "Who wants pie?" Every one of them grabbed a plate as Mark shoved a big piece on each one. They stood around the kitchen island, eating the pie, and continuing to talk.

"My wife is going to kill me if I get out of here, and I'm fat!" Billy said with his mouth full. "And being that I'm out for the season, I'm not working out like usual."

"Are you out because you're in here?" asked Deacon as he grabbed a piece.

"No, man. I tore my ACL. That's why I started using Vicodin... and I couldn't stop." He pulled up his pants leg to show them the scars from his surgery. "See? Three separate surgeries and the last one is when it all went downhill."

"Wow. Will you be able to play again?" Nick asked as the three of them gazed at Billy's scars.

"I should... if they still need me next year. I'm going to be a free agent next season, and I'm getting older, and now I'm injured. I'm not optimistic about my chances," Billy said. "Sucks, too; all I ever wanted was to play in the World Series. Looks like that's never going to happen now."

"Sorry, man," Mark said.

"Yeah, that's life. I had a good run, though, right?" Billy tried to sound positive. And he was right. How many people get to live their dream of playing Major League Baseball? It was a dream his parents had always encouraged. Being from Puerto Rico, they wanted Billy to have all of the opportunities they never did. And he had.

"Hey Mark, didn't you get addicted to Vicodin after getting injured on the set of a movie?" Nick asked.

"No! I don't know why people believe everything they read. I've never even *had* Vicodin!"

CHAPTER
Thirty-Eight

DEACON TOOK a bite of the pie and devoured it as the others took their pieces off the counter. The other guys watched him and were amused by him eating the whole piece without even taking a breath. Deacon looked up and saw the look of astonishment on their faces as he licked his plate. He laughed uncomfortably. "That pie was better than sex."

Mark laughed. "Man, when is the last time you got laid? Pie is good, but it isn't *that* good!" The other guys laughed.

"It's been months since I had sex, and I guess it wasn't very good, either," Deacon said.

"You guess?" Mark asked.

"Well, my wife came out of the bedroom a few minutes afterward and screamed at me, 'Do you even know where my clitoris is?' and I looked at her and asked, 'Where'd you have it last?' Then she said, 'It hasn't moved in fifteen years!' Then like a week later, I got served," Deacon said bitterly, and all the guys laughed out loud. "I mean, she was always *misplacing* stuff…" and they laughed harder.

"Deacon, I've got some magazines in the nightstand that might help you," Mark said.

"You have girly magazines in rehab?" Billy laughed.

"Hey, they don't want me to have sex for a year!" Mark said.

"I don't think Deacon needs magazines; I think he needs a map!" Nick laughed.

"GPS," Billy said. The three guys were laughing, but Deacon was not.

"Don't kick a guy when he's down," Deacon said defensively.

"Ah, he's right. C'mon guys, the poor man's getting divorced," Mark said. He slapped Deacon on the back and went to the fridge to pour drinks for everyone.

"I'll tell you what... the worst thing about getting divorced. I really miss my wife and kids," Deacon said, reminiscing.

"Well, that's not for me. I can't see me ever being tied down to one woman," Mark said as he poured four cups of water from a pitcher.

"You think you've got it all figured out, Mark? Because you can have any woman at any time? Well, I was like you once, and I'd rather go home to my wife than a stranger," Billy said.

"If I had a wife that looked like yours, I'd go home to her every night, too," Mark said.

"Good thing she knows what a pig you are, otherwise I'd worry about her running away with you," Billy said as he picked up a glass of water and drank it.

"Hey, I've gotten a nasty rap," Mark said. "You know, if I could find the right one, maybe I would stick around. What I do know is that I can't be with any women who drink." Mark said as he downed his glass of water.

"I need to find a woman who doesn't drink, too. I can't be sucked into this old life anymore," Nick added, "I can't be around someone like me."

The men agreed.

"Speaking of which, Mark... Summer's coming here

tomorrow, so if you could make yourself scarce, we'd appreciate it," Billy said.

"Get some, Billy," Nick said, and the other guys snickered.

"Hey, that's my *wife*," Billy said.

"All right, man. We'll take off when she gets here," Mark said.

The guys finished up their pie and drank their water and went back to playing cards. Mark and Billy dominated the table. "Hey, we should go to Vegas together," Mark said to Billy.

"No way! Summer will kill me if I trade one addiction in for another."

"C'mon, how much trouble could we get into in Vegas?" Mark asked.

"Dude – I *know* you're not serious right now," Billy said.

"Yeah, I think you two going to Vegas would end very badly," Nick said.

"Me too," Deacon said as he threw his cards down.

Deacon looked at Mark, "Do you think my wife left me because I couldn't satisfy her? I mean, would a woman be so superficial?" he asked.

Mark put his arm on Deacon's shoulder with one hand and held his cards in the other. "Look, women are complicated. They're like roses, so delicate and beautiful; they're soft and smell great. They seem so perfect, and just when they have you where they want you…"

"Yeah?" Deacon asked.

"They stick their little thorns into your flesh until you're bleeding in multiple places, asking what the hell you did to make them turn into a cactus with no warning."

"Three aces, huh!" Billy trumpeted loudly as he revealed his winning hand.

Mark tossed his losing hand onto the table.

"Agh!" said Nick, throwing down his hand in disgust as Billy scraped all the chips over to his side of the table.

"You have issues," Deacon said.

"We all have issues, or we wouldn't be here," Nick chimed in.

"I don't have issues. I just don't see myself getting so wrapped up with one woman that I let my world revolve around her," Mark said.

"Of course not, because that would mean your world wouldn't revolve around you anymore. Mark my words, my friend, you will meet a woman who turns your world upside down, and when that happens, boy do I want to be there!" Billy said.

"Me too, and I hope she has a friend for me," Nick said.

"I just want my wife back. It's been thirty days since I've heard from her. I wonder if she'd even take my call," Deacon said.

After a few minutes, Nick and Deacon went upstairs to their room. Mark and Billy hatched a plan to visit Deacon's wife before they left rehab to plead Deacon's case. It was one thing for her to reject Deacon's phone calls, but they doubted she would deny a visit from Mark Taylor and Billy Hernandez.

CHAPTER
Thirty-Nine

ANOTHER DAY DOWN, and it was time again for his individual therapy session with Beverly. He actually thought it was possible to have the life he always wanted – the life he *deserved*. And for once, he believed the people around him were pulling for him and wanted it to happen.

He walked right over to the sofa and lay down. Almost immediately, he broke down, unable to stop crying.

"Did you have a bad night?" she asked.

"I had a dream about my dog, Angus."

"Is someone watching him while you're in here?"

"He died right before I came here. It was my fault. When I went on my last bender, I passed out at my house and left the door unlocked. Angus got out and got hit by a car."

"I'm so sorry," she said.

"Yeah, me too. Angus died because of my drinking."

"Maybe he gave his life so you could have yours," she said.

"I think he did. He was like that. He always seemed to know what I needed." He laughed a little through his tears. "I loved that stupid dog like he was my kid."

"I hope you take this opportunity to make a life change, Mark."

"That's why I'm here. I *want* this."

"You can *have* it," she said with a smile.

At the end of that session, Mark was exhausted from all the emotional upheaval. He walked back to the apartment to take a nap.

When he walked into his bedroom, Billy was sitting on the bed with his eyes shut, holding his bible and a rosary. Mark tried to sneak back out, but Billy heard him though he never opened his eyes.

"And Lord, please bless my friend, Mark, who needs your direction even though he pretends he's an atheist." Billy slit one eye open, trying to peek at Mark. "Lord, please forgive him for being such a stubborn jackass. I know that you've put us in this room together because I am obviously much wiser, not to mention better-looking than him…"

"Do you really think you should use the word *jackass* when you're talking to God?" Mark asked.

Billy laughed and stood up. "Yeah, probably not. It's easy to backslide when you're around."

"Oh, don't you hit me with that God stick too! I'm sick of it. Every piece of literature, every poster, and every session tries to convince me this elusive *God* will make me sober. Where was this God when I made all those mistakes? If he's real, why doesn't he show up until rehab?"

Mark had spoken to Billy a few times about his faith, and Billy was more than willing to share about it. Mark was hesitant to discuss religion for two reasons. He didn't want Billy to get offended if he made a joke. But more importantly, he didn't want Billy to get the impression that Mark wanted to be converted. He definitely wasn't buying into any of it. In fact, he called it nonsense. He didn't understand why, if there was a God, he would allow so many bad things to happen. Not just to Mark, but in general.

Mark valued Billy's friendship, and if Billy felt like he needed the crutch that he called *God,* he was willing to let him have it and not tell him how stupid and naive it was to believe in something or *someone* that you couldn't see. What really didn't make sense to Mark was if there was a God, why couldn't Billy stop drinking on his own? Shouldn't he be able to pray to his God Almighty and be delivered from his demons? But whatever, Mark was content to have made a friend whom he was convinced would be a friend for life.

The next day, at appointment time, Mark bounded down to Beverly's office. He was actually looking forward to their session. He got there while she was making a cup of coffee from her credenza. He entered her office and sat in his chair. He didn't want to lie down this time. She came in to find him looking at a picture of an attractive woman in her mid-twenties.

"She's cute," Mark said, holding the frame in his hands.

"She's off-limits," she said, shutting her door with her foot as she stirred her cup. "Coffee?"

"No, thanks. Is that your daughter?" he asked as he put the frame down.

"Mmm-hmm."

Beverly sat down.

"You don't think I'll make a good son-in-law?" he asked with a smile.

"I think you'll be great… for someone *else's* family!" They both laughed.

"So let's pick up where we left off a few days ago." She looked at her notes. "We were talking about a serious girl-friend when you said, *'It wasn't right that we were together.'*"

"Oh. Well, I was very young."

"How young?"

"Twelve."

She chuckled. "And you say you were in love with this girl?"

"I was. Completely."

"What grade were you in?"

"Sixth."

"It was puppy love, then?"

"No, it wasn't. I mean – that was my first time."

"You had sex with her?"

"Yeah. I kind of compare every woman to her."

"You had sex at twelve?"

"Yeah."

"Wow, that's really young to have sex."

He let out a little laugh. "I didn't think I was ready. I didn't know where anything went. My parents never talked to me about sex."

"It was her idea then?"

"Yeah, it wasn't her first time. I mean... she was *married* and everything," Mark said casually.

Beverly's eyes widened. Which, of course, was really inappropriate. You're not supposed to show that kind of emotional response when you're counseling someone. She just sat there and stopped taking notes for a minute while Mark continued.

"My parents used to send me over to her house to mow her lawn or pick weeds. They had no idea what was going on there."

"It sounds like they trusted her. Your parents must've liked her. She never gave them any cause to worry?"

"I guess not. And I was totally in love with her. I thought I was going to marry her. She was putting these ideas in my head. I really thought she loved me. What did I know? I was just a stupid kid. I mean, here's this woman – a *real* woman, not like the girls in school – who wants me. And she wants to do things with me that the other girls aren't doing. I liked it. She made me feel special. You know? This adult said she *needed* me."

"Where was her husband?"

"Mr. Potter?"

"Yes, Mr. Potter."

"He worked a lot. He was never home," Mark said.

Beverly was shaken by this information. "Did anyone ever find out?"

"Yeah, turned out she was banging this other kid in my neighborhood. So, she didn't love me after all. Her husband came from work early one night and caught her in their house with another kid. He beat the crap out of both of them. I was glad he didn't catch me there. He put her in the hospital."

"So, they both did jail time?"

"She did. I had to testify at her trial."

"And your parents, how did they handle all this?"

"I don't know. We never talked about it. I mean, they were at the trial and everything, but we never talked about it after that."

Beverly sat back in her chair. So many things made sense. It was clear that Mark had a lot of unresolved issues from childhood. The stuff he never talked about with anyone. Mark confided in her that at the time of the trial, he had some court-appointed counseling sessions, but he never discussed it after that. He had never told anyone. Not the women he dated, not anyone outside of his parents, no one knew. Imagine carrying that around since childhood? It was no wonder he was such a mess. How could he trust anyone again?

"You have a habit of picking abusive women."

"Was that a question?"

"No. You seem to have a history of abusive partners. I mean, if the tabloids are true. Your girlfriends physically and verbally abuse you."

"I guess. I never had a relationship that wasn't volatile on some level."

"You've never had a 'normal' relationship then because mental and physical abuse is something that is not part of a normal, healthy relationship."

"I know."

"What kind of women are you attracted to?"

"I love all kinds of women."

"Well, let's talk about traits. What kind of character traits do you like?"

"She has to have a nice ass and big…" he cupped his hands.

She interrupted. "Okay, those are *physical* traits, Mark. C'mon. You have to think other things are important. Like if she's loyal, respectful, funny, considerate… things like that."

"I never thought about it. It's not like I have to work for it. I mean, women are pretty easy. They come on to me all the time. If they're willing to give it, I'm going to take it."

Mark spent the rest of his session telling Dr. Winthrop stories about the relationships he'd had. Some made her laugh; one made her cry, but most made her glad she never had to date Mark Taylor. He was sitting on the chair with his hands behind his head, elbows out like he was on a hammock talking about the weather when the next client knocked on the door.

"Okay, Mark. That's all the time we have today."

He smiled. "Hey, you know what? I actually like talking to you now. I feel better."

"I'm glad. I want to focus on building your character, Mark, so we can prepare you to have a mature and lasting relationship, okay?"

"Sure," he said half-heartedly as he walked out the door.

CHAPTER *Forty*

BEVERLY SAT THERE for a few moments looking at the door even after Mark disappeared. So many things made sense to her now. Mark was insecure, vulnerable, and depressed. Funny, isn't it? People who have big egos can sometimes feel inferior. God only knows what's really going on in someone's head.

Some people think it may not be a big deal for a guy to have sex at such a young age. Not only was his body not fully developed, but he wasn't emotionally mature, and whether he realized it or not, it did permanent psychological damage to him. Unbeknownst to him, it had hindered every relationship he'd ever had, hanging over him like a dark cloud. For it to end the way it did, with an arrest and trial, it didn't reinforce the idea that Mark could ever have a normal relationship. He didn't even know what normal was. There was no courting. There was no taking time to get to know someone. Why bother? In Mark's mind, relationships *were* sex, and women certainly weren't making that difficult for Mark. How would this man find someone to love when he never had to?

There were still two weeks left, and those guys in Room 207 acted like they had known each other all their lives.

Therapy was helping all of them, but maybe no one more than Mark. He knew when they left that place, they would forever share a bond and a friendship like no other Mark had ever had. For the first time, Mark felt like someone had his back and would be there for him, no matter what.

On the day of his next individual therapy session, Mark looked at his watch and wondered what he'd wind up discussing with Beverly as he made his way down to her office. When he shut the door behind him, she grabbed a coffee and sat down with her notepad.

"How are you today?" she asked.

"I'm okay. I had a bad dream last night," he said. He'd chosen the sofa today. It felt good to lie back and relax.

"What happened?" she asked with concern.

"I was on the set of *The Trifecta*. It was the last episode that Dominic was on. He told me he was going to do it."

"You mean, commit suicide?"

"Yes," he said, then sighed. "Ugh. I hate even thinking about this. I don't want to talk about it."

"You brought it up. Are you sure you don't want to discuss it? I know you were close."

"Do I have a choice?" he asked, looking over at her. She just looked at him and wiggled her pen over her notepad. "Fine. No one saw it coming, okay? We all knew he was having financial problems, but we had no idea he was going to end it all."

"So, he didn't say anything about what he was going to do?"

"Not at all... I thought that when people are serious, you usually don't see it coming anyway."

"Why do you think some people take their own lives?" she asked.

Mark finally picked his head up and looked at her, the pen poised above her notepad. He rolled his eyes. "You're going to want to write this down," he said.

She pressed her ballpoint to the paper and listened intently.

"Ready?" Mark asked.

"Yes!" she said with anticipation.

Mark exhaled loudly, "How the *hell* do I know?"

She looked up at him.

He stood up. "You think all famous people are the same? We all come from different places, have different families, different lives. I don't know what was going on in Dominic's head that made him think there was no other way out. How would I know? You think we tell each other about our feelings? We *don't.* There are few people you can actually trust in this world... and he had a beautiful wife and children." Mark clenched his fists and looked up to the ceiling. "What I wouldn't give to have someone who loved me like she loved him. God, it almost *killed* her!"

Beverly hadn't seen Mark get that emotional.

Mark lay back down. "Is that what you wanted to hear? I don't know why some people who look like they have it together, fall apart. All I know is that when you're a star, you give the public everything, and they still want more. I'm not the man everyone makes me out to be. Maybe I don't want to be. Maybe sometimes I just want to be Mark Taylor, from South Carolina, son of a real estate investor. Sometimes I just want to be normal." He sat up and leaned forward on the sofa and put his hands in the prayer position but rested his forehead on his thumbs and his elbows on his knees. "Honestly, Beverly, I don't know what the hell *normal* even is anymore."

Mark just sat that way as tears rolled down his face. Beverly threw her notepad on the desk, walked over to the sofa, and held him for a few minutes.

When the session ended, Mark went to the coffee shop and drank a huge cup of coffee and bought the newspaper. His eyes were red, and he didn't want to go back to the apartment, feeling like he needed to explain his appearance. The other guys had done their share of expressing emotions there, but Mark's a tough guy. No one's supposed to know that he has real feelings under that tough exterior. So, he made small, meaningless conversation with the other people in the coffee shop and finally went back to his apartment to have dinner with the guys. He was looking forward to being with the guys tonight. It had been a tough session for him.

Perhaps that was because Dominic was the first close friend during Mark's career that died, or maybe it was because the two of them had a lot in common. They both suffered from depression. When regular people get depressed, it's one thing. But when a celebrity gets depressed, they can't just stay in their house and not come out. When someone famous is suffering, everybody knows. It may not come out like they're unhappy. It may appear that their life is just out of control. And that may show up in the form of drinking and one-night stands, or anything they can find to cram into the empty hole in their hearts.

CHAPTER
Forty-One

MARK WENT UPSTAIRS to the rooftop deck, and his roommates followed. That's where most of the residents spent their free time when they weren't in their apartments. They had a huge outdoor kitchen with tables and sofas. It was like a party up there – a *sober* party. There was a beautiful view of the city and quietness. The furniture was in happy colors to make you forget where you were, and they were close enough to smell the salty ocean air. Mark went up to the edge, closed his eyes, and spread his arms out as his white linen shirt blew in the breeze. He inhaled as a cool breeze came over them.

The guys looked at each other and went over to Mark.

"What's going on?" Nick asked.

"I'm going to stay sober this time," Mark said with confidence.

"Yeah, well, we'll read all about it if you don't," Nick said, and the guys laughed.

"I'm serious. I'm not going to let myself wind up being another tragic Hollywood story," Mark said. "I chose this life, and it's time I learn how to deal with it."

Billy smiled. "It's not easy being in the spotlight, but it's definitely where you belong, Mark."

"I feel like I want to pray for you, Mark. Is that okay?" asked Deacon apprehensively.

Mark looked at Billy, and Billy nodded.

"Yeah, okay, Deacon," Mark said.

The three guys put their hands on Mark as Deacon prayed. Many of the other residents came forward and prayed too. Mark heard the words but felt mostly, he felt more and more hands-on him. When he opened his eyes, there were dozens of people surrounding him. He felt an uncomfortable calmness, a sense of peace and serenity he had never experienced before. Mark said, "I'm going to make it," under his breath, and smiled at everyone.

Mark looked at the other three guys, who were now sitting down, watching Mark pace back and forth. He spent about five minutes on a spontaneous motivational speech filled with hand gestures, talking about the meaning of life, and how he was never going to drink again. When he was done, he let out a sigh and sat down, grinning. The guys looked confused.

"What's up, guys?" Mark asked.

"We didn't bring any food up here," Deacon said as he watched some of the other residents eat, "and we're hungry!"

"Well, come on then, let's go out to dinner – on me. Let's see what's happening on Fifth!"

"Hey, if Mark's going to buy dinner, what are we waiting for?" Billy asked. The guys all got up and walked to Fifth Avenue.

They picked a Japanese restaurant and sat down. A lot of people came to their table asking for Mark and Billy's autographs. Some of the fans asked Nick and Deacon who they were. Nick felt comfortable saying, "Nobody!" but Deacon didn't like that response.

"Hey, I'm somebody!" Deacon said.

"I don't think these chicks are looking for someone to do their taxes," Nick said.

"Yeah, they're looking for a good time!" Billy said.

"Well, *math* can be fun," Deacon said, and the guys let out a big laugh.

"No wonder you drank!" Billy said.

As the night went by and the traffic picked up, the guys got into a conversation about women and money. Billy was the only one in a relationship. Deacon didn't talk about his marriage much, and Nick and Mark had never been close to marrying anyone. Their longest relationships were laughable.

"I can't find a woman who likes me for me," Nick said. "As soon as they find out my parents are rich, that's all they care about. They just want me to buy them stuff. It's not like I have money."

"I'm glad I met my wife when we were in high school. I know the money doesn't matter to her," Billy said.

"And, your wife is hot, man. You're lucky to be with someone that long and still have her look hot," Mark said.

"Being rich has allowed us to get her some enhancements," Billy said with a smile as he cupped his pecs.

"That's nice," Deacon said sarcastically. "If you can't find the perfect woman, you can *build* her," Deacon said.

"Don't get me wrong. I loved her before. She said it was for her anyway," Billy said.

"Yeah, right! You're a ballplayer. Everyone knows you guys screw around. She's trying to keep you whipped." Nick said.

"Well, then it worked, because I take my marriage vows very seriously," Billy said. "I don't even look at other women."

Just then, a beautiful woman walked by and said, "Hi, Billy. I'm a big fan."

Billy gave her a smile and said, "How you doing, baby?" and winked at her.

All the guys raised their eyebrows and laughed as she walked away.

"What? It's all public perception. She's not even that hot," Billy said as he watched her walk away. "Give me a break; I've been with the same woman for fifteen years!"

"Wow! I haven't even been with the same woman for fifteen months!" Mark said.

"I can count all the women I've slept with on one hand. I'm not a man-whore like some people at this table – Mark!" Billy said.

Deacon suddenly got very interested in the conversation. "How many women do you think you've been with, Mark?" Deacon asked and leaned in for the answer like it was a secret that Mark had been with a lot of women.

"I don't know, a couple of hundred?" Mark said with a shrug.

"*Hundreds*?" Deacon asked, shocked by his answer.

"Man, how has your dick not fallen off yet?" Billy asked, and all of them started laughing.

"You're like a human trampoline," Nick said.

Just then, a pretty brunette came into the restaurant with Mike Sanders, who was a pitcher for the Red Sox.

"Check her out," Nick said.

"When you're Mike Sanders, you can pretty much have all the pretty women you want," Billy said.

Mike gave Billy a nod as he pulled out his date's chair. Billy nodded back. The woman looked at their table, and her eyes widened when she saw Mark. Then they narrowed, and she gave him a foul look. The guys all laughed, except for Mark.

Billy slapped Mark on the back. "I wonder what number *she* was!" Billy said.

Mark looked back at the woman. For some reason, she *did* look familiar. He didn't feel animosity towards her. But he did know her, somehow. As the guys ate their meals and talked, the time slipped by. Mark occasionally glanced at the woman with Mike Sanders. Billy noticed it and leaned over, saying quietly, "You really do know her, don't you?"

"Blackouts," Mark said, sipping his iced tea. "I have a lot of nights that I don't remember. But I wish I could remember *her.*" He set his glass back on the table.

Just then, Mike Sanders and the woman with him stood up abruptly. Mike Sanders got right in her face, so she slapped him so hard on his right cheek that it left a handprint.

Mark jumped out of his chair. The woman stormed out of the restaurant, and Mike chased her. Mark went after them. By that time, it was dark, and all he could see were crowds and headlights. He had no idea where the couple had gone. Mark looked up and down the sidewalks on both sides but didn't see either of them. He did see a blue Audi R8 pull out in a hurry, and then he saw Mike Sanders standing at the curb, cursing and waving his arms at the car. So, Mark smirked and went back into the restaurant. Mark walked back to the table and sank back into his chair.

"Man, what did you think you were going to do?" Billy asked as Mark sat back down.

"Yeah. Mike Sanders is a *big* guy," Nick said.

"*Every* guy is a big guy compared to you, Nick!" Billy said.

"I don't know," Mark said. "I just… there was something about her."

"Well, I, for one, have had enough excitement. What do you say we call it a night?" Deacon asked. The guys agreed, and Mark paid the check, and they left. Nick and Deacon walked ahead of Mark and Billy. They had separate conversations, and Billy wondered what was really going on in Mark's head.

There was nothing really, except a lot of regrets. He honestly couldn't remember who that woman was, and it really bothered him. He assumed they had never been lovers;

otherwise, she probably would've slapped *him* instead of just scowling at him. Mark had *so* many regrets.

CHAPTER
Forty-Two

THE NEXT DAY during their free time, Billy and Mark pulled out of Recovery Road onto US-41 and hit the road to Deacon's house in Bonita Springs. Deacon didn't know anything about what they were doing. Mark didn't want him to talk them out of it. Even though he hadn't known Deacon long, he knew Deacon loved his wife, and she'd help him stay out of trouble.

They got to her house, and a teenage girl answered the door, all giggles. Deacon's wife, Monica, called from the other room, "Who is it?" But the daughter was a little too smitten with Mark to answer, so her mom came to the door. She opened the door even wider and wiped her hands on her apron, which was covered with powdered sugar. She was a little round woman with tiny arms and legs. She had ashen skin and wore outdated pink lipstick and blue eye shadow.

She was blushing and looking down instead of making eye contact with the guys. Mark thought she looked like a human doughnut with pearls. Good thing, she had a friendly personality. Although, it wasn't like Deacon was a looker himself!

"Oh my, it's Mark Taylor," she said as her young son came

running up. She extended her sugar-covered hand, and Mark shook it and then wiped it on his jeans with a smile.

"Billy Hernandez!" her son squealed, and Billy stuck out his hand for a high-five. "What are you doing here?" the boy asked as he smacked Billy's palm.

"We're friends of your dad," Billy said.

"Why?" asked the son, not understanding why his accountant father would have such cool friends.

Mark and Billy laughed. "May we come in?" Mark asked.

"Of course, where are my manners?" Monica said as she ushered them into the living room.

"Can I talk with your mom alone for a few minutes?" Mark asked the kids.

"Why don't we throw the baseball in the back yard for a few minutes while they talk?" Billy asked.

"Throw the baseball with Billy Hernandez? Yes!" the kid said as he grabbed his glove and a ball. Billy followed him outside. "No one's going to believe I played catch with Billy Hernandez!"

"We'll take a selfie with my iPhone, and I'll text it to your mom," Billy said.

Mark and Monica sat down and looked at the teenager, who was just sitting there, giggling.

"Honey, can you go back to the kitchen and finish your homework?" Monica asked.

She didn't say anything, just stared at Mark over her shoulder as she walked out of the room, bumping into the furniture on the way. Mark smiled at her, and she giggled even harder.

"I'm confused. What are you doing in my home? You know – this is so weird, we just saw one of your movies, and now you're here in person!" Monica smiled and put her hand on her forehead and laughed.

Mark sat forward. "Look, I know you and Deacon have had your problems..."

"Who?"

"Derek, sorry. We call him Deacon. Anyway, he loves you. All he's been talking about the whole time is you and the kids. He'll do anything it takes to make it work," Mark said.

Monica got up and started pacing. "I know you don't understand, Mark, because you've only known him a short amount of time, but he does this… he screws up and then apologizes and says he's going to change. I can't live with constant disappointment. And it's not just me – he always lets the kids down. I need some stability in my life, and so do they."

Mark got up and held her elbows at her crossed arms, "I know you're taking a chance on him. I know he's let you down. But the man I know loves you and doesn't want to let you down anymore. You think you're taking a chance of him disappointing you, but what if you're taking a chance at happiness?" And then he flashed that killer smile, so convincing.

She smiled a little. "You think he's changed this time? I can't take another disappointment. If he lets us down again, I'll kill him."

Mark squeezed her elbows, "If he lets you down this time, *I'll* kill him!"

After about a half-hour of Mark's closing argument, she agreed to let him come home. Mark told her it was going to be an adjustment, and it would be hard at first, but that they would be a family again and a stronger one at that. When Billy came into the house, she hugged Mark, and they left.

On the ride back, Mark and Billy talked about Monica. Billy said her son was a cute kid. He knew all of Billy's baseball stats, so Billy liked him even more. "They're a nice family. I hope we did the right thing," Billy said.

"If she didn't still love him, she wouldn't have agreed to take him back. I hope he doesn't disappoint us," Mark said.

"Wow, man. I'm really proud of you. You're acting like you care about people," Billy said with a smile.

"Monica's nice." Mark hesitated like he wanted to say something.

"Yeah, but she's built like a doughnut!" Billy said.

"That's mean, dude," Mark said, but then he busted out in a hard laugh. "That's why I don't eat empty carbs!"

They went back to the apartment and picked up Deacon and took him to Saks at the Waterside Shops in Naples. Mark and Billy picked out a cool outfit for him and made him get a good haircut. They went out to eat and then went back to the apartment. Then they sat him down and told him everything he would ever need to know about women and what makes them tick... or purr. Then Mark added some personal experience, everything you could explain without drawing pictures. Actually, there were pictures, but Mark's no artist, so they were more like stick figures. You can't really get someone to grasp the idea of anatomy when you're using stick figures.

Deacon tried to tell them he wasn't interested in hooking up with a woman. Mark tried to convince him that's not what this was, but he didn't believe it until Mark and Billy dropped him off at a very exclusive restaurant on Fifth Avenue in Naples where his wife was waiting for him with a big smile. Mind you, it wasn't as big a smile as Deacon would wind up giving her later, but that too was thanks to Mark and Billy.

The next morning, while the guys were eating breakfast, Deacon practically danced his way into the kitchen. The guys laughed at his dramatic entrance, complete with a girly twirl that made them all hoot with laughter.

"Someone got some last night," Nick said.

Mark was about to take a bite of a doughnut. It was just lingering on his lips. He shut his eyes and opened his mouth and then... Deacon *had* to start talking.

"I did. I did. A gentleman doesn't kiss and tell, but I will say this… she was very open-minded last night," he said with a sigh. "You know I did that thing that you…"

Mark opened his eyes and looked repulsed as he pulled the doughnut away from his face, "Okay, we're glad you had a good time, but we don't need to hear the play-by-play, man, okay?"

"Please, *no*!" Billy laughed, "I mean, it's your *wife,* man. But I'm glad you got some." Billy and Mark exchanged looks and smiled. Mark shook the doughnut at Billy.

"Want it?" Mark asked.

"No, my doughnut-eating days are over!"

"I'll eat it!" said Deacon as he grabbed it out of Mark's hands.

"We knew you would," Mark said as he and Billy laughed.

"Am I missing something?" Nick asked.

"No!" said Billy with a sly little smile.

CHAPTER Forty-Three

LATER THAT NIGHT, after Nick cooked the guys dinner, Mark asked if they wanted to go and walk around on 5th Avenue. They all agreed, but Nick insisted on changing his shirt. When he came down the stairs, he had a t-shirt that read, *'I'm with sober'* and had an arrow pointing to the left. The guys laughed.

"Nice shirt," Mark said.

"Thanks, I got it downstairs in the gift shop," Nick said proudly.

"Hmm. Now, if we could only decide who's going to walk to the left of you," Billy said as he and Mark scrambled for the door and walked well ahead of Nick and Deacon.

They had to walk a couple of blocks to get over to where everything was happening. They could hear music blaring from some of the restaurants, and they noticed a crowd at one bar in particular.

"Hey, they're doing Karaoke there!" Nick said, "Let's go."

"C'mon, man. What are you – a chick? You like listening to people howl like dogs?" Billy asked.

"I'll go. I love Karaoke," Mark said.

"You would. You can actually sing," Billy said.

The guys looked at Deacon, who said, "I'm game if you are. But I'm not sure we should be going to a bar. Everyone's going to be drinking but us."

"It'll be fine. We have to get used to being around people drinking," Mark said, convincing everyone to follow his lead. The bar was packed. There were so many people there that everyone was touching. People were excited to see Mark and Billy walk in even if they did have two anonymous souls in tow.

A table opened up right in front of the stage, and the people standing by insisted on giving it to the celebrities. Mark and Billy thanked them, and the four guys sat down. The waitress came over, smiled at the guys, and asked them what they were drinking. Nick and Deacon both ordered Cokes. Billy asked for water, and Mark ordered a San Pellegrino. She smiled at Mark again before she left the table.

"Man, you have it so easy," Nick said to Mark.

Mark just shrugged and smiled. A few minutes later, some attractive women sitting at the table next to them asked Mark if he was going to sing. He hadn't intended to, but he was sick of listening to people who couldn't sing absolutely destroy good songs. Mark told the guys he was going to sing a song, so he got up to look at the song selection, and he started smiling as he picked the one he was going to sing.

Billy stood up while a terrible singer was on stage. "I gotta take a piss, I'll be right back."

"Hurry up, Mark's almost up," Deacon said.

Billy hated Karaoke, so he didn't really care. "Okay, Deacon."

Nick watched Billy walk away and then turned his attention to Mark, who was talking with the women at the next table. Then Nick turned to Deacon.

"You think Mark's going to be okay? It'll be a lot harder for him when we get out," asked Nick with genuine concern.

"Mark's been through a lot. But I *think* when it comes right down to it, he'll use good judgment."

Just then, the DJ called Mark on stage and announced, "Now performing for you, the one and only, *Mark Taylor*!"

The crowd went crazy. No group was louder than the women a table over. Mark said, "Thank you," into the microphone and the music came on.

Deacon looked at Nick as the track started. "Why do I know this song?"

"Yeah, I know it too," Nick said, and as he started to remember the lyrics, Mark began to singing…

"I want a new drug…" by Huey Lewis and the News.

Deacon looked at Nick and groaned.

"What were you saying about Mark's good judgment?" Nick asked with his arms folded, shaking his head.

Deacon shrugged and put his left hand on his forehead for a few seconds and laughed uncomfortably.

Billy came back to the table and shouted, "Go, Mark!" and sat back down. Nick and Deacon looked at Billy in disapproval as Billy started moving his shoulders in time with the music.

"What?" Billy asked.

Mark jumped off the stage with the microphone and started singing to the women at the table near them while they pawed him. When the break came in the song, one of the women yelled to Mark, "Mark Taylor, where are you sleeping tonight?"

Billy, Deacon, and Nick all turned to the lady and yelled, *"Rehab!"*

Mark shrugged his shoulders and smiled and got back on the stage to finish the song. Everyone clapped, and then Mark went back to the ladies' table and finished his conversation. One of the women gave Mark her phone number on a napkin. Mark then came over to the guys and sat back down.

Nick said, "Nice song choice, Mark."

Mark just laughed. That song never really was about *drugs* anyway… that's just Mark's sick sense of humor.

Deacon said, "I wonder what it would be like to trade places with you for a day. I've never had a woman throw herself at me. I wonder what that would be like."

"You know, I'd actually like it if someone gave me a challenge," Mark said.

"Why?" Nick asked.

"I don't know." Mark looked around the room at the women who were giving him the eye. "I get bored easily," he said as he slammed his glass of water down on the table.

"I don't think I'd *ever* get bored of women throwing themselves at me," Nick said, "and those chicks are hot!" The guys stood up, and the women at the next table tried to convince Mark to go home with them, but he apologized and said that he was out with the guys. When they started walking back to rehab, Mark ran ahead of them and threw the napkin with the woman's phone number into a trash bin.

Nick put his hands on his head. "No! Why would you do that?"

"Did you see how much she drank while we were there?" Mark asked, "I can't be with someone like that now."

"I wouldn't have thrown her number *away*!" Nick said.

"Come on, man, I can't keep making the same mistakes over and over," Mark said.

"Good for you, Mark," Deacon said. "You need to find a nice church girl."

The other guys started laughing. "Yeah, that's what Mark needs… a *church* girl," Billy snorted.

"Hey, I like that idea. I'll just get one that Deacon goes to church with… they know how to have fun at *his* church," Mark said, joining in the laughter. Deacon didn't appreciate that comment.

It was hard to believe, but those eight weeks went by pretty fast. The guys were confident, and now they had friendships that would solidify their new life decision to remain sober. Everyone who was wrapping up their stay was getting emotional. It was a big graduating class, and they all made preparations for their friends and families to see them earn their sobriety medallions and walk away clean.

The last session with Beverly was also emotional for Mark. After two months, she'd gotten to know him well. She got to the heart of Mark Taylor, and few women can say that. She was confident that Mark would be able to love someone once he learned to lean on people who had already walked down the road he was on.

They smiled at each other as he sat down. "I can't believe it, but I'm actually going to miss you," he said.

"Me too. Honestly, I feel like you've grown up a lot in the last two months."

"I don't know about that. I mean… of course, you made me see why I do some of the things I do. But let's not go crazy." Mark crossed his legs and put his hands behind his head with his elbows in the air. "So, what do you think, doc? Am I cured?" he asked with a sly smile.

"Cured?" she asked with a laugh. "Sorry, Mark. Nothing is ever that easy."

"But as far as women…?," he asked. "You got any advice?" The smile disappeared as he folded his arms and listened intently.

"Mark Taylor is asking my advice about women?" She found this amusing. "Wait a minute, I want to make a note of *this*," she said with a laugh. "Yes, I do have some advice, Mark. Find someone who doesn't drink, someone who's not in the entertainment business, someone who is educated and financially independent. And most of all, find someone who doesn't jump right into bed with you."

"Oh, is that *all*?" he asked sarcastically.

"I'm just trying to help, Mark. I want you to succeed, I want you to walk out those doors and not come back… *ever*!"

"Well, that makes me feel *good*," he said sarcastically.

Beverly laughed. "Of course, we'd love to have you back as a guest speaker, but not as a *resident*!"

"I know. I was just kidding. I will take your comments under advisement and be more particular about the women I spend time with," Mark said with a little smile.

Beverly wasn't convinced. "Mmm-hmm," she said, making a little scribble in her notes.

The rest of the session was spent talking about Mark's new friends from rehab and his goals for when he left.

CHAPTER
Forty-Four

AFTER THEIR LAST group A.A. meeting, Mark, Billy, and Nick decided to go out to dinner. Deacon went out to eat with his family. The guys walked over to Fifth Avenue and found an Italian restaurant. They sat down and placed their order with the waitress, and started talking.

"I can't believe rehab is almost over. I can't believe I'm saying this, but I'm kind of depressed. It's not going to be the same without you guys around," Nick said.

"Well, I, for one, am glad I don't need any more time in rehab," Mark said.

"I'm ready to get home to my wife. It's been tough for her with all the media crap," Billy said.

The food arrived, and they started eating. Billy took a few bites of his calzone and then put his fork down. He wasn't even done chewing before he started talking. "Nick, I swear, man, you make better calzones than this guy. You should be running your own restaurant."

"Really? You think so?" Nick said.

Mark agreed. "I've had better pizza than this in California. He's right – you should be running your own restaurant."

"C'mon, I didn't even go to culinary school, guys," Nick said.

"Formal education is overrated." Mark leaned across the table and said quietly, "A lot of people don't know this, but I've never taken an acting class in my *life*."

"That explains your last movie," Billy said, laughing. Mark just gave him a dirty look, which made Billy smile even more.

"Besides, my parents would never give me the money I needed to get started, "Nick said.

"I would!" Mark said, "I have some money saved from *The Trifecta*."

"Me too, man. I'd give you some start-up money. I believe in you," Billy said. "No, *we* believe in you."

Nick got choked up. "I can't understand why you guys have faith in me," he said as the guys started getting emotional.

"We don't have faith in you, man; we have faith in your calzones. Oh my God, no one makes food as good as you!" Billy said.

Nick reached into his wallet. "Well, I wasn't going to do this until tomorrow," he said, "but since we're here, Mark, take this." He handed Mark a business card with a woman's name and number on it.

Mark looked at it. "Who's this?"

"Oh, just one of the most brilliant producers on Broadway. And by the way, she's a huge fan!" Nick said.

"Is she cute?" Mark asked.

"Very, but she's also my cousin, so I warned her about you. All you have to do is sign the papers, Mark. She wants to cast you as the male lead in the hottest new Broadway musical.

Mark got really choked up. He waved the card around. "This is a singing part?"

"Yup. You were the first choice too."

"You deserve it, man," Billy said.

"We're both going to expect tickets on opening night!" Nick said.

"I'm back!" Mark said, "This is exactly what I needed. You Yankees have to stop being so nice, or I'll have to get rid of my confederate flag," he said, staring at the card.

"Awe, you guys are much better at waving the white flag, anyway!" Nick said as he and Billy laughed.

Mark didn't even lookup. "Nothing you can say can bring me down. This is awesome!"

The guys did some shopping on Fifth Avenue and then went back to the apartment. He couldn't blow his money on booze, he may as well have fun buying stuff he didn't need. He thought it would make him happy, and it worked temporarily. He relished the thought of being back at work and seeing his name in lights on Broadway. Even though that had never been his dream, he sure could envision it now. Maybe New York would be the new beginning he needed. After all, if you can make it there… well, you know.

Billy came into their room while Mark was packing. "Hey man, we're going to stay in touch, right?" he asked, trying not to get emotional.

Mark stopped packing and turned to Billy. "Are you kidding? I promise I will come to see you when you play the Marlins. The field isn't too far from my house. You could even stay with me if you want."

Billy hugged Mark. And not a manly pat on the back either – a real hug with girly emotion. They embraced each other like brothers mourning the passing of their younger, stupider days and welcoming their new futures. "Of course, man. We need to keep each other on the straight and narrow, right?" Mark asked.

"Yeah," Billy said with some hesitation. He never confided it in Mark, but Billy was nervous about falling back into the same routine once he was out.

The apartment phone rang, and Nick answered it. "Hey Mark, it's your agent," Nick shouted across to the living room, holding the phone out to Mark as they walked toward each other.

"Hello?" Nick and Billy only heard Mark's side of the conversation. "Oh, they do?" Mark asked, grinning at the two men watching him. "For the Super Bowl?" He gave a thumbs-up. "Yes. And let me know. Thanks!" Mark hung up the phone.

Billy and Nick couldn't wait to hear what the phone call was about. "C'mon, man, don't keep us waiting," Nick said.

Mark tried to act humble. "Oh, nothing. *Mercedes* just offered to star me in their Super Bowl commercial for next year! I guess they liked the publicity from me driving the McLaren."

Billy hit his arm. "That's great, man. See? You're getting your second chance."

"That is so cool. So, are you getting Super Bowl tickets or what? 'Cause I know you'd take your two best friends with you, right?" Nick asked as he motioned to Billy and himself.

Mark looked up, surprised, and said sincerely, "Yeah! You guys *are* my best friends! Yeah, I will definitely take you guys to the Super Bowl next year!"

The three of them continued to talk and watch TV. Mark was on cloud nine. He couldn't have been happier. He saw a glimmer of hope for his career. Maybe he would make it. Perhaps he could avoid doing dinner theater with his name on the marquee as someone who used to be someone. All the things he had been so worried about were no longer a concern. Maybe Tinsel Town hadn't yet extinguished Mark Taylor's star.

CHAPTER
Forty-Five

MARK HAD FORMED A PRETTY good relationship with all the employees from the grocery store down the road and decided to order a cake from there. He wanted to celebrate sobriety and cheer up some of the people who were nervous about going home and encourage those who had just arrived.

Mark made the phone call to the grocery store and spoke with someone at the bakery. "Hey, it's Mark. I want to order the biggest cake you have for a party."

Mark thought the girl on the other end of the phone sounded cute. *Everyone* sounded cute to Mark. "What flavor?" she asked.

"Oh, I don't know what everyone will want," he said.

"We can do one-half vanilla and one-half chocolate," she said.

"Yeah, that'll work," he said.

"What do you want to be written on the cake?" she asked.

"I want it to say *Happy Sobriety* in blue, with sprinkles and crap."

"Okay." She repeated the order back to him. "You want the full sheet cake, half vanilla and half chocolate with cream cheese icing, and you want it to say, Happy Sobriety in blue writing with colored sprinkles?"

"Yeah, that's good. And you can have it here tomorrow for our last night?" Mark asked.

"Sure, no problem, Mr. Taylor. We'll deliver it as soon as it's ready."

"Thanks!" Mark hung up the phone and made his way up to the rooftop kitchen. Everyone else was already there having sweet tea and appetizers. Billy was in a hammock, and someone was playing island music. Mark went over to Billy. "Hey, man, did you bring the chicken?"

"Yeah, it's already on the grill," Billy said.

"Is that what smells so good?"

"Someone's grilling shrimp and making jambalaya," he said.

"You going to miss this place?" Mark asked.

"When I'm traveling with the team…"

"Right. I can't wait 'til I get out, and the reality of not having any sober friends will set in," Mark said.

Billy gave him a fist bump. "Well, you got one, man."

They all ate dinner, and then a few guys went back to Mark and Billy's place to play cards. They ate chips and drank soda and laughed about living a healthy life. Mark wondered what life would be like in Hollywood now. He realized that it meant no more going to all the places that used to tempt him beyond his control. He worried if he would ever have a normal life again. Not that his life was exactly normal – but it was what he knew. And it would surely be different now. At least he had Ted and Margaret next door. They'd be there if he needed them.

He could now he could make a fresh start, in his perfect house. He'd managed to salvage his career after all. Maybe everything would be okay, and he could lead the life he'd always wanted. There might even be a shot at finding someone he could love.

Could he ever be a man that someone could rely on? A man that someone could trust? He wanted to be. He knew there was no such thing as unconditional love, but the reality of being alone made it seem more vital than ever before. And there would be no bottles waiting at home to comfort him. Ted made sure of that.

Mark slept great that night and woke up excited about the ceremony. It was his last night at Naples Recovery Center. Ted and Margaret had promised to be there to see him get his medallion and then drive him home. Mark felt strong. He didn't even think about the possibility of getting emotional at the ceremony, but he did. And that was okay. He'd never worked that hard at anything, but sobriety literally meant life and death for him. No more mornings waking up next to strangers, or with his head pounding, and no more headlines that damaged his body as well as his reputation. He was a new man.

Mark took a hot shower, and as the water rushed down his body, he decided to live each day as his last. He would savor every significant moment and be glad to be alive. He still wasn't sure about all the "God" stuff he'd been fed at Naples Recovery Center, but something made him wake up to life. Something had made him realize he had to change if he wanted to live – really live – and he was grateful for that. He relished the thought of being married and having kids.

He knew he wasn't ready, but he also knew that marriage might be the one thing that would keep him stable. He had to find someone who didn't drink, someone who could keep him grounded. But for now, he was content just knowing where he was in the mornings. He liked reading the paper and drinking his coffee. He was amazed by the simple things in life. He no longer wanted to strangle little birds chirping outside his window, he wanted to know what kind of birds they were and what made them sing their happy little songs. Life was different. Life would be good from now on!

The day went as expected, nothing that special, but Mark was happy. He was sober, and he liked the way it felt. He had meaningful conversations with new residents and encouraged them. He went into all the staff offices and thanked them for the work they did. He bought some of the staff flowers and wrote kind notes to people.

Mark Taylor was a changed man. He was a good man – the man who had been fighting to get out for all these years had finally arrived. The end of the day came, and Mark went down to the main meeting room where the other residents and family members were gathering. Mark, Billy, and many other residents were waiting for their medallions. Ted and Margaret waved at Mark. One of the volunteers came up to Mark and whispered, "The cake was just delivered. I put it in your kitchen."

"Thank you," Mark said to her with a huge smile. Mark didn't get a chance to look at it, but he wasn't concerned. He was so happy that he and Billy were getting their sixty-day sobriety coins. He was also glad that Billy would be able to go home with his wife. Those two were on the phone every moment they could be. Mark was envious and hoped he would find a woman who could love him like that. Everything else seemed to be falling in place. Dane gave a short speech and then handed out the coins and made a few comments about each resident.

Mark gave him a big bear hug and couldn't stop admiring his coin, the way women look at their engagement rings. He closed his hand around it and brought it up to his chest. Everyone clapped. Tears welled up in his eyes. Then Billy was clutching his medallion, hugging the counselor, and then hugging his wife. After the ceremony, everyone went up to the outdoor kitchen and started talking and laughing. After everyone ate, Mark went to their apartment to get the cake and brought it up to the outdoor kitchen. He opened the box to inspect the cake while the others were looking over his shoulder and laughing.

Mark looked down at the cake. It read, *"Happy Sobriety in Blue with Sprinkles and Crap."* Mark burst out laughing and realized he should've ordered it in person. But it didn't matter a bit. He cut the cake, and the newer residents came up to all the graduates with hugs and handshakes. In less than two hours, Mark realized he would be back in Miami.

CHAPTER
Forty-Six

AFTER THE CEREMONY, Deacon's wife came up to Mark and stood uncomfortably close to him. She was almost touching him, but she had her back to him and talked under her breath like she was passing him classified information.

"So, Mark, Deacon tells me I have you to thank for all of his new techniques," she said as Mark drank some water and looked around the room. Mark was *really* uncomfortable now. He could feel color coming to his face, and his cheeks were burning. She continued, "I guess I don't have to imagine what it's like to have sex with Mark Taylor because I kind of *did.*" Mark started coughing on his sip of water. "And you were *terrific,*" she said as she walked away. He stood there frozen and tried to shake off her comments. He was glad she scurried away because he had nothing to say to that!

Billy noticed the odd exchange from across the room and came over to Mark. "What was that all about?"

"Monica just said that when she was having sex with Deacon, it was like she was having sex with me."

Billy laughed as they watched Deacon, who was standing with Monica on the other side of the room. "Look at that guy; he's like a rock star to her now." Deacon was holding a doughnut with a napkin. He lifted it up in a salute to them, which made Billy laugh even harder.

"Don't even say it," Mark warned him.

And then Monica caught their eye. She gave them a little wave, and they waved back hesitantly.

"I can't believe you had sex with her. That's your friend's wife, man," Billy said with a huge laugh.

A female resident overheard Billy as she walked by and said, "God, you're such a *pig*, Mark."

Mark shrugged. "The good news is I feel like I can go another ten months without having sex now."

Summer came up just in time to save Mark from any more of this conversation. She gave Mark a hug. "So, are you ready to face the real world again?"

"I have never been more ready."

"I'm proud of you, man. You promise that we'll stay in touch, okay?" Billy said as they gave each other a fist bump.

"Definitely, man. You can stay with me when you play the Marlins. I'm not leaving Miami until August."

"And miss a chance to stay at the Holiday Inn?" Billy joked. "I'm going to run back to the room and grab my bags, and then I'm headed home."

"Yeah, me too. I'm just going to say some quick goodbyes, and I'll be up in a few." Mark said.

Mark took a few minutes to exchange phone numbers and say goodbye to the other residents and the counselors.

Beverly came up to him and opened her arms. "Goodbye, Mark. I hope I *never* see you again."

"I hope I never see you again either," he said, and they both laughed. He hugged Dane and met some of the spouses of the residents. Feeling somewhat overwhelmed by his emotions, Mark went up to his room just in time to catch Summer and Billy making their way down the stairs with Billy's stuff. "Oh, let me help you with those," Mark said, grabbing the bags from Summer.

"Thanks," she said as they made their way down the flight of stairs. They walked over to her car, and she popped the trunk. Mark started to load the bags in, and Summer looked at the two of them and got teary-eyed. "Come give me a hug, Mark," she said as they embraced. "I'll let you two say your goodbyes."

"Bye, Summer," Mark said, his eyes following her to the driver's side.

"I'm glad you have her," Mark said, envying him. "It must be nice going home to someone."

"Are you telling me Mark Taylor is getting sick of being single?" Billy asked.

"Maybe. One day at a time, right?" Mark said.

"Definitely, but I want you to keep one thing in mind," Billy said thoughtfully as he put his hand on Mark's right shoulder. Mark listened intently for the forthcoming advice. "Deacon's wife has a *sister*," Billy said. Both men erupted in laughter.

Mark shook his head. "I can't believe I'm actually going to miss having you around."

"C'mon, man." Billy leaned in for a hug. "I love you, man."

Mark patted his back and stepped back. "Me too."

Billy walked around to the passenger side and opened the door."I'll call you soon, Mark."

"Sounds good, man," Mark yelled back and waved as they drove away.

As Mark was giving away his last hugs, Ted grabbed his bags, and he and Margaret made their way out to the car.

Mark came out and got in the back seat. "Thanks for being here. I hope it wasn't hard on you, sitting through that ceremony, Ted," Mark said.

"Why would it be?" Ted asked as he pulled out of the parking lot.

"It must've brought back a lot of memories of when you stayed here."

Ted and Margaret laughed. Mark didn't understand what was funny. "Ted didn't stay here, Mark – *I* did!" Margaret said.

"But, Ted, when I made fun of 'Recovery Road' you said you had been on it before."

"I did. But I never said it was for *me*!"

"*You're* the one in recovery?" Mark asked Margaret. He was astonished, and he leaned forward inquisitively.

"Ted said if I didn't go, he was going to leave and take our kids. I knew I had to make a choice," she said. Mark couldn't picture her drunk. She was so *lovely*. He never would've guessed that *she* was the one with the drinking problem. She explained that people with addictive personalities have to pick up new habits when they drop their old ones. "I had to do something because Ted said I only had one chance, so every time I wanted a drink, I'd plant something."

Ted said, "That's why our lawn looks like a jungle!" Margaret gave him a dirty look. "Sorry, honey," he said, "you'll never see our house featured on HGTV."

She sat there in silence and looked at him again, "Well, maybe as a house that got a surprise make-over," she said as Ted and Margaret both laughed.

Mark smiled at this playful exchange between them, and he sat back and thought about all the plants in their yard and realized she's *still* planting them. Mark knew maintaining his sobriety was going to be a permanent battle, but it was nice to know there was someone right next door in the fight.

CHAPTER
Forty-Seven

MARK WAS off to New York! Mark Taylor's name was in the lights of Broadway. Boy, that's a sight he never thought he'd see. He was excited about the future. As he spotted New York's skyline out his plane window, he wondered how long the show would run. He decided no matter what, he wouldn't read any reviews. No need to bring him down. He was going to live in New York again. That's something he swore he would never do, yet there he was, and he was actually happy about it.

Unfortunately, the show only ran for six weeks before it was canceled. But three good things came from the run: Mark got rave reviews from a ruthless *New York Times* critic, he got an offer to replace the lead in another action film called *Mortar Man* right away, and he managed to escape one of the harshest winters in New York history!

After the movie was completed, Mark came back to his Miami house for a week. He was scheduled to start shooting a film in New England the next month. For now, he was happy to be home and check on Robert. Margaret and Ted had taken outstanding care of him. Margaret noticed Mark working on the landscaping around his house. Margaret was working on hers too. She saw him kneeling on the ground planting a little tree and waved. She walked over towards him and rested her arms on the fence that separated their yards. She took her gardening gloves off.

"I see you bought some plants!"

"I did," he said as he covered up the roots with soil. "It feels good to get out into the sun."

"How are you doing?" she asked.

"Good," he said as he got up and brushed the soil off his hands onto his cargo shorts. "I'm doing what I'm supposed to be doing. So, that's new," he said with a smile.

"It gets easier, Mark."

"It does?" he asked optimistically.

"Sure, until something terrible happens. And then you may struggle, but if you surround yourself with the right people, they'll get you through it. And when you're ready to sponsor someone, it'll be even easier to stay sober because they'll be depending on you to keep them clean."

Mark walked over closer to her. "Do you think it's a coincidence that I moved into the empty house next door?" he asked.

She smiled. "Oh, Mark, there's no such thing as coincidence."

"That's what I keep hearing."

"You're not ready to admit that God's in charge, huh? It's hard to believe that there's someone besides Mark Taylor orchestrating all the events in your life."

"It *is* hard to believe."

"Our lives are a big puzzle, Mark. But somehow, the pieces all come together. You may not even see or feel it happening, but you'll look back one day and see how everything in your life was woven exactly together for his plan."

"Okay…" he said skeptically.

"Well, you're not ready to see it yet. Maybe when you're

married, you'll look back and see the glimpses of your future in your past."

"What, like an ex-girlfriend?"

"No! They're exes for a reason. But when you find the one, you'll understand that your paths crossed at exactly the right time."

Mark looked at her in disbelief. "Okay, Margaret."

"Ted's grilling steaks tonight. You want to come over?" She didn't wait for his response. "Six?"

"Yeah, that sounds good. Thanks."

Margaret walked away, and Mark wondered if it really was a coincidence that he'd moved in next door to Ted and Margaret. It certainly was strange that she was living in recovery and knew the one rehab that could actually help him. But he wasn't ready to embrace the whole "God's in charge" thing. How could he be? How could we have free-will and still be in his charge? It didn't make any sense. Mark believed he made things happen in his own life. He only believed in God when he needed somewhere to place blame. He wasn't about to give God credit when he had built his own career. He auditioned for that play in college. He moved to New York for that soap opera. And then he got offered *The Trifecta*. He had chosen to do *Don O'Malley* in Miami, where he finally got cleaned up. Mark was the one making all of that happen. Why give credit to "God"? After all, God was absent when Mark called on him.

When you've got it all, it is hard to believe that something or someone is bigger than you. That would mean the things that happen are out of the sphere of your control. And who wants to admit that they're not in control? Certainly not Mark. But maybe he was starting to believe there was someone else controlling some of the pieces.

The next week, Mark was off to New Jersey for four months. Again, Ted promised to take care of everything while he was gone and assured him he wouldn't let Robert die.

Mark's recovery wasn't perfect; there were still moments when he thought about drinking. But then he'd start thinking about some of the things that happened while he was under the influence. He knew life was meant to be more. He vowed he would never take that road again and would get rid of anyone who stood in the way of his recovery.

Some of that was easier to achieve than he had thought it would be. Many of his "friends" were no longer talking to him. And the ones that were kept offering him alcohol or asking if he wanted to get high. People who have never had addiction problems don't understand that sobriety is a total lifestyle change. You not only have to change your habits – very often you have to change your friends, your job, or your school. When you clean up, you change everything – or you fail. And Mark *couldn't* fail. It had to work this time, or he would be finished, and he knew it.

Most people don't understand addiction, and it's ironic because most people are addicted to *something* nowadays. Sure, it may not be whiskey or pot, but it's something: porno, cell phones, or social media. Everyone's addicted; they just don't understand what an addiction really is. At least Mark knew what his weaknesses were. The trick now was not falling into the same traps that had ensnared him all his life.

CHAPTER Forty-Eight

FOUR MONTHS LATER, when Mark returned from his film project up north, the doorbell rang almost as soon as he came in from the garage with his suitcases. It was a delivery guy with a package. He wasn't expecting anything, and it was from an address in New York that he didn't recognize. As soon as he signed for it, he opened it up and pulled out a book. It was called *The Declan Diaries,* and it was written by Claudia. He opened the jacket cover and smiled. She had signed his copy. As he flipped through the pages, he read the dedication: "To Mark Taylor, The Real Hero of This Story."

Mark quickly walked into the house and sat down. He started to read and realized that in the way she had written it, it was going to be perceived that Mark was only out for justice for the victims. He was portrayed as the only one who couldn't be bought off. He was a hero and liberator and truth-seeker. It was total *bull*. After all, Mark had been more concerned with how the scandal would affect his career. Yeah, he felt terrible about the victims, but most of his actions were for self-preservation. Isn't it nice when we do something self-serving and don't get caught?

Mark read the book in a few hours, and as the book became a best-seller, his phone started to ring and never stopped. No one thought of him as a chauvinist pig anymore. He was a *hero* now. It was no coincidence that the next year Mark Taylor got voted *The Sexiest Man Alive*. Everyone loves a hero… well, someone appearing to be a hero. On top of the excellent publicity from the book, several women Mark had met at the women's shelter were interviewed on a national "news" show on a major network spewing on about how selfless Mark was and what a changed man he was. Wow. He couldn't have paid for all of the publicity he was getting. It's never been hard for Mark to live up to his reputation. However, when the publicity is suggesting that you've become a champion of women's issues, you'd better be careful! Because as we know, the media loves to build people up, but they *really* get off on tearing them down!

As time went by, Mark remained very close to Billy and Nick. Mark popped in occasionally to enjoy Nick's success running his restaurant in Miami. As a free agent, Billy was picked up by the Red Sox and was training in Fenway South in Fort Myers. That wasn't too far for Mark, about two hours from Miami. Mark made the drive over when his schedule allowed. The guys got together whenever they could. And they all enjoyed their new lives. Sure, it was tough when the pressure of being in the limelight got to Billy and Mark, but they made sure never to miss an A.A. meeting, even when they were out on the road. And Nick met someone at the restaurant who didn't drink and knew how to handle him. More importantly, they were in recovery and *happy*.

Mark was still unlucky in love but lucky at the box office. He wound up starring in the second highest-grossing movie ever. And he wasn't the only lucky one. Nick opened two new locations for his restaurant in Miami and Boston.

Later in the year, Billy was ecstatic that Mark and Nick were in Fenway to watch Game Six of the World Series against the Cardinals. Billy came out of the bullpen in the last inning and grinned at Mark, who sat behind home plate wearing a Red Sox hoodie. Then he looked at Nick, sitting next to Mark. Nick was still a Yankees fan and had the poor taste to wear a NY hat to Fenway. Billy just shook his head when he spotted him.

When the game ended, security helped Mark and Nick down onto the field to celebrate. "I can't believe you didn't get your ass kicked wearing that hat, Nick!" Billy said. They all laughed and hugged each other. It wasn't just a victory for Boston. It was a victory for sobriety, and they were all in it together.

A few minutes after the cheers started to die down, several members of the press noticed Mark and ran over to ask him some questions. One reporter yelled, "Mark, are you in town, shooting a movie?"

Another one stuck a microphone in his face and asked, "Mark is there any truth to the rumor that you're going to play Curt Schilling in a documentary?" Mark shook his head. He had no idea what the reporter was referring to.

And another one yelled, "Mark, have you always been a Red Sox fan?" That one just made Mark laugh.

"I must have because I've never liked Yankees!" he responded with a big smile.

Mark ignored the rest of their questions. "Hey, today is not about me, it's about the Red Sox winning the World Series. This rebel loves the Red Sox! Who knew?" Mark grinned and gave Billy a high-five. The reporters moved on to the players and left Mark, Nick, and Billy standing there.

"It's not about you, huh?" Billy asked.

"No, and it's hard to admit that!"

Billy slapped a new "2013 World Series Champs" hat on Mark's head and led his friends into the clubhouse to congratulate the team.

One of the players grabbed Nick's hat and threw it in the trash. "Hey! You can't do that!" Nick protested.

Another player said, "You're a friend of Billy's?"

"Yeah."

The player put a new hat on him. "Then, you wear *this*." A little crowd of large men had formed around Nick, so he decided it would be stupid to protest. Nick was a relatively small guy, after all, and always claimed he was a lover and not a fighter. He smiled and said thanks, then scurried to catch up to Mark and Billy, who were in the middle of the celebration.

Afterward, the three of them went back to Billy's house to watch ESPN. Billy had done an interview after the game while Mark and Nick waited outside for him. The guys were waiting for it to come on. Nick and Mark hadn't known that Billy and Summer were having problems, but they'd thought it was strange that she wasn't at the game. And then the reporter doing the interview mentioned it, asking if their marital problems were alcohol-related. What a jerk! Leave it to the media to get off topic when there was a positive, exciting story to cover.

Billy exhaled, and his shoulders sunk down as he looked at the guys. "Sorry, man. That guy was way out of line asking you that right then," Nick said.

"Yeah, that was pretty unprofessional," Mark said.

"He told me they were going to edit that part," Billy said.

"That's so unlike the media *to lie*," Mark said. "Is everything okay with you and Summer? Where is she, anyway?"

Billy said she had gone to her mom's house for a couple of weeks to think about things.

"We didn't even know you were having problems. You're not using again, are you?"

"No, our problems are strictly baby-related. We can't get pregnant."

"Sorry, man. I didn't know you guys were trying," Nick said.

"I could pinch-hit for you," Mark said with a laugh. After all, *I've* never used steroids."

"You jackass. You know, I've never been able to shake those rumors? And no thanks, I know where that thing has been. You're not sticking it in *my* wife."

CHAPTER
Forty-Nine

MARK WAS home in Miami for a few weeks in between projects and noticed his new neighbors, the Millers, moving into the house next door. He decided to be friendly and bring a houseplant over to them. He knocked on the door, and when they opened it, they were pleasantly surprised to see Mark Taylor standing there holding a plant with a ribbon on it.

"Welcome to the neighborhood," Mark said with a smile as he handed off the plant.

"Oh, thank you!" the woman said, grabbing it. "I'm Glenda, and this is Henry."

Mark shook Henry's hand as Glenda held the plant.

"Please, come on in," the husband said as he motioned for Mark to enter.

"Oh, thanks, but I have to be somewhere. I just wanted to drop in and say hello."

"Well, we sure do appreciate you coming by," she said.

Mark started to walk away, and then he turned around and snapped his fingers. "By the way," he said, "they do trash pick-up on Thursdays, yard debris and recycling on Monday.

Feel free to come by if you all ever have any questions or need anything."

Henry stepped out of his house and looked over at Margaret's yard, which was almost completely covered in plants by now. Henry pointed and asked, "I do have one question – what's up with the jungle in the neighbor's yard?"

Mark just shook his head and said, "Tree huggers!" Then he smiled and walked away, and with his back turned, he yelled out, "I hope you recycle!" Mark knew it wasn't his place to explain why Ted and Margaret's lawn looked like what Floridians call "Old Florida!"

Mark was box office gold. He managed to stay in recovery the whole time, even with the bouts of bad press and bad break-ups. He had a new lease on life and a new image. Even his football team was doing better! He started a classic car collection with the money from his last movie, and Robert was as green as ever!

Mark made an appearance on *The Tonight Show,* and it was a hilarious interview. A famous NY publishing house was so impressed; they offered Mark a multi-million dollar book deal to write his memoir. Mark came up with a title that summed up the last ten years. Because he'd had so many blackouts, he called it, *"Hi. My Name is Mark… Who the Hell Are You?"* It would cover the timeframe from college through his recovery. Mark decided to leave out some of the stories and a lot of the details. Mark had already given enough of himself to the public. What they don't know, they just imagine anyway.

In between projects, Mark went back to Miami to shoot the pilot for a television series called "Miami Dade" as a favor to someone who gave him his comeback movie role. It was a police drama… oh good. There aren't enough of those on TV! Mark had no intention of returning to television.

Usually, when successful actors return to television, it's because they have a family and want a more routine schedule, or their movie career didn't pan out like they thought it would. As you know, Mark was nowhere near the point of settling down and having a family, and he was very successful in his movie career. Besides, he liked traveling and new adventures of being abroad, even for short periods. It just wasn't as wild anymore. But on the bright side, he took a lot of pictures and could actually remember what happened on his journeys.

Mark still had no luck in the love department, but he was used to being alone now, and he was okay with it. He finally realized it was better to be alone than with someone who made him miserable. It became progressively more challenging to find someone who didn't do all the things that Mark used to do, and Mark knew he couldn't ever be with someone who drank again. So he did what you're supposed to do. He started carefully selecting who he would go out with from that point on.

While he was in Florida making the pilot, he visited people and places he hadn't seen in a while. On top of the list was Beverly from rehab. He wanted to drop in and tell her he was doing fine. Besides, he had a few advance copies of his book and wanted to personally hand-deliver them – primarily since he'd dedicated the book to the staff. He drove to Naples and saw the green street sign on Recovery Road, and it made him smile.

He walked into the front office, with books in hand, and everyone came out to give him a hug. All the counselors were the same. Some of the volunteers had changed, but he recognized most of the faces. The director of the facility, Maggie, knew Beverly was in between clients, so she wanted to walk Mark down herself. She peered around the door into Beverly's office and announced, "There's someone here to see you." Beverly looked up, and Maggie smiled and walked back to her office.

"Hi," Mark said with an almost bashful smile.

"Mark Taylor!" She threw her pen down, got up from

behind the desk, and practically ran over to him. He gave her a quick hug. "How are you? Sit down!" she said, gesturing to the chair next to her. He sat down and handed her his book. She took it and read the title out loud and laughed. "Did you think of that title yourself?"

"I didn't have to. I actually said that quite a few times," Mark said with a laugh. He opened the book to the dedication page. "Look at the dedication."

"To the staff on Recovery Road." She got choked up and looked up at him. "Thank you."

"I didn't even have to think about the dedication. God, my life has changed so much since I walked through these doors three years ago."

"So, what's in this exactly?" she asked, flipping the pages.

"Not *everything.* I couldn't. There are some things the world doesn't need to know about me. But I did put in most of the ups and downs of the last seven years."

"Well, there have been plenty of those." she looked at her watch. "I have a patient coming in about twenty minutes, so you'd better tell me everything fast! What are you up to now?"

Mark gave her a smile. "I just got done filming a television pilot in Miami, and now I'm heading to Fort Myers Beach to shoot a movie."

"How long are you going to be there?" she asked.

"About four months."

"What movie are you in?"

"*Man from Buckingham.*"

"Oh, that was a great book." She wiggled her eyebrows. "So, anyone special in your life?"

He shook his head. "No. I haven't been with anyone in a while. I've been so busy. I don't know how I'd find time to balance a relationship with the amount of work I'm getting."

"If you found the right person, you'd find the time."

"I'm just traveling so much. I don't know where I'd meet someone to get serious *with*."

"Uh oh," she said with a smile.

"What?" Mark asked.

"That's usually when you find someone… when you least expect it."

He scratched his head. "I feel like I'm ready, you know? Like for the first time, maybe I'm ready for a real relationship now."

She smiled. "I'm really proud of you, Mark. I just want you to keep in mind that you need to find someone who will complement you."

"And she has to be *hot*," Mark said.

"Maybe you should find someone who will make you laugh. You need a little laughter in your life."

"Do you know how hard it is to find someone funny *and* attractive?"

"Maybe just concentrate on the funny part?"

"You know what? You're right; I don't care about how she looks."

Surprised and proud, she said, "Really?"

"Sure, I'll just have her turn the lights out!" he said, laughing. She gave him a pretend punch.

"I'm glad you're doing well, Mark." Then she held the book up. "And thanks for this. It means a lot."

As Mark was about to leave, another counselor popped her head in the door and announced that Beverly's friend, wouldn't make it because of a weather delay. They would have to find a last-minute speaker. The woman batted her eyes at Mark. "What do you think?" Beverly asked.

"I think… I'm your guest speaker tonight."

"Can you come to dinner after? You know we usually take the speaker out for dinner. There's a great new French restaurant on Fifth."

"Oui, allons manger!" Mark said with a smile and a bow.

He could tell from Beverly's blank stare that she didn't understand. "I said, 'Yes, let's go eat!'"

"Well, I understood the *'oui'* part," she said sarcastically. "I'll have to meet you over there."

"Sounds good," Mark said with that movie star smile. As he opened the door to leave her office, her next appointment walked in. When the woman looked up and saw it was Mark Taylor, she got almost delirious. She got a foolish grin on her face and said, "Hi," with a sigh of adoration.

Mark smiled at her, "How's it going?" he asked in passing.

"Great!" she said breathlessly, and then she realized it wasn't great – she was in *rehab*! But his back was already to her. "I mean – it's okay. I'm in rehab, so not great." She was so disappointed. She knew she sounded like a star-struck idiot.

CHAPTER *Fifty*

A LITTLE WHILE LATER, Mark stood in front of the group while Dane gave him a nice introduction. Dane got a little choked up when he sat down and saw Mark in front of the group. He was like a proud father. Mark had left the nest and come back as a success story. They don't all come back that way. Mark was a little nervous, but he got over it quickly when he received overwhelming applause.

Mark looked around the room at the excited faces and wondered what he was going to say to the group. Mark Taylor was not who they were expecting. It's not very often that you get a star, in the prime of their career, in rehab discussing their flaws and humanity. He exhaled to compose himself and decided to just speak from the heart.

"I just want to thank you all for inviting me…" he looked down at his watch, "… an hour ago." Everyone laughed. "My name is Mark Taylor, and *I* am a person living in long term recovery. I just want you all to know, I was sitting right where you are now, three years ago. I felt depressed, alone, and ashamed. I was out of control, and I let my drinking come before my work, my relationships, and my happiness. See, I didn't understand that there are certain things in this life that

I *could* control. I could no longer blame the media, my girlfriends, or my football team for my drinking. There is such a stigma in our society about dependence. It's not something we're supposed to talk about. I mean – everyone knows we have a problem. Millions of Americans live with addiction, and yet we're supposed to sweep it under the rug and pretend it's not there. I know you have a lot of regrets. I had them too, but I'm glad to say the only regret I have now is that it took me so long to get real help. I stand in front of you today, a different man from the one who stayed here just three years ago. I love life. I get up every day and think about who I can help today by sharing my struggles. Is it you? I've been where you're at and came out on the other side. I no longer wake up wondering what I did the night before. I wake up savoring every moment. What's it going to take for you to take your life back? It took me losing everything; my image, my career, and my dog. I was so unreliable; some directors didn't want to work with me, so I wound up making a couple of bad movies that went straight to DVD! Hollywood is a lot like high school, and if you're not drinking or doing drugs, then you're not cool, and you won't fit in. And when you're sober, they certainly don't want you bragging about it and ruining it for the rest of them! It took me hitting rock bottom to realize that I could only go up, and it was a lonely climb, my friends. Because guess what? The friends who helped you get wasted no longer want to stand by while you get sober. But I did it, and you can too. You *have* a choice. What kind of life do you want? You have the power to change it right now! *I did*. And, if Mark Taylor can stand in front of you a changed man, then there's hope for everyone in this room. Forget about what you did *yesterday* – what are you going to do *tomorrow*?"

The End

Mark's Rehab Schedule

Naples Recovery Center Schedule

Resident Name: Mark Taylor

Room: 207

Length of Stay: 8 weeks

Week Ending: March 24, 2011

Monday - Friday

6:00-6:30 am Wake up

6:30-7:00 am Medicine/Vitamin Supplements

7:00-7:30 am Breakfast

7:30-7:45 am Free Time

8:00-8:15 am Meditation

8:15-9:15 am Serenity Group

9:15-10:15 am Lecture and Process

10:15-11:15 am Anger Management

12:00-12:45 pm Lunch

1:00 – 1:45 pm Biofeedback/Relaxation Therapy

2:00 – 2:45 pm Tobacco Education

3:00 – 3:15 pm Meditation

3:30 – 5:00 pm Individual Therapy

5:00 – 6:45 pm Dinner/Fellowship Time

7:00 – 8:00 pm A.A. Meeting (except Fridays, movie night)

8:15 – 8:30 pm Fellowship / Medication

Saturday – Sunday

6:00-6:30 am Wake up

6:30-7:00 am Medicine / Vitamin Supplements

7:00-7:30 am Breakfast

7:30-9:45 am Free Time

9:45-10:00 am Meditation

10:00-11:00 am Spirituality Group

11:00-12:00 pm Relaxation Therapy

12:00 – 1:00 pm Lunch

1:00 – 3:00 pm Visiting Hours

3:00 – 4:30 pm Individual Therapy

The 12 Steps

The Twelve Steps:

1) We admitted we were powerless over alcohol – that our lives had become unmanageable.

2) Came to believe that a Power greater than ourselves could restore us to sanity.

3) Made a decision to turn our will and our lives over to the care of God as we understood him.

4) Made a searching and fearless moral inventory of ourselves.

5) Admitted to God, to ourselves and to another human being the exact nature of our wrongs.

6) Were entirely ready to have God remove all these defects of character.

7) Humbly asked Him to remove our shortcomings.

8) Made a list of all the persons we had harmed and became willing to make amends to them all.

9) Made direct amends to such people wherever possible, except when to do so would injure them or others.

10) Continued to take personal inventory and when we were wrong promptly admitted it.

11) Sought through prayer and meditation to improve our

conscious contact with God, as we understood Him, praying only for knowledge of His will for us and the power to carry that out.

12) Having had a spiritual awakening as the result of these steps, we tried to carry this message to alcoholics and to practice these principles in all our affairs.

*From the Alcoholics Anonymous website: *www.aa.org*

If you or someone you know struggles with addiction, *you are not alone.*

Hazelden Betty Ford Foundation (toll-free)

(800) 831-5700

References and Help

Hazelden Betty Ford Foundation (toll-free)
(800) 831-5700

To find A.A. meetings in your area,
visit the websites below:
www.aa.org

Alcoholics Anonymous – *aa.org*
Al-Anon – *al-anon.alateen.org*
Hazelden Betty Ford – *hazeldenbettyford.org*

Drugs and Alcohol 101
By Debbie and William Shooter

Opening Our Hearts, Transforming Our Losses
By Al-Anon

Paths to Recovery
By Al-Anon

Healing and Hope
By Betty Ford

The Anonymous People (movie)
manyfaces1voice.org